FIC   Gerson, Jack.

       The Whitehall
       sanction

DATE			

© THE BAKER & TAYLOR CO.

the WHITEHALL SANCTION

the WHITEHALL SANCTION

A Novel

JACK GERSON

Beaufort Books, Inc.
New York

Fic

R00400 99308

Copyright © 1984 by Jack Gerson

Library of Congress Cataloging in Publication Data

Gerson, Jack.
　　The whitehall sanction.

　　I. Title.
PR6057.E72W5　　1984　　　　　　823'.914　　　　　83-22330
ISBN 0-8253-0198-X

Published in the United States by Beaufort Books, Inc., New York.

Printed in the U.S.A.　　　　　　　First American Edition

10　9　8　7　6　5　4　3　2　1

To the memory of my mother and father

PROLOGUE

At the beginning there were words murmured at the edge of the grave.

Of these, some consisted of the usual, conventional phrases, uttered with the obligatory shaking of heads; regrets at the passing, ruminations on the premature ending of a life. Since the deceased was in his middle seventies these phrases contained a degree of exaggeration which could only be interpreted as politeness. There were tears too, not in profusion since there was no immediate family to exhibit the degree of their loss. But rather there was occasional watering of the eyes, in one case a single track down the well-powdered cheek of a female whose relationship, while of long standing, had been in a secretarial capacity.

And there were the other words. These were uttered in lower tones than even respect demanded and mostly on the walk back from the edge of the grave. They were furtively allowed to fall from the corners of the tight mouths of men in expensive suits, heads bowed together in a manner denoting a secret intimacy. They barely reached the intended ears before the sound was lost in the gusts of wind that caused the rain to slap loudly against the leaves of the sentinel trees lining the cemetery path.

As they reached the line of official cars drawn up like black beetles in single file these men foregathered briefly with a silent shaking of hands, some covert nods and finally there was a scramble for the cars as the density of the downpour of rain increased. The cars took off smoothly, almost silently, a seemingly melancholy procession away from the proximity of death.

One figure had lingered by the graveside ignoring the rain. A man in his seventies, he stared intently at the hole carved from the earth. It was as if he felt the necessity of separating himself from the official expressions of mourning to say his own silent farewell.

After a time, becoming aware of his solitude, he straightened up, seemed to force himself erect and, grasping the ebony stick on which he had been leaning, he waved it towards the grave in a manner of salutation not without respect. Then, turning, he walked slowly down the now deserted path towards the car-park and the cemetery gates.

He walked, still deep in thought, eyes on the pebbled track in front of him. Now, he thought, is the dangerous time, the narrow corner beyond which lies the Castle Perilous. He grimaced briefly at his own literary allusion yet he believed it was apt. He could tell himself he was out of it now, removed from all arenas of action. Still he had noted some of the faces at the graveside and had shivered at the recognition of what might be − no, was − behind the bland expressions, the solemn facades.

Carteret, for that was his name, sighed, an expression of weariness mixed with a sense of frustration. The Rear-Admiral was dead and Carteret feared that with his death floodgates would open; actions which he could only suspect might come to pass. He walked across the car-park and headed towards the gates using the ebony stick to ease the stabbing pains of age that racked his body. God, give me back the strength of youth, he thought. Then he could have taken action. Now he was simply an old man in a wet month waiting for warmth. He could only wait, hoping that somewhere someone would perceive the threat and action would breed reaction. Then he might be of use. It was the one thing left that he cared about, to be of use.

Some distance past the cemetery gates Carteret was approaching a row of small shops when he became aware he was being followed. He had been staring at the shop fronts, the stone of their facade soot-begrimed, the windows edged with dust. Against the frontage of a newsagent's, warped boards sported crumpled posters for Sunday papers, two days out of date. It seemed to Carteret symptomatic of the city, indeed of the whole country; there was a feeling of decay, of lack of care, a hopelessness.

It was when he looked away from the shop fronts across the road that he saw, out of the corner of his still-keen eyes, that he was the subject of scrutiny. There were two of them, deliberately assuming an air so nondescript as to be instantly recognisable to the trained observer. They were standing together on the opposite side of the road, hatbrims obscuring foreheads, bodies close together as animals huddling for warmth.

As he continued to walk they drew apart and walked with studied nonchalance in the same direction. Occasionally they spoke and one of them, the older and taller of the two, gestured towards a shop window as if commenting on the contents. It was not a good performance.

This man, the taller one, Carteret recognised. With the passing years he had aged, the once boyish features matured; yet the walk, and what he could see of the face, was unmistakable. He was from the sub-section, one of Buller's boys. In the old days they had been known as the 'heavies'. Carteret wondered momentarily if the nickname was still retained. It probably was. Little changed in the Section operational pattern and in the *patois* of the Section.

Now past the row of shops Carteret found himself approaching a narrow access road between two blocks of tenements. Deliberately he stepped from the kerb seeming to be about to cross. Then, with surprising dexterity for his age, he swerved sideways into the narrower road. As he stepped from the sight of his followers he flattened himself against the tenement wall, coming to an abrupt halt and causing a female passer-by to glare at him with suspicion and quicken her pace. No trust anywhere he thought, and rightly so.

His shadowers, on seeing him suddenly disappear from their view, hesitated and then the younger of the two sprinted energetically across the road, pulled up just before he reached the corner and, assuming his previous nonchalance, turned into the side road. At once he came into contact with the ebony stick held horizontally across the pavement, waist

9

high. Carteret, the stick held out, was leaning against the wall.

'Excuse me,' said the younger man, eyes moving nervously.

'Why?' responded Carteret.

'What?'

'You're following me.'

'A mistake.'

'Certainly,' the old man smiled. 'Yours.'

The younger man looked around, embarrassed, searching for his companion.

'I'm an old hand, you know,' Carteret went on. 'Know all the tricks. Can spot a good shadow easily. You're not very good.'

'A problem?' The older of the two followers had turned the corner and stood facing them.

'This gentleman seems to think we are following him,' the younger man explained, his face flushed.

'Can never be too careful these days,' the older man replied, attempting an easy smile. 'But you are mistaken, sir.'

Carteret stared up at him. The face was now in full view, the eyes a bright blue, like those of a newborn child.

'Oswald,' he said. 'Willie Oswald. You're one of Buller's heavies. Know you anywhere.'

'I'm afraid you have the advantage of me.'

Oswald was always well-spoken in the old days. It was a carefully cultivated accent, the result of a great deal of work to obliterate the East End harshness. It was also intended to disarm the listener.

Carteret lowered his stick now. 'You know me, Oswald. I was on the interview board when you came into the Section. I voted against your admission. But I was outnumbered.'

'What do you want, old man?'

'I asked your friend. Why follow me?'

Oswald shook his head sadly. 'Sorry. You're mistaken.'

'I told him that,' the younger man cut in. 'I told him. A mistake.'

'Don't make 'em,' Carteret insisted. 'Not in forty years.'

'Why should we follow you?' Oswald asked with a grimace.

10

'That's a Jewish joke,' Carteret forced a smile. 'Why do you Jews answer a question with a question. Who's asking a question?'

The younger man looked at Oswald. 'You're not Jewish?'

Oswald ignored him. 'You're getting old, Mr Carteret. Fanciful. Jokes aren't so funny. Of course, we were at the Admiral's funeral. Then we were just walking.'

'Oh, then you do know me now, Oswald,' Carteret said quickly.

'I do just remember you now.'

'But I didn't see you at the funeral.'

'We're trained to merge into the background. You know that. You were one of our teachers.'

Carteret ground the tip of his stick into the cracked pavement. The old interrogation game. Counter with irrelevancies. But who was playing the game? Oswald or himself? Have to bring him back to the point.

'Who told you to follow me?'

'That would be admitting we were following you,' Oswald replied and Carteret realised the grimace which had remained on the man's face was actually an attempt at a smile.

'But let me ask you another question,' Oswald went on. 'What brought you out of retirement today?'

The answer seemed so obvious Carteret had no hesitation in replying. 'The funeral. Last respects to an old colleague.'

It sounded sincere because it was sincere.

'No other reason?'

A breeze sprang up quite suddenly, there was a flurry of rain again and a sodden piece of torn newspaper danced along the pavement and draped itself around Oswald's shoe. He shook it off without glancing down but it made Carteret aware of the untidiness of the street, of unswept paving, discarded cigarette packets in the gutter. It was an ugly street, an unsalubrious district.

'You were talking to Harrington,' Oswald said, a simple statement.

Was I talking to Harrington? Carteret thought. I certainly saw him on the walk towards the graveside. Yes, he had said something to Harrington, a greeting, a reflex enquiry as to his

11

wife's health. And Harrington had replied, some kind of conventional response which he had barely heard. And why should he not talk to Harrington? They were almost the same generation, had worked in the Section for twenty years. Of course, Harrington was a little younger, would still have a year or two before he retired.

'What's wrong with talking to Harrington?' The question was rhetorical. He'd always been on good terms with Harrington. Everybody in the Section had. After all Harrington had no career ambitions. Therefore there was no internal political rivalry. He'd run the communications room for most of those twenty years and been happy to do so.

'This is a waste of time,' Oswald's companion broke in impatiently.

Oswald ignored this. 'And Harrington spoke to you?'

'He would do,' Carteret shrugged. 'It would be polite.'

'He spoke to you, perhaps gave you a message?'

'No.'

'Could have. An old friend. An old member of the Section.'

'We passed the time of day.'

Oswald stared at him in silence for a moment, then hit him. It was a strong direct blow with the back of the hand and it struck Carteret on the cheekbone, jerking his head to the side, causing his eyes to fill with tears. The tears were not of pain or fear but of shock. The blow jarred through his head and produced a momentarily delayed pain. The old man would have lost his balance but for the steadying support of the stick.

Carteret was surprised. Not that he believed Oswald and his companion were not capable of violence, he knew they were; indeed violence was the function of Buller's 'heavies'. But the blow seemed at once unprovoked and pointless.

'He did give you a message!' Oswald repeated – a statement, not a question.

'He did not. And I was not aware that the Section encouraged common assault.'

He was prepared for the second blow and had moved imperceptibly to feel the wall at his back and gain support. It

12

was a mistake. The younger man hit him this time, in the stomach and the wall accentuated the force of the blow. Pain shot through his body and he found himself gulping for breath. At the same time, he thought, they could so easily kill me. At his age the next blow could be fatal.

The two men continued to stare at him as he slid down the wall, choking in his throat as he struggled to regain air. He sat on the pavement with relief, trying to ignore the pain.

'You see, if there was a message, you'd tell us eventually, Mr Carteret,' Oswald said in kindly tones. 'You'd tell us and you'd remember you are retired and you want to enjoy your pension. So, if there was a message, you'd be honest and you wouldn't be tempted to tell anyone else, would you?'

There had been no message and he was winded and aching and there was no point in replying even had he been able to do so. He stared bleakly up at the two men with disbelief in his eyes. This was not happening, there was no point to it, it was some kind of waking nightmare.

Through the pain he heard the younger man say, 'Do we finish him?'

'Not in our brief,' Oswald replied. 'We had to see what he would do, we had to find out if anything was passed, and we had to discourage him.'

Then Oswald knelt down and put his face close to Carteret's. Carteret became aware of a trace of stale tobacco on the man's breath.

'Can you hear me, Carteret? Nod a little if you can.'

Carteret did so, finding the movement painful.

'Fine. Now I'm inclined to believe Harrington said nothing. But if he did you're going to forget it. We could kill you but we're not going to do that . . .'

From a distance Carteret heard the younger man's voice. 'Why the hell not?'

'Because he's an ex-member of the Section and questions might be asked,' Oswald replied and turned again to the figure on the pavement. 'We don't want that, not now. But if you misbehave, we will. And under the protection of the Section. You know the routine. An accident. With extreme prejudice.'

13

Carteret heard the words despite the pain that was still with him. What were they talking about? He wasn't on the other side, he wasn't a defector or some double selling information to both sides. He was an old man retired, gone to seed, left with memories, most of which came under the Official Secrets Act.

Oswald was still talking. 'You have to forget everything Harrington said to you. Or didn't say to you. You see we might not even have had to talk to you if you hadn't seen us on your tail. We could have ascertained your culpability or otherwise without even speaking to you.'

'Ascertain your culpability,' Carteret found himself repeating the phrase through dry lips. Where did they dig up phrases like that? The eroding influence of official jargonese on conversation. There was a newspaper article there that wouldn't offend the Official Secrets people.

'Culpability,' Oswald went on. 'So now we just underline our point and then you are left alone. You just tell anyone who comes along you've been mugged by a couple of niggers. You understand? Two niggers. Say anything else and you come up against solid concrete.'

Oswald took two paces back and nodded to his companion who carefully stepped forward and kicked Carteret twice on the side of his body. This time he was slammed against the wall and, before he blacked out, he thought they've gone too far, they've forgotten my age and they've killed me. The thought gave him a fleeting satisfaction that they would be in trouble for killing him. Then came the darkness.

He recovered consciousness after what seemed like several hours but was, in fact, four minutes later.

Oswald and his companion had gone and Carteret found himself crawling across the pavement towards the gutter, hands wet and muddy. One side of his body was on fire with pain and his eyes were misted. At least he was alive, he thought, but for how long? Was death going to be a long drawn out process of pain and hospitals and the unpleasant smells of departing mortality? And then he had the thought that he had not been followed for himself but because of Harrington; because of what Harrington might have said but

14

didn't. And the question was, what could Harrington have said that would cause his own people to be so concerned?

Despite the pain he was intrigued. And at once the process of rational thought reassured him. He was not going to die. At that moment he felt a hand on his shoulder and, forcing himself to half turn he stared, dazed, into the eyes of a uniformed policeman.

PART ONE

1

James Ryder drove out of London on a misty spring morning in April. He always remembered later the feeling of relief he had at leaving the metropolis. The city, it seemed to him, was decaying, dying under a watery sun. The streets seemed dirty, gutters strewn with the flotsam of the previous night; crushed cigarette packets, torn fragments of newspaper, and all the residual debris of living.

Even in his own neighbourhood of South Kensington, outside the expensive block of flats in which he lived, the tarmac of the road was cracked, potholes appearing amid the paving stones of the kerb. And, on the journey outwards, the facades of the buildings seemed to be begrimed, in places the stucco had fallen away revealing the ugliness of jerry-built construction.

Time was when London was a city of charm, even of beauty. Now the decadence and the poverty of spirit of the second half of the twentieth century had eroded the beauty, deformed the charm.

God, Ryder thought, a philosophical morning it was to be. He was escaping for a time to the north and he could not simply be glad to escape; rather he had need to ponder on what he was leaving behind. Yet in two weeks when he would be forced to return, he would probably welcome the homecoming. The familiarity of London, of his London, gave him a sense of security. He would be no longer a stranger and, despite a comfortable life, financial stability, few obligations or worries, he needed that security. It reassured him, gave him a sense of identity.

James drove fast, but with care, along the M1. He enjoyed

17

driving, took pleasure in the power of the old but beautifully preserved Jensen. And as London receded behind him he began to relax, enjoying the air, cool on his face from the open window, the sight of green fields on either side of the broad strip of motorway. He could reflect, too, on the fact that he was on vacation and was leaving behind a successful antique business which would be run efficiently if, he told himself not without a degree of conceit, lacking his personal flair for an occupation he actually liked.

There had been worries, problems in the past establishing himself and there had, too, been the traumatic ending of his marriage to Jennifer. But all that was gone now and even the scars of Jennifer's departure were healed. She had married again, someone in the City who had kindly removed the financial burden from his shoulders and assumed it for himself with, James had heard, as little success as he had. Jennifer's problem had always been in her never-ending search for novelty in life. During their marriage she had never succeeded in settling down and he believed it was still so. But now he could even feel sorry for her.

Of course there had been other relationships with women since Jennifer. But never with the same intensity of feeling. Perhaps he had never allowed himself a repetition of the kind of emotion which had nearly destroyed him. He had built up an emotional barrier and taken care to mend any incursions that threatened to overthrow that barrier. Now there was Sybil who, like himself, had her own wounds and maintained her own barrier. Although separated from her husband, she had avoided divorce, using her indeterminate status as a protection and an avenue of escape when necessary. She and James were friends, even lovers on occasion, but without ties, each always able to retreat to prepared positions. It was a most suitable arrangement. At forty-two years of age, James could enjoy solitude whenever he so desired.

Now he was driving on a leisurely trip which would take him eventually to Inverness where, in a week's time, the contents of an old and once great house were to be auctioned. He was in no hurry, determined to relax on the outward and return journeys, stay at decent hotels, eat good food, perhaps even get some fishing in, in Scotland.

He was approaching the first motorway café when he remembered that he had omitted to make himself any breakfast. He enjoyed the comfort of his flat in South Kensington but the kitchen he avoided as much as possible. His respect for good food, combined with his awareness of his own shortcomings, placed his kitchen beyond the pale, except for the making of tea, coffee and the occasional plate of scrambled eggs. Not that motorway cafés had any remote connection with good food, he told himself. Still there was coffee and they couldn't do much damage to a bacon roll. Smiling to himself he swung the Jensen into the inside lane and drove up the access road into the car-park.

He edged the car into a space beside a blue Capri, distinguished by the number of dents on its bodywork, switched off his engine and got out. His right leg ached and he was aware that he was limping more than usual. The limp was the result of an attack of polio in his early teens, fortunately the only memento of the one serious illness he had ever had.

The interior of the café was awash with the debris of convenience foods, the air heavy with the smell of stale cooking fat. James decided to skip the bacon roll and settle for a cup of coffee. He sat at a corner table with his coffee, aware that the café was cluttered with motorists, all seemingly talking at the tops of their voices. Above the strident tones of forty loud conversations, somewhere a speaker poured unlistenable-to music on top of the neon-lit room, a distant cacophony of ugly, undistinguished sound.

At the next table, a loud child stridently protested at the contents of the plate in front of him, and the child's parents equally stridently insisted on the beneficial effects of the food. James felt inclined to take the child's part.

Beyond the table in the opposite corner of the room his eye was caught by a splash of colour, a slim, scarlet scarf around the throat of an attractive woman. Indeed it was the only splash of colour in her outfit which consisted of a well-cut grey jacket, matching skirt and a white, polo-necked pullover. But it was her face that drew him to her. Clear-eyed with high

19

cheekbones, a delicate nose, dark hair, pulled back from her forehead and gathered at the nape of the neck, framed her features, the pale skin smooth and without blemish.

There was something familiar in that face, James told himself. We've met before, he thought, but where? Perhaps she was a customer; she had the intelligent look of someone who might care for antiques. Or perhaps he'd met her at some party in town.

Her eyes settled on him briefly with no hint of recognition as she sipped a large cup of coffee. Then, suddenly she rose and made her way through the tables to the exit. Pity, he thought, she looked nice. He smiled to himself. What a weak word 'nice'. Ineffectual, almost uncomplimentary in its suggestion of compromise. He turned back to his coffee.

Ten minutes later he walked back to his car, the pain gone from his leg, the limp imperceptible.

The bonnet of the blue Capri was up and she was standing staring down at the engine, the intelligent face frowning, annoyed at its lack of comprehension.

It was a gift from the Gods.

'Can I help you?' The time-honoured question sounded too obvious.

She did not look up. 'Do you know anything about car engines?'

'To be honest, not a lot.'

'Then your question was a waste of breath.'

'I can always try.'

She handed him her car keys and he sat in the driving seat of the Capri, switched on the engine. It spluttered and then started. He looked out of the driving window at her, questioningly.

'Try putting it in gear.'

He did so. There was a sound of grinding metal. He tried second gear. The grinding sound was even louder and more unpleasant. He looked up into the clear eyes which seemed to be grey. Or was it the reflection of her outfit?

'Gearbox. Sounds as if it's gone.'

'Damn!' She swore in a whisper. 'I should have had it

looked at. I should have thought. ... ! How long do you think it would take to repair?'

James shrugged and stepped out of the car. 'Ask them. Sounds like it needs a new gear-box. I should say at least a twenty-four hour job.'

She frowned, irritated. 'Leave it. Perhaps I can hire a car around here somewhere.' She kicked the off-side front tyre. 'The AA can earn their money and collect it sometime. Mechanisms! I get so angry when they don't work.'

James accompanied her back into the motorway café. The girl behind the newspaper kiosk was not helpful.

'Have to go to Northampton to hire a car, I reckon. Northampton would be the place.' She turned to another girl in an overall who was arranging magazines on a stand. 'Northampton, Lily, that would be the place to hire a car.'

Lily who had blonde hair tinged with purple shrugged. 'Why ask me? I couldn't even afford to hire a bicycle. Not with my old man. Reckon he drinks a Rolls Royce a year in the pub.'

They strolled back to the car-park.

'Look, I could run you to Northampton. Further, if you like,' James ventured.

'I was wondering how long it would take you to make the offer,' she responded with a smile. 'My name is Nora Matheson.'

'James Ryder.'

'I know. We have met, you know.'

He had been sure the face was familiar yet still he could not place her. This, he found surprising. He usually remembered attractive women, prided himself on his memory in that area.

'I should remember,' he stammered, suddenly awkward. 'But I don't.'

'Not very flattering. I should be hurt. But since you are giving me a lift, I shall forget the wound to my vanity.'

She took a small attache case and a briefcase from the Capri and transferred them into the rear of the Jensen. She then climbed into the passenger seat, not without an appreciative look at its interior.

'Nice,' she said, her lips pursing into a small smile. 'Very. Part of the image? Successful antique dealer and man about town?'

He sat in the driving seat beside her.

'Perhaps. But I happen to like driving it, too.'

They didn't speak again until they were out of the car-park and on the motorway heading north.

'Where?' he asked. 'And when?'

'Oh, let me see. Two years ago. Maybe three. A party at Sarah Shaw's place in Chiswick.'

He remembered the party. A theatrical affair, but then Sarah Shaw was a successful young actress. It was at least three years ago and he'd been invited with his wife. They'd still be together then although the time of parting had been close and they were fighting that night, the kind of fighting husband and wife did among strangers, under the breath mutterings, iced stares, tinges of sarcasm when forced to address each other. It was not surprising he had little memory of meeting Nora Matheson.

'I don't think you and your wife were getting on too well that night,' she broke in, as if reading his thoughts.

'You're very perceptive.'

'Not really. Too obvious. Anyway perception is part of my job.'

'Which is . . . ?'

'I'm a journalist.'

The name should have been familiar too. Nora Matheson, he'd seen it often. Once a week. In the feature columns of one of the better Sunday newspapers.

'You're that Nora Matheson?'

'Is there any other?'

'The Sunday Times!'

'The "In Depth" column. Investigative journalism. Full of interest, fun and old Capris that break down just when you need them.'

'I read you. Once a week. Faithfully.'

'Nice to know there's still fidelity in the world,' she went on, a slightly bitter smile on her face. 'And how is your wife? If I remember rightly we were all introduced at Sarah's party but she was more responsive than you.'

'We're divorced now,' he responded quickly, anxious for no reason he could admit to clarify his situation. 'I think that party was the last time we were actually out together.'

'Then I forgive you for not recognising me. You must have been under a strain.'

James pursed his lips grimly. 'More than that. A weight of concern. Contrary to popular opinion breaking up and divorcing can be traumatic even when you're glad to be rid of the marriage.'

Nora replied 'ow quiet tones. 'I know. Been through it myself. The mang er. Still, one recovers.'

James took his eyes off the road briefly and found himself looking into her eyes. They both laughed. At once he felt at ease, relaxed; she was no longer a stranger. They had divorces in common, a bond of experience.

Nora settled back into the passenger seat and lit two cigarettes, handing him one.

'Are you still in antiques?'

'It's a living.'

'You are a master of understatement, Mr James Ryder.'

'I try. For the benefit of the Inland Revenue.' His eyes were now fixed on the ribbon of road stretching ahead and the car cruising at a steady seventy miles per hour. 'You still doing the "In Depth" column?'

'Very obsessively. Uncovering social worms under national rocks. I'm a dedicated woman.'

'I've always wanted to meet one. What worm is taking you north this time?'

She did not reply at once but stared at the dashboard of the car, her brow creased into small furrows.

'Probably nothing,' she finally replied. 'We get a lot of crank stuff. Have to look into it all. This time it's a disgruntled ex-civil servant. Thinks he's on to some horrendous plot. Phoned the paper in London and asked if I'd come and see him. And it had to be today.'

Again the frown. 'Funny. We offered to pay his fare to London but he turned it down. That's why I'm going to see him.'

'Because he wouldn't come to London?'

'Because he seemed to be genuinely afraid to come to London.'

Again they drove in silence for some minutes. Nonetheless he was conscious of her presence, of the subtle fragrance of her perfume, of the attraction he felt towards her. And something else. A feeling within her of concern was transmitted to him and, with the concern, a subdued excitement.

He broke the silence. 'You think he's genuine, this character?'

'You get a feeling for the real ones, the people who have something serious on their minds.'

'Where exactly are you going to interview him?'

'Chester. But if you drop me at Northampton, I'll hire a car. It's on the paper.'

James took a deep breath.

'I'll take you to Chester.'

'There's no need – '

'I'd like to. I'm on a kind of vacation. Have to be in Inverness in a week for an antique auction. But the rest is holiday. I take you there on condition you have dinner with me after you've seen your man.'

'Conditional, eh? I warn you I'm a big eater.'

'Good. Then you're on. We head for Chester.'

Two hours later they drove into the outskirts of Chester.

James had always remembered Chester with affection from childhood visits to the old town. He had a clear recollection of the old Elizabethan-style houses that leaned into Eastgate Street narrowing the view of the sky but lending their own warmth to the pavements. He remembered, too, the excitement of the small boy walking the old city walls, imagining himself beating off strange, child-imagined invaders. His father had visited the town often on northern forays for antiques and James and his mother had often accompanied him.

Yet now the suburbs seemed strange, not unlike those of London, and again James experienced the feeling of viewing a decaying society. Was it in him or did it exist? He could not be sure but it did breed within him a feeling of melancholy like the aftermath of a bereavement, the death of someone close and beloved.

'I have the address here.' Nora Matheson broke into his thoughts, her voice efficient as she drew a piece of paper from her handbag. 'Totnes Street, off Wrexham Road.'

'You know how to get there?'

'I'm afraid we'll have to ask.'

They received very precise directions from a tired policeman sitting in a panda car and ten minutes later they turned into a narrow street lined with rather ugly red brick villas, the debris of middle-class architectural taste from the twenties.

'Number thirty-five,' Nora indicated with a distinct lack of enthusiasm. 'That's it.'

James drew the car up at the kerb.

The windows of the house – which stood behind a ragged hedge and a small, neat, precise and unpleasant plot of sheared grass – were dark, possibly with dust, and at their edges heavy plum red curtains hung, lank and crumpled. The house itself, semi-detached, seemed to cling to its Siamese twin forlornly, for support. A green iron gate, the paint peeling, opened onto a thin gravel path, threadbare in patches where the gravel had dispersed, permitting the occasional stubble of weed to creep through.

Nora stared at the facade in silence for a moment as if depressed by the view.

'Would you like me to come with you?' James offered, feeling sorry for her.

'Come to the door. Just to make sure he is there. But I'd better do the interview alone. Otherwise they sometimes clam up.'

She stepped out of the car and stood for a moment still gazing at the house.

'Do you want your briefcase?' he asked.

She smiled at him shaking her head. 'No. No briefcase, no notebook. If you take notes that sometimes intimidates them. The secret is, rely on your memory and conduct the interview as if you're simply having a chat. See, I'm good at it.'

'I believe you,' he replied, joining her on the kerb.

After a moment they walked forward together, James

opening the gate for her. The gate responded with the expected creaking of rusty hinges.

They arrived at the heavy wooden door with its small segment of stain-glass panelling at the top. A brass bellpush at the side of the door was tinged with verdigris. Diffidently, James pressed it. They waited.

'Look,' he said. 'I'll go into the town centre and book into the Grosvenor Hotel. Will you be . . . staying the night?'

She smiled up at him, grey eyes mischievous. 'I'll have to, won't I? Anyway I hate night trains.'

'Fine. A table for two for dinner and . . . '

'Two single rooms.'

He returned the smile. 'Of course.'

The distant sound of footsteps came from behind the door.

'Shall I call back here for you?'

'I don't know how long I'll be. I'll phone for a taxi.'

The door opened to reveal a thin young man, hair cut short, nervous, questioning eyes staring at them. He was dressed in a pair of creased flannels and a fair-isle pullover over an open-necked shirt.

'Yes?' he said, a slight stammer in his voice.

'Mr Skinner, I'm Nora Matheson,' Nora replied with a disarming smile.

Skinner was dutifully disarmed. He opened the door wider and, as he did so, he seemed to give a small sigh of relief.

'I've been expecting you.' The nervous eyes turned on to James. 'I thought you would be alone.'

'Mr Ryder was good enough to give me a lift. He's not waiting.' She hesitated, decided introductions were in order and nodded towards James. 'James Ryder . . . Roy Skinner!'

But Skinner had turned away from James and gestured to Nora to enter.

'See you later then,' James said, feeling awkward, and turning walked down the path. The door closed behind him.

Ryder's reception at the Grosvenor Hotel was smooth and efficient. He signed in and was shown to a pleasant room on the second floor. He was assured that the other room for his companion when she arrived was just next door. A searching look at the receptionist at this point revealed no hint of anything other than the smoothness and efficiency he had already noted.

Left alone in his room he unpacked another suit, laid it on the bed and going into the bathroom ran himself a bath. He was relaxed in the soothing warmth of the water ten minutes later and lay back contemplating the evening ahead with pleasurable anticipation. He liked Nora Matheson, or what he had seen of her. She seemed good company, intelligent and with a sense of humour. And she was a good-looking woman. Strange phrase, he thought, to apply to a woman. Good looking was more the descripion one applied to a man. Yet it was right for Nora. She wasn't beautiful, perhaps she verged on being pretty, which was a word he hated in that it sounded weak as a descriptive term. No, she was good looking with a hint of sensuousness in her looks which he found very attractive.

James was not an overly conceited man; he knew he was attractive himself to some women and to others, well, he had learned to accept that whatever chemistry was between two people sometimes did not function. He also held out no expectations of more than a pleasant dinner, a couple of liqueurs and a friendly good night, with the prospect of making an arrangement to have dinner at a future date.

It was when he came out of the bathroom, a towel draped around him, that he noticed that the porter had not only placed his own case in the room but had also deposited beside it Nora Matheson's small attache case and her briefcase. He was about to ring down to reception and ask the porter to transfer them to her room next door when it struck him that she would obviously ask for them on her arrival and he would therefore receive due warning of when she would be ready for dinner.

He drew a rather crumpled dressing gown from his own case, slipped it on and settled on the bed, not before removing his suit to the wardrobe. He opened the *Guardian* which had been on top of the case and started to read. But after a short time he allowed the paper to slip from his hands and he lay back, closing his eyes. Although it was only late afternoon he had driven at least a couple of hundred miles, part of the

27

journey with his leg paining him, and a short sleep seemed the ideal way to pass the time until Nora arrived.

In sleep he dreamed. The face of the man Skinner peered at him through the side of the door. Nora moved forward and the door opened as if beckoning them to enter. Then he seemed to drift after her into a long, long, dark hall. Skinner was now beckoning, the nervous eyes illuminated somehow in the darkness of the hall. James moved forward but Nora was no longer in front of him and the walls of the hall seemed to become narrower and narrower. Around him he was aware of a mist which seemed to dissolve into granules of dust, floating in front of him. Then the hall opened out and to his right was an old-fashioned Victorian hatstand, identical to the one he remembered as a boy which stood in the hall of his father's house. It was devoid of headgear but under the hat hooks was a compartment for walking sticks and this was filled with sticks and canes of every description, from the ebony cane with the silver handle that his father had once owned to a single gnarled length of wood with a carved handle.

James turned away quickly, dismissing memory, and found himself facing a heavy door which stood ajar. He stepped forward and, pushing it open stepped into the room beyond. Inside he stopped, standing motionless, amazed. The room which he had expected to be like the drawing room in his childhood home was empty; four walls, a bare electric light bulb, the room lacked furniture, fireplace or windows. There was only dust gathered in small piles in the corners of the room. Above him, cobwebs stretched from the bulb and flex to a ceiling patterned with cracks. Then at once he was aware of a rancid smell, the odour of decay, no, more than decay, corruption. Can one smell corruption? he thought and then knew he could and was doing so.

He called out. He called out her name.

'Nora!'

It echoed around the walls of the room, as if it had become some vast echo chamber. He spun round to move back to the door but there was no door. And the dream had become a nightmare. Fear flooded in upon him.

He started to fight his way out of sleep still gripped by the nightmare and yet aware that it had no reality. He forced himself to rise to a surface of consciousness but it seemed a long struggle to drag himself away from and beyond the four walls of the empty room.

He came awake slowly, damp with the sweat of fear and the effort of forcing himself out of the dream. He found himself lying on top of the bed shivering despite the perspiration, fearful that he might slip back into sleep.

He sat up knowing he'd had a nightmare, a rare occurrence since he had been a boy, and yet almost at once the memory of the empty room seemed to fade, dissolve in his mind until he could remember only the terror and not the reasons for that terror.

He found himself staring at the windows of the room with some surprise. It had been daylight when he had fallen asleep but now darkness had fallen, a darkness tinged with the yellow of a distant street lamp.

James looked at his watch. It was eight o'clock in the evening.

He dressed quickly and rang the reception desk.

'I'm sorry, sir, Miss Matheson has not checked in yet.'

Concern was there at the edge of his mind as he went downstairs and, leaving word at the desk of his whereabouts, he entered the cocktail bar and ordered a Cinzano.

Time passed. His concern grew. If Nora had changed her plans she would surely have phoned him or at least left a message. He had her attache case and briefcase in his possession and she surely would not have left Chester without these.

He looked again at his watch.

Five minutes to nine.

He switched from Cinzano to gin and tonic and sat huddled in a corner of the bar from which he could observe the door and beyond that part of the reception desk. If she arrived he would see her. He thought then of the little she had told him about visiting the man called Roy Skinner. A disgruntled ex-civil servant, that was how she had described him, who had phoned London with some kind of secret information. Skinner had rejected the offer of an expenses-paid

29

trip to the capital, insisting she visit him, maintaining he was afraid to come to the city. Nora had mentioned, too, the amount of crank calls she received in her professional capacity. Yet for some reason she had seemed convinced Skinner was not one of these but was genuine.

Yet if she was mistaken . . . if he was not merely a crank but some kind of dangerous crank, what position had she placed herself in? Concern was no longer at the edge of his mind but was gradually taking over. He gulped what was left of his gin and tonic and, rising, went out of the bar.

'Still no messages, Mr Ryder, and no sign of Miss Matheson,' the receptionist told him with a trace of impatience. She was a dark girl, flawlessly made up, with just a trace of a Liverpool accent in her voice.

'If she does arrive will you tell her I've stepped out for a short while. I won't be long.'

'Of course, sir.'

This time the young woman gave him an unmistakable look bordering on pity. As if she were saying, 'Face it, you've been stood up.' His irritation at this was assuaged only by something else in her face, a vaguely inviting look as if to let him know she might be available later for consolation.

He drove out of the hotel car-park and headed for Totnes Street.

It was ill-lit with old-fashioned street lamps alternating at considerable intervals on each side of the road. Some of them were unlit, out of order. The hedges cast long shadows across the kerbs. The street was deserted.

Number thirty-five was in darkness as James brought the Jensen to a halt at almost the same spot on which he had parked that afternoon.

The rusty gate duly screeched as he opened it and walked up to the front door. The windows of the house stared blindly at him, dark eyes embedded in the red brick stonework. He rang the bell.

Somewhere in the depths of the house he could hear the bell ring out. As he waited impatiently a thin drizzle of rain started to fall from a night sky that was darkening over. He stepped closer to the door as spots of rain settled on the shoulders of his suit. He rang the doorbell again. There was no sound after the bell rang out.

The rain became heavier and James found himself leaning on the door. A growing feeling of dread had come over him. There was obviously going to be no reply to his now persistent ringing and he began to fear for Nora. God knows, he had only glimpsed Skinner briefly but the appearance of the young man could hardly be called prepossessing. Could he be some kind of psychopath who had perhaps developed a fixation for the woman journalist? Apart from her by-line every Sunday in the newspaper, there was often a photograph beside her articles. And on occasions he remembered she had appeared on television news programmes. These things seemed to happen too often in this sickened society.

James leant against the door and to his surprise it swung open. The lock had been off the latch all the time. He stepped into the dark hall and as he did so he experienced a feeling of déjàvu, a stirring in the back of his mind, something to do with his hotel room and something in the dream.

He reached out in the darkness, his hand groping along the wall and after a moment he found the light switch and pressed it down. The hall was flooded with yellow light.

It was a small narrow hall, much narrower than that of which he had dreamt. A staircase ran up one side of the hall to the upper floor and on either side of him were doors. A thin strip of worn carpeting ran the length of the hall ending at a third door presumably leading to the kitchen region.

James pushed open the door on his left and entered the room, switching on the light as he did so. It was obviously a living room and though he was almost prepared to find it devoid of furnishings he did see that it was in fact cluttered with furniture, a small room filled with rather ugly furniture dating from the nineteen thirties. A sofa faced a small grate in which the cold ashes of a fire lay. On either side of the grate were matching armchairs, the seams of one split and a wisp of stuffing protruding. Against the wall opposite the fireplace was a display cabinet in ugly stained wood. Inside it were a number of dusty ornaments, some badly designed china animals and some electro-plated salvers. A bookcase at the

31

side of the fireplace was half empty, the shelves holding a number of well-thumbed paperbacks and some cheap hardback novels which looked as if they were pre-war publications. The rest of the room seemed filled with occasional tables, more ornaments, an ancient radio and, to James's surprise, no television set – but he found a small portable one in the other room across the hall – a tiny room also containing a desk, an upright chair and a more modern easy chair.

The kitchen at the rear was also small and ill-equipped. An ancient gas cooker faced an equally old refrigerator which was empty. A pint bottle of milk stood on a small table beside two cups and a teapot. A quarter of the milk had been used and the cups contained cold dregs of tea. The only food in the kitchen was a few tins of stew and macaroni in a cupboard.

Upstairs, there was a dusty bathroom and two bedrooms, one of which contained a large bed covered in a dust sheet. Indeed all the furniture in this bedroom was draped in off-white dust sheets and the room had obviously not been used for some time. The second bedroom contained a single divan bed, the bed clothes roughly made up. On top of a chest of drawers was a small bottle of aspirins and a washbag and shaving kit. Beside the bed was an open suitcase filled with men's shirts, a creased suit and two pairs of corduroy slacks. Underneath these were articles of underwear, socks and handkerchiefs. This case was the last thing James looked at, going through it as if he might find among its contents some explanation for the disappearance of Nora and Skinner. Because the house was empty.

James came down the stairs, looking for a telephone. There was none.

He left the house and drove straight to Chester Police Headquarters.

2

'Time was,' said the detective sergeant. 'When it was easy. You knew all the villains and you could keep the kids in order with a cuff on the ear. Before my time, though. My dad was a copper and he told me it was like that.'

He smiled, a young man, probably barely thirty. He was dressed in a rather worn sports jacket and flannels. Detective-Sergeant Hastings, Harry Hastings as he insisted on informing James Ryder as he had ushered him into the CID room.

'Now of course it's all broken up,' Hastings went on. 'The ruddy amateurs have taken over from the professionals. Amateur burglars, amateur thugs. No respect, you see, no respect for society. Of course what can you expect? They think they're part of society. Think everybody's bent. Times you think they're right too.'

He stood up collecting the sheets of paper which comprised Ryder's statement.

'Mind you,' he said as an afterthought. 'This is a new one. Your little business. Probably nothing in it, you know.'

'I think there is. Miss Matheson *has* disappeared.'

'You're not a kid, Mr Ryder. You know women do things like this. Sometimes it's a come-on. Look for me, chase me, Charlie, keep the old interest going. Other times, well, they've gone off with a new boy friend.' Hastings grinned, an element of assumed compassion in the grin.

'I'm afraid it's not like that,' James insisted. 'Miss Matheson and I were casual friends. There was no need – '

'But you did have a dinner date with her?' Hastings cut in.

'Yes, but – '

'Maybe she changed her mind. Didn't fancy it after all. Gone off with this Skinner character.'

'Look, sergeant, you have my statement. Do you intend to do anything about it?'

James stared at the papers in the sergeant's hand. He had told his story exactly as it had happened to the best of his recollection. The sergeant had typed it up, referring to him occasionally to check the details, and he had signed the typed statement. During the period of an hour James had found himself becoming impatient with the police procedure.

'Shouldn't you be doing something right now?' he had demanded of Hastings.

'We have to have the complete picture, Mr Ryder,' Hastings had responded quietly, the low tone of his voice deliberately pitched to reassure the over anxious complainant.

Well, now they had the complete picture and the damn detective sergeant still seemed in no hurry. James wondered what would have happened if he had discovered Nora's dead body in the house on Totnes Road. Would they still have demanded a leisurely statement, or would there have been the rush to cars, the cawing of police sirens and the appearance of officers of prestigious rank?

'Well now, Mr Ryder, if you'll wait here, I'll take this away and see if we can't get a little action.' Hastings smiled again as he spoke. 'Meanwhile I'll have them send you a cup of tea. And there are some papers there if you want to pass the time.'

Hastings indicated a pile of papers on a chair at the desk next to him; then he turned and went out leaving James in the now deserted CID room. James looked around, at the same time wondering how he could be expected to read newspapers under the circumstances.

The room was oblong and contained four desks, the tops of which were all uniformly untidy. Each had a typewriter and various bundles of papers in seemingly haphazard piles. The walls of the room were painted a light unpleasant green colour and were broken up by a number of nails on which were clipped more bundles of papers. A notice board of worn green baize dominated one wall and it was adorned with formal-looking memoranda and two 'Wanted' posters, one showing a rather out of focus photograph of a sad, ordinary looking man. Underneath the photograph was a physical description of the man and the additional information that he was wanted to assist the police in their enquiries into the murder of his wife. The sadness in the picture of the man somehow reflected the sadness of the room to James.

After about ten minutes a uniformed constable entered carrying a mug of tea and a plate containing a sandwich. He placed this at James's elbow.

'I hope you take sugar, sir. I took the liberty of putting in one teaspoonful.'

James nodded his thanks. The sight of the sandwich made him realise he had not eaten dinner and despite the strain he felt he was under he became aware of the fact that he actually was hungry. Nevertheless he couldn't resist questioning the constable.

'Will the detective sergeant be long?'

'I couldn't say, sir.'

'But surely there's some urgency?'

'I wouldn't know, sir. CID matter, I believe.'

The constable withdrew with what passed for a reassuring smile. James sipped the warm sweet tea and ate the sandwich which contained a thick slice of passable cold ham. After a time he found himself reaching over and taking a newspaper from the top of the pile. It was a local morning paper and contained little he had not already read in the *Guardian*. The second paper on the pile was the *Sun* which he ignored but underneath it he found a smaller paper which turned out to be the *Police Gazette*. It seemed to contain nothing but photographs of wanted men and, below the photographs, a list of their convictions. The first of these was a grainy photograph of a sullen-looking man. It appeared that he had previous convictions for a long list of offences which included burglary, armed robbery, grievous bodily harm and shop-lifting. His name was given as Lewis Alconbury, aka Lewis Ash, aka Lloyd Aston. He was thirty-two years of age. James could only reflect that his life, despite its comparatively short length, had been varied and energetic. He did find himself surprised at the variety of crimes listed, having always believed that criminals usually specialised in one or two types of crime. Perhaps, as Hastings had said, the amateurs were taking over indeed.

Nearly half an hour passed before Hastings returned. He came into the room, the fixed smile again in place.

'Sorry to have kept you,' the smile said. 'I think we might take a run up to Totnes Street. Have a look at this house, eh?'

'There is nothing there,' James said, getting to his feet.

'Never know. Trained eye and all that. Might spot something.'

'Are you doing anything else?'

'Don't you worry, Mr Ryder. Steps are being taken,' Hastings replied ushering him out of the CID room. 'We'll go in our car, eh? You can pick up yours later.'

Hastings sat in the rear of the car which was driven by another plain-clothes officer and bore no insignia to show it belonged to the police.

'CID car,' Hastings explained. 'Times we don't want them to know who we are, eh?'

The *eh* at the end of every sentence was beginning to irritate James. A psychologist would say it signified lack of confidence in the sergeant, a need for reassurance. Or perhaps it was simply that the man was so used to asking questions that he could not help turning simple statements into small interrogations.

The driver, who was introduced briefly to James as Detective-Constable Reardon, drove fast and with considerable expertise. He also ignored the speed regulations. In seven minutes they drew up outside the house in Totnes Street. The rain had stopped but the damp pavements still reflected the yellow glow of the occasional street lamp.

The house was exactly as James had left it, the front door still ajar, the rooms untouched.

James had to admire the speed and thoroughness with which the two detectives went through the house. They covered each room, opened drawers, glanced into cupboards and eventually came together with James in the hall.

'Nobody here, right enough,' Hastings said. 'But

36

somebody's been today. You can tell from those tea cups in the kitchen.'

'I did notice them,' James responded in mild supercilious tones.

Hasting grinned with a kind of appreciation and turned to Reardon. 'I thought the beat man was going to be here.'

'They did call him.'

'I wish to hell he'd hurry up!'

The detective sergeant returned to the sitting room where he browsed around the room reminding James irresistibly of a dog sniffing the air as if it would tell him something.

Eventually the beat constable, a large middle-aged man with a lined face, clumped into the house.

'Sergeant?'

'Odham, isn't it? What do you know about this place?'

The constable ran the back of his hand across his nose. 'Used to be owned by an old lady, I think. Missus . . . Missus . . . Skinner, that was it. She died.'

'So who owns it now?'

'Left it to her son, far as I know – '

James cut in. 'Skinner. That's the name.'

Hastings sighed wearily. 'I do remember you saying that, sir.' He turned back to the constable. 'And he lives here . . . ?'

'No, sir, least not very often. Works in London, I believe. We were asked to keep an eye on the place since it was mostly unoccupied.'

'Mostly?'

'The son, Mr Skinner did come up occasionally. But I think you'll find the local key holder is a solicitor in town.'

'Name?'

'Wilkins and Webb, I think. The station would confirm that. I've never had cause to have to call on them. I check the locks now and then – '

'Today? Last night?'

'Not for a few days, sir. I remember once checking and finding the house occupied. Last summer. It was Mr Skinner. I ascertained it was him.'

'Did you meet him?' James asked rather to Hasting's annoyance.

37

'Oh, yes,' the constable replied. 'Young fellow. Twenties. Bit pimply, if you know what I mean.'

'That's him,' James nodded at Hastings.

'I did think it might be. All right, now I think we'll go back to the station. You'll stay around here, constable. Reardon, you'll phone the key holder. Get him round here to lock the place up. And have a word with him about Mr Skinner.'

They arrived back at the police station and James was again left on his own in the CID room. He looked at his watch. It was past midnight. A faint hope stirred within him that when he went back to the hotel Nora would be waiting, indignant at his reporting to the police.

Hastings eventually returned, his face serious.

'Well, Mr Ryder, we have been making enquiries. Mr Webb, the solicitor . . . of Wilkins and Webb . . . he has informed us that he has no knowledge of Mr Skinner returning from London – '

'But I met him!'

'Possibly. He has his own key and could have been there. On the other hand he does usually inform Mr Webb when he comes up to Chester. As far as he knows the house was locked up. You didn't by any chance break the lock, eh, Mr Ryder?'

James stood up with some deliberate show of indignation.

'I told you the door was open. And Skinner was there this afternoon. Miss Matheson came to Chester to interview him.'

Hastings was silent for a moment staring downwards contemplating his foot.

'Yes, well, if it wasn't open, the door of the house at Totnes Street, we could have you for breaking and entering.'

'Wait a minute – '

'However you did come to us of your own accord so at this stage there is no question of that, eh? I suggest you go back to your hotel . . . the Grosvenor, isn't it? And maybe you'd like to call back here about ten tomorrow morning.'

Suppressing his rising indignation at the suggestion that he may have broken into the house, James nodded.

'I will do that. But meanwhile I hope you'll find Miss Matheson.'

Hastings finally smiled again. 'Or perhaps you will. Perhaps she'll have turned up at your hotel.'

Hastings' hopes were not to be realised. A dull-eyed night porter informed James at the reception desk that Miss Matheson had not turned up. James went wearily to his room.

Undressing, he donned his pyjamas and lay on top of the bed smoking a final cigarette. It all seemed so stupid, hc told himself. Just over twenty-four hours ago he had left London determined to pass a relaxing two weeks untroubled by business concerns or any other worries. Yet now he was involved with the police, had met and lost an attractive acquaintance (one whom it was true he could hardly recall meeting in the first place), had spent an interminable time sitting in a drab untidy CID room and had been virtually accused of breaking and entering a dreary, dusty house. Perhaps none of it had really taken place; perhaps it was part of that barely remembered nightmare he had experienced earlier in the day. Then again, had he really had a nightmare? There seemed no certainties, as if weariness blurred reality.

James yawned, finding difficulty in keeping his eyelids from closing. He stubbed out his cigarette in a glass ashtray on the bedside table and climbed under the bedclothes. A momentary fear of sleep assailed him, a trace memory of the nightmare. He dismissed this from his mind. His exhaustion was too complete, too all-embracing to allow for resistance.

It was as he leant over to extinguish the bedlight that he again saw, beside his own luggage, the attache case and briefcase. These at least assured him of the reality of Nora Matheson. Unfortunately he had omitted, both in his statement and his talk with the police, to inform them of his possession of these articles. Still, there was his ten o'clock appointment at the police station. He could produce them if he wanted to. But did he want to? He shook his head to dispel his fatigue for a few moments longer. Why should he not want to hand these items over to the police? They would go some way to proving his story. Yet somewhere in the corner of his mind was a warning signal, a caution that he should not hand over his only evidence. But he could not, at this moment, for the life of him think of any clear logical reason why he should not do so.

He rose from the bed and, swaying slightly, moved across to contemplate the luggage. It was a large attache case, more like a small overnight bag, certainly too large to fit inside his own suitcase and be effectively concealed. Another question came into his mind. Why should he want to conceal it?

He shrugged and turned to the briefcase. It was small, slim, expensive; and it was locked, a clip on the zip fastener stretched over and secured into a strong metal slot in which there was a keyhole. He picked up the briefcase, studied it and, with his thumb, tried to push the clip open. It would not budge. Lockfast, he supposed the police would have called it. Yet locked as it was it could fit into his own large case.

He knelt down, lifted a neat pile of clean shirts and placed the briefcase under the shirts. He replaced the shirts and closed the case. For a reason he was unable to rationalise, this gave him a sense of security. At least some of the evidence was concealed. He returned to the bed, pulled the sheets over him and switched out the light.

This time James Ryder slept a deep, dreamless sleep.

When he again opened his eyes it was as if he had merely closed them for a few moments. Yet the room was flooded with sunlight. He reached out for his watch on the bedside table and blinked at it wearily. It was ten minutes to eight. The night was over.

Within half an hour he had washed, shaved and dressed. In the hotel dining room he realised how hungry he was and ordered what was described on the menu as a full English breakfast. While he waited for this he studied the *Daily Express* which was the only morning paper left at the hotel kiosk.

The news was predictably bleak. Five hundred men had walked out of Leyland's over some ill-described dispute. A block of flats had been demolished in error by an over-enthusiastic local council. Three murders had taken place the previous day, the most horrendous of which was that of a small child savagely beaten to death by a complete stranger. The pound was strong but the trade balance showed a large deficit. And a politician of some stature was once again denouncing the Soviet Union. The only spark of optimism in the newspaper was an editorial telling readers that Britain would be great again and how right the politician was to denounce Russia. James found it all equally depressing. It was as if the country lived in some idyllic dream and the news stories around the editorial referred to another place and another time.

By nine o'clock, James had finished his breakfast and, with an hour to pass, he decided to take a stroll through Chester. The sun was still bravely struggling to shine through more threatening clouds and the air was pleasantly warm. Chester, James was glad to see, still retained a great deal of its superficial charm. It was only when one came close to the buildings did one notice the usual (for a Londoner) graffiti scrawled or sprayed on half-concealed walls, obscene mutterings in paint and chalk against the society that bred the instigators themselves.

It was when he decided to take a walk along the walls of the old city that James first realised he was being followed. A tall bulky man with a round fleshy face peering out from under a grey soft hat, he wore a rather crumpled raglan coat. James had first noticed him when he had stopped to study the window of an antique shop and the man, who had been prepared to walk on some yards behind James, was suddenly forced to stop and look into the window of a building-society office which contained nothing to see except a gaudy notice advertising rates of interest. When James moved on and then at once changed direction, climbing a narrow stairway that led between the buildings onto the wall of the city, over his shoulder he saw the man hesitate at the foot of the stairway, shuffle his feet awkwardly and then follow him up onto the walls.

Strolling for some hundred yards along the wall, James observed the man ambling in the same direction, pausing occasionally to stare over the wall, simulating an interest in a distant gasometer. It was an unconvincing performance.

James quickened his pace only to observe obliquely his follower do the same. Reaching a small turreted shelter with

41

steps leading down to street level, James stepped behind a wall, effectively concealing himself from view. The follower speeded up, ran past James through the shelter and stopped as he realised his quarry was no longer on the wall in front of him. Swinging around on his heels the man ran back into the shelter, his eyes fixed on the stairs leading downwards. There was no one on the stairs. The man hesitated again, puzzled. James stepped from behind the wall and tapped him on the shoulder.

'Did you think you'd lost me?'

The man swung around and James found himself peering into small dark eyes, barely visible due to the pressure of his flabby cheeks.

'I beg your pardon?' The question was uttered with some histrionic skill, containing elements of surprise and puzzlement.

'You were following me?' James enquired assuming a lightness of tone he did not feel. Indeed he was conscious of his own nervousness and his hands trembled slightly at his side.

'I'm afraid I don't know what you are talking about,' the man replied, a hint of cockney in his accent.

'You've been following me for some time. I'd like to know why?'

'Look, I've been talking a walk, sightseeing. I've never seen you before in my life . . . '

The man turned away moving towards the steps but James reached out and gripped his shoulder.

'Wait a minute!'

'Mister, let go my shoulder or I'll call a policeman. You know, that could constitute assault.' The man spoke suddenly with authority.

James loosened his grip, feeling slightly foolish. Could he have been mistaken? Were the events of the previous day making him paranoiac? He had always felt self-confident in any situation he had encountered, assured that he could handle whatever came along in life but now there were cracks appearing in that very self-assurance and the knowledge of them made him feel gauche, awkward, embued with nervous uncertainty. God knows he'd encountered little of what seemed like melodrama in his life but now it appeared to surround him. He did not like the sensation.

His antagonist took another step away from him and looked him up and down, an appraising glance.

'You can get arrested for accosting people, mister,' the man said with a hint of a sneer on his lips. 'Anyway I should be more careful if I were you.'

It was then that the man made his mistake.

'You see,' he went on. 'In your position you don't want to get in bad with the police again, do you?'

James hesitated, momentarily unsure of what he had just heard. Then he realised he hadn't been mistaken, this man had indeed been following him. *In bad with the police again,* that's what he had said. And that meant he knew what had happened the previous day. There were, too, elements of a threat in that final sentence.

The man had now turned away and was starting to descend the stone steps. James moved after him.

'Wait! Tell me what happened to Nora Matheson?'

'Who's Nora Matheson?' the man replied continuing his progress towards the street.

James drew level with him halfway down. 'Tell me!' he insisted.

The man stopped, the small eyes staring at James without blinking.

'You've lost her? Whoever she is, that was very careless. But then maybe she wanted to get lost.'

James felt a rage rising within him. He reached out and grabbed the lapels of the raglan coat. Exactly what happened next he could never be quite sure of. The fat cheeks loomed large in his vision for a moment, then he felt an excruciating stab of pain at each elbow and he was propelled backwards against the cold stone wall of the passageway. This was immediately followed by a sharp blow to the solar plexus and James found himself gulping desperately for air. He managed to stay on his feet albeit supported by the wall but continued to gasp and choke for some moments. Flashes of light crossed his vision and when they finally faded he began to regain control of his breathing again. At the same time a feeling of humiliation came over him. He hadn't been in a fight since his schooldays and then at least he had put up some kind of a show. But now he realised he had been disabled swiftly and expertly without being given even a small opportunity to retaliate. And there was another emotion too, one of self-disgust, not so much at his inability to retaliate as at the fact of being physically mishandled.

He raised himself from the wall, shivering imperceptibly. His assailant had gone, disappearing into a milling crowd of morning shoppers at the foot of the steps. James descended slowly to street level still shaken and aching at his elbows.

At five minutes to ten he entered the police station having regained something of his composure. Yet a feeling of shame mingled with a growing anger. James Ryder did not like anger, especially within himself. It indicated to him his own potential lack of control and he hated the idea of being unable to control either behaviour or emotion.

Once again he was shown into the CID room which was in the same state of disarray as it had been the night before. And again he waited.

The police, James noticed, seem to make a habit of being unpunctual. Or perhaps they used time as a tactic, a way of weakening the confidence of whoever had to wait on their pleasure. James, on this occasion, waited for just over half an hour before Hastings entered followed by a tall immaculately suited man who looked like a bank manager. This, Hastings informed him, was Superintendant Beddoes.

'Well, Mr Ryder, you've kept my men on the hop,' said Beddoes in low modulated tones.

'Isn't that the purpose of having a police force?' James couldn't resist replying smugly. 'To help citizens with problems?'

'If the problems are genuine, of course.'

'Mine certainly are. Miss Matheson has disappeared. And so has Skinner.'

Beddoes shot a glance at Hastings who seemed to shrug.

'Your facts are not accurate, Mr Ryder. We have been in touch with Miss Matheson's editor in London. Miss Matheson, according to him, is in Paris.'

James felt a chill creeping into his body. He prepared himself to anticipate unexpected information. His own previous smugness was overwhelmed by a greater sense of smugness emanating from the two detectives.

'Left for Paris yesterday,' Hastings chipped in, determined not to be left out of the act.

'In that case, she almost certainly changed her mind since I met her on the motorway!' James insisted.

'That might have been possible,' Beddoes went on calmly. 'But for the fact that the Paris office of the newspaper confirmed that Miss Matheson arrived at Orly yesterday and is now presumably following up a news story about the import and export of lamb. Apparently the French are at it again, breaking Common Market rules.'

The chill now embraced James completely. He started to shiver and, to control this, he forced himself to reassert his position.

'Everything I told Sergeant Hastings was true. Miss Matheson was here yesterday. I suppose it is possible she could have flown to Paris overnight although I can't see her doing it without informing me!'

'But according to you, you hardly knew her. Of course, we can't rule out the possibility that you met someone posing as Miss Matheson – '

'It was Miss Matheson! I met her before and . . . and I've seen her photograph in the newspaper.'

Beddoes sighed as if forced to tolerate a spoiled child.

'Anyway, what about Skinner?' James pressed on.

'Ah, yes, Skinner. According to the department he works in – he's in the civil service, you know – Mr Skinner was at work the day before yesterday and is now on a short period of leave.'

'Then he could have been at the house yesterday!'

'He could have been except that there was some query regarding his work and a colleague contacted him at his London home. He has a flat near the British Museum.'

'He was seen in London?'

'No. He answered the telephone at his flat. Yesterday afternoon.'

'But he was here . . . !'

'You've met Mr Skinner, too, then?'

'I told you. Yesterday afternoon.'

Beddoes smiled, a gleam of triumph in his eyes. 'If you met anyone, you met someone calling himself Skinner.'

'If I met anyone . . . ?' James was indignant, but it was a studied indignation. 'Are you implying I've been lying?'

'I'm not implying anything, Mr Ryder. I don't have to imply anything,' Beddoes continued in the same tone. 'I'm just pointing out holes in your story a tank could be driven through. Now I don't know whether you're lying or the victim of some pointless hoax. But you know it!'

'I've told you the truth!'

'Your truth, then. There are different varieties. In my business truth is like Heinz's fifty-seven — '

'For Christ's sake, I told you, I gave Nora Matheson a lift. I left her at that house with a man who said his name was Skinner. And now they have both disappeared!'

Beddoes paced the room for a moment in silence. Perhaps, James thought, he's reliving his days on the beat. Plenty of time to think. And this one needed to think. Finally, he stopped pacing and swung around on his heels and faced James.

'Sergeant Hastings did tell you you've laid yourself open to a charge of breaking and entering?'

Anger warmed James, took away the chill in his body.

'Great!' he spat out the words. 'Charge me then! Because, if I am the victim of some kind of hoax, you people are part of it. And you're going to look very strange in court. Because you'll have to explain why I came to the police after my breaking and entering exploit. And Sergeant Hastings did come back to the house with me. Are you going to charge him too?'

Hastings went red in the face.

'And there is something else,' James went on. 'When I left the hotel this morning I was followed. A tall man with a fat face. Would he be part of your hoax?'

Beddoes and Hastings looked at each other. And Beddoes gave a slight nod as if James's statement had confirmed something in his mind.

'Mr Ryder, I believe you were going on holiday?' Beddoes said. 'Well then, go on holiday. Leave us alone. We're busy people. The crime rate in this city, as in others, is rising. We haven't time to deal with pointless hoaxes. Or gentlemen with paranoiac tendencies.'

James took a deep breath. Control, that was the thing. Not to allow his anger to take over. Not to give them excuses or fuel their belief in his instability.

'May I go?' he asked from between clenched teenth.

'Surely,' Beddoes made an attempt to sound avuncular. 'And when you do get back to London, look up your Miss Matheson. If she's back from Paris, of course.'

James turned on his heel and walked out of the CID room. Beddoes stared after him, a thoughtful expression on his face.

James was some two hundred yards from the police station when he realised he hadn't mentioned Nora Matheson's two cases. The previous night his inclination had been not to mention them to the police but this morning they had slipped his mind. There was no conscious intention of keeping them from the police. And now, if he did tell them about the cases it would go some way to proving his story. He turned back towards the police station determined to take Superintendent Beddoes to the hotel, present the two cases to him and enjoy his discomfiture.

To reach the main entrance to the police station he had to retrace his steps across the entry to a yard in which police cars were parked. As he reached the entry he automatically looked inwards to ensure no traffic was about to come out. At the rear of the yard was another entrance to the police station, a wooden door painted the regulation green colour. In front of this door three figures were standing deep in conversation. James came to a halt. He recognised them at once.

Hastings was standing slightly to one side, listening respectfully. Beddoes was engrossed in discussion with the third man. James could not mistake the height and the plump features of the man who had followed him that morning. After a moment Beddoes and this man shook hands amiably. James stepped back quickly out of their vision. He felt now there was no point in returning to the police station. If there was a conspiracy then obviously the police knew much more than they were willing to tell him.

He walked quickly back to the hotel.

His mind was full of questions. Why had the man followed him? And what connection had he with the police with whom he was obviously on good terms? If they were merely checking up on him by having him followed why not admit it? Questions, too many questions. And at this moment they all pointed to the conclusion that the police were trying to cover up the whole business.

Obtaining his key from the hotel receptionist James went straight to his room. As he unlocked his bedroom door he found his hands were trembling again, a nervous reaction. He told himself he needed time to think.

At first the room seemed exactly as he had left it. The bed had not yet been made up, the bed clothes rumpled and untidy at the foot of the bed. It was only after a visit to the bathroom, where he filled and drank two glasses of water, that, oncoming back into the room he noticed Nora Matheson's attache case was missing.

He stood in the centre of the room, looking around nervously. Then he opened his own case and lifted the pile of clean shirts. The briefcase was still there.

Someone had entered the room and removed the one obvious piece of evidence that linked him with Nora. Fortunately, they had not thought to search James's own case, presumably believing Nora had only been carrying one case.

His first instinct was to telephone reception and inform them his room had been entered and part of his luggage had been stolen. His hand was on the telephone when he had second thoughts. The hotel would automatically call the police and James had no doubt he would again be faced with at least Hastings if not Beddoes. And again he could be accused of lying or further indulging his fanciful story. If he mentioned he'd seen them in conversation with the man who had followed him, they could easily deny it or tell him he was merely mistaken.

A kind of panic took hold of him. He wanted to be away

from Chester, away from the memory of that dark empty house of the previous night, away from the false sympathy and underlying suspicion that emanated from the two police officers.

He sat for some minutes on the edge of the bed, forcing himself to remain calm. There were explanations, he was sure. Nora Matheson would reappear probably with some innocuous explanation for her disappearance. It had to be so, he insisted to himself. Yet he knew it did not explain everything.

Eventually he decided he would move, get away from his hotel where his presence was too obviously known. He would find some small quiet hotel not too far from Chester and there he would think it out, resolve his next move. He would check with Nora's editor in London by phone. After all he had only Beddoes' word for it that Nora was in Paris. He had to find out for himself.

He packed quickly ensuring the briefcase was still between his shirts, locked his case and presented himself some twenty minutes later at the reception desk where he paid his bill.

'You did book a second room, Mr Ryder,' the receptionist, this time a pale-faced young man, reminded him.

'Yes, I did. I'll pay for that too.'

'Your friend didn't turn up?' There was the trace of a sneer in the man's rather ingratiating smile.

'I always take two rooms,' James responded with a heavy edge of sarcasm. 'Comes of having a split personality!'

The smile on the receptionist's face became glacial. He handed James a receipt and beckoned the porter to take his case.

'No need,' James insisted. 'Both of us are strong enough to carry it.'

The Jensen was in the hotel parking area in the same spot he had left it the previous night on his return from the police station. The sight of it brought him a kind of reassurance. It had crossed his mind that, if his car had been stolen, he would have had even greater problems. Doubtlessly Beddoes would have insisted he came to Chester by train.

James carried his case to the rear of the car, unlocked the boot and opened it.

The body was squeezed into the boot and lay twisted on its back, a large crumpled doll, eyes staring sightlessly up at James. And one inch above the eyes in the centre of the forehead was a small blood-encrusted hole.

Despite their brief meeting the previous day James recognised him at once. The body in the boot of the Jensen was that of the man he had been introduced to as Roy Skinner. Skinner was quite dead and had been so for some time.

3

Most people hold an image of themselves that is often at variance with the truth. Yet it is a necessary image essential to preserve not merely their self-esteem but their very confidence in facing life. James Ryder had always considered himself to be an urbane, sophisticated man, perhaps he would admit slightly vain, but with a knowledge and experience of his world that was reasonably comprehensive. He had never questioned his courage since he had never been put to the test of having to demonstrate it existed. In all of this his judgement was reasonably accurate. But he would be the first to acknowledge that this assessment applied only to his personal world; that there were other adjacent worlds which he read about in newspapers or, on rare occasions, viewed from a distance.

With the discovery of the body in the boot of his car, James felt he had been catapulted into one of those other worlds. Indeed he had begun to suspect he was entering this other world when he had gone into Skinner's house for the first time the previous eveing. And he had received additional confirmation of this suspicion when he was assaulted that morning. He was unused to physical violence and now it seemed he could be in a world where not only violence but violent death was commonplace.   •

As he stared down at Skinner's body he knew for certain that his comfortable world had deserted him. He was in another place.

He closed and locked the boot of the Jensen. Placing his suitcase in the rear seat of the car he sat behind the steering wheel and lit a cigarette. He needed time to think.

The normal sensible course of action would be to go at once to the police. He had seen too many films, read too many novels in which there would have been no plot if the hero had at once gone to the police. Yet he could not forget his reception at the police station less than an hour before. And particularly he could not forget the amiable conversation he had seen in the yard between the man who had followed him and Superintendent Beddoes; the man who had so expertly disabled him and the superintendent who had dismissed his story of the disappearance of Nora Matheson with equal expertise.

He had been told Nora Matheson was in Paris and had been there since the previous day. This he knew to be untrue. He had been told Roy Skinner was in London and yet the man he knew as Roy Skinner was lying dead in the boot of his car. So why were the police lying?

James Ryder was no heroic character, he told himself, no trained investigator. He was an intelligent man in early middle age, reasonably well-educated with a knowledge of antiques, perhaps even, he prided himself, an expert on Meissen china. He was ill-equipped to handle the situation he found himself in. And yet there was within him a sense of old-fashioned gallantry. He owed Nora Matheson something, not because he knew her well or because he was in love with her, although he could not deny his attraction to her, but because of an old fashioned sense of duty. If asked to define that sense he would have been unable to do so. It was as if Nora had placed a degree of trust in him and he was under an obligation to live up to that trust. It was necessary that he should find out what had happened to her. Since the police had not only proved themselves unhelpful but also suspect in their attitude, he could only proceed on his own.

He stubbed out his cigarette, switched on the ignition and drove out of the car park. He headed for the M6 motorway and once beyond the city boundary increased speed until he was touching eighty miles an hour. But after a few minutes he slowed down to under seventy, aware that he could not afford to be stopped by a police patrol. It did occur to him that whoever had placed the body in the boot of the car might well have informed the police and road blocks could be out.

In this he was mistaken. He had a clear run to the motorway but on reaching the access road he began to have second thoughts. His expected course of action would be to proceed north or south as quickly as possible. There was a logic there. He would be expected either to return to London or proceed north, his original destination. He must not make the obvious move. He drove over the motorway heading east.

Time to think out his position, that was still his most pressing aim. He would have to rid himself of Skinner's body but this, he could not do in safety until night and the cover of darkness. And he had to open Nora's briefcase. If there were any leads to her disappearance they would be connected with the story on which she had been working. There had to be information on this in the briefcase. Otherwise he faced a dead end.

As he drove, another thought came to him, one he had avoided, wanted to ignore. If Skinner was dead then perhaps Nora, too, was dead. The bullet hole in Skinner's head had placed him in a nightmarish situation. If Nora, too, had been killed then the nightmare had no end. Believing in a conspiracy of some kind was bad enough but now murder had been committed because of this conspiracy. And whoever was behind it would have even fewer scruples about killing a second time.

The nightmare closed in. He stared at the road ahead automatically now, his mind clouded with fear. He took a corner barely concerned with steering the car and his offside front wheel thumped onto a grass verge. He reacted instinctively pulling the car back onto the road aware that he must regain his concentration. He told himself Nora Matheson must be alive because he wanted her to be.

The countryside became a stretch of bleak moorland and as the car climbed upwards the sky darkened and it began to rain. By the time he had reached the crest of the hill, the rain was flowing down the windscreen of the car, carving deltas of water across the glass.

Below him the road curved downwards to a large town nestling in a great hollow. A glance at his roadmap indicated the town was Macclesfield. By the time he reached the town itself, the rain was slanting down, turning pavements into liquid mirrors reflecting the rows of small houses.

In the town centre he found a small commercial hotel and in a yard behind the nondescript facade he parked the Jensen. Reassuring himself the boot of the car was still securely locked, he grabbed his suitcase, threw a raincoat over his shoulders and ran through the downpour into the hotel.

The room was small and not particularly clean. A hand-basin had been rubbed lightly over with a cloth but still bore traces of a waterline of scum. The bed was narrow and a depression in the centre bore witness to many previous occupants. The porter, a grey little man, indicated that the bathroom was at the end of the corridor.

James divested himself of his raincoat hanging it in the large dusty Victorian wardrobe and, opening his suitcase, sat on the edge of the bed contemplating Nora's briefcase. He tried the lock of the case. He exerted some pressure on it but it held fast. He searched his pockets, produced a bunch of his own keys and one by one tried fitting them into the lock. None would fit.

He rose and went to the window. The rain still poured down and he found himself peering through the splattered glass into a dim, empty main street. After a moment a pedestrian scurried by clinging to the side of the building opposite as a defence against the downpour. James felt unutterably weary although it was still only early afternoon. His stomach ached slightly where he had been struck that morning. He lit a cigarette and lay on the counterpane of the bed trying to relax. What the hell, he asked himself, was he doing in a drab hotel in Macclesfield, a fugitive from God knows who, with a corpse in the boot of his car? If it hadn't been so terrifying it could have been ludicrous. A day ago he had been a respectable dealer in antiques, a successful one, with no particular problems. Certainly he had been hoping that in the next two weeks he might make it with an attractive female, at the least a new companion on his holiday. But it was a casual thought, one that would never have disturbed him. And he had met Nora Matheson who more than fulfilled his hopes. And who had, albeit involuntarily, propelled him into his present horrendous situation.

He stubbed out his cigarette on a convenient, if cracked, bedside ashtray and swung his feet off the bed. There was a time for action, had to be a time otherwise he would never find his way out of the frightening labyrinth of events. That time was the present.

Searching through his jacket pocket he found the small penknife he carried with him. He had endeavoured for some months to break the cigarette habit by smoking a pipe and the knife had been useful to clean the pipe. However he had quickly returned to cigarettes and the pipe lay now unused in a drawer in his flat. But the knife had stayed with him.

The blade was stained with tobacco and fairly blunt. He tried the tip of the blade in the lock of the briefcase without success. All he succeeded in doing was scratching the leather. Nonetheless that gave him the answer. He jabbed the blade viciously into the leather and after some minutes of twisting and pressing, the blade went through the leather. Further pressure tore the leather and eventually he had created a rip some six inches in length. He was able to reach in and pull the contents of the briefcase out.

Lying on the bed in front of him was a notebook, the cheap reporter's variety. It was filled with shorthand notes. The headings were, however, not in shorthand and gave him some clue to the subject matter. The first of these headings was 'North Sea Oil. Dissipation of Profits'. He flicked through the book but if there was anything to link it to Skinner he was unable to decipher it.

Besides the notebook he had extracted several sheets of

paper, many of them blank, a number of letters and copies of letters with *The Sunday Times* printed at the top of each sheet. There was a letter too from a rival newspaper, a friendly epistle from a features editor making tentative advances to *Dear Nora* in the event that she ever decided to cross Fleet Street and change her job.

The last item from the briefcase, James found, held what he was looking for. A leather-bound diary it contained under the previous day's date one word: *Skinner*. Towards the end of the notebook after the dates ran out there were several pages with the word 'Memo' printed at the head. Under the first of these were a number of scribbled notes, fortunately not in shorthand.

Roy Skinner, 29 years. Civil Servant in the Home Office. Checked this with registry. Telephoned twice. Claims to have information which he insists should be published *in the national interest*. Repeated this twice. Under some sort of nervous strain. Possibly a crank.

There followed a space of two lines. Then further notes.

Second telephone call. Insists he is genuine. Refused to come to London. Fear. Agreed when I suggested he might be contravening Official Secrets Act. Again insists in national interest. Suggested I check on what happened to man called Harrington. Conversation ended with the following: 'It started when the Rear Admiral died and Carteret retired. Harrington knew. He was an executive in the section' (what section?). May be worth trip to Chester. Check on Harrington and the section. . . .

Again there was a space in the notebook to the foot of the page. James flipped the page over. At the top of the next page she had written one on top of the other:

The Section?
The Rear Admiral?
Harrington?
Carteret?

Below this was a scribbled note. 'Check these with C. Pincher or Ronnie Mansfield.'

Lighting a cigarette, James stared at the last two names. Pincher? Chapman Pincher was the *Daily Mail* authority on espionage and counter-espionage. And Ronnie Mansfield? Ronald B. Mansfield, author of *The Intelligence Menace,* a book James had read some years before. So a minor civil servant in a state of terror phones an investigative journalist, mentions The Section, the Rear Admiral and two names, and this sends Nora Matheson to two of the foremost authorities on espionage in the country. And the man who started it all was dead in the boot of James' car with a bullet in his head.

James Ryder, what the hell have you got into? How many times in the last twenty-four hours had he asked himself that question. He took a long draw on the cigarette and looked again at the notebook. The rest of that page was empty. Again he turned a page. More brief and cryptic notes.

Rear Admiral: Six months ago Rear Admiral Sir Arthur Morris, Retired, died of a heart attack at the age of sixty-eight. *Retired?* But was he? No other rear-admirals died recently. Check Morris.

Harrington? Several in civil service. All healthy. Newspaper report, April 9th. George Stafford Harrington fell under a tube train in Holborn Station. Coroner's verdict, accidental death. Minor news story in Times and Daily Telegraph. Occupation: *Civil Servant.* Is this Skinner's Harrington? Check with Skinner.

The final note in the book was on the next page. Nora had scrawled in handwriting that indicated some haste, 'Pincher in Washington. See Mansfield after Chester.'

James closed the notebook and returned it to his suitcase with the other papers from the briefcase and lay back on the bed.

The rain still rattled the window pane. He stared at it registering that the downpour seemed unceasing. He thought, where was Nora? Was she alive or was she lying somewhere, like Skinner with a small round hole in her head. At least

56

the notes gave him some leads as to the story she was working on; not very satisfactory leads, he had to admit. A dead Rear-Admiral, something called 'The Section', and two names, one of which might also belong to a dead man. No, they were not exactly enlightening. Still there were the two journalists, Pincher and Mansfield. They might be able to help. He had no choice but to return to London.

No choice? What the hell was he thinking about? He had told himself earlier he was no detective. He should get rid of Skinner's body; more, he should go to the police, show them the body, answer as best he could their questions and get out, go on to Scotland as he had planned. But would they let him go? The body was in his car and he had driven away from Chester. He could say he'd just discovered it and driven straight back. But then he had made a statement saying he had met Skinner. Therefore he would undoubtedly be under suspicion. And he did not trust Superintendent Beddoes. Too friendly with the follower who had virtually beaten him up. Furthermore none of this would help to find Nora Matheson.

It all amounted to the simple fact that his freedom would be less restricted if he continued on his own, experience or no experience as an investigator.

Closing his suitcase, he donned his still damp raincoat and went down to reception. The receptionist who was chewing gum expressed some surprise at his early departure.

'You hardly been here an hour!' she exclaimed, her front teeth clogged with chewing gum.

James responded with a muttered excuse about remembering an urgent appointment in Manchester. Manchester sounded reasonable and should the police trace him as far as Macclesfield, the mention of Manchester might temporarily mislead them. He paid a bill for one night's board without demur which obviously surprised the girl and, struggling again through the rain, placed his suitcase in the back seat of the Jensen and drove off.

He did not head for the motorway but driving south east he followed road signs to Leek and Derby. After about ten miles he passed through Leek and the rain began to lessen, the downpour turning into a misty drizzle. Beyond Leek he turned into a secondary road and the mist thickened. After about three more miles, he brought the car to a halt on a grass verge beside a ditch. The road was narrow and on each side were hedges beyond which were fields stretching into the mist. And if there was any sign of human habitation nearby the mist effectively hid it.

Steeling himself for an ordeal he was dreading, James stepped out of the car and walked round to the boot. Unlocking it, he hesitated before grasping the handle and opening it. Like most people he was unused to the sight of death and particularly of violent death. He stared at the boot for some seconds watching the fine rain pattern the metal, gather into rivulets and run downwards to drip onto the road.

Finally steeling himself he twisted the handle of the boot and raised it, an illogical idea flashing through his mind that the body might have gone, that his previous viewing of it might have been some mirage, a temporal aberration. It was not so. The man he knew as Skinner lay as before concertinaed into the boot, knees drawn up. One of the eyelids, previously open, seemed to have sagged with the movement of the car and the dead face now seemed to be winking up at him.

Manipulating one arm under the legs and the other under the waist, James lifted the body clear of the car. It seemed surprisingly light but then Skinner appeared to be a comparatively thin man. The head now hung awkwardly back and as James moved towards the ditch it lolled sideways and he had his first view of what had been the back of the head. James had heard and read of the damage done by a bullet but was not prepared for what he now saw. The hole in the forehead, as he had noted before, was small, a black dot encrusted around the edge with blood. But the area where the bullet had exited was another matter. The back of Skinner's head was nonexistent. In its place was a gaping hole surrounded by dried blood, bone and a whitish substance. The sight of this caused James to gag and he had to stand, the body in his arms for some seconds gasping for breath, fighting off the inclination to vomit.

Recovering himself he staggered to the edge of the ditch and tumbled the body from his arms into a flowing stream of watery mud. The body settled into the mud face downwards and James turned quickly away.

As he walked back to the car he felt as if he had committed some irredeemably irreverent act. He was not a religious man, indeed he'd always considered himself an agnostic but the throwing of the body into the ditch clashed with all the accepted *mores* bred into him since childhood. He was innocent of the murder of Skinner but in the method of disposing of the man's corpse it seemed to him there was a callousness which imbued him with an overpowering sense of guilt.

He drove away at speed as if distance from the spot would lessen the guilt. And after a short time the feeling did give way to one of relief. He was no longer carrying a dead man. Then another thought occurred to him and again he stopped, drawing into the entrance to a field. The mist still surrounded him blotting out the edges of his vision. Getting out of the driving seat he reopened the boot. It was with a sense of relief that he noted there were no signs of bloodstains in the interior. The only indication that a body had been there were two indentations in the rubber mat lining the floor of the boot where Skinner's heels had rested.

James climbed back into the driving seat and drove on.

Of course he knew Skinner had been killed elsewhere and with the nature of the gunshot wound must have died instantaneously. Therefore there should be no reason for bloodstains or the inevitable fragments of bone which such a shot would have left. But the placing of the body in the boot of his car had been a deliberate decision after the murder. Why? To incriminate him, that seemed obvious. Who would want to incriminate him? The people who had taken Skinner and Nora. But the police believed that Skinner was alive and well and living in London. Unless they could be convinced otherwise? Or the man in the boot was not Skinner? Or the man in London was not Skinner? Damn the questions! James could admit to himself he had never liked puzzles. How the hell had he landed in the middle of a living, breathing, deadly puzzle. God, there was more sanity in one small beautiful Dresden figurine. Give him inanimate objects any time.

59

He seemed now to be driving along interminable, twisting country roads wreathed in the still-prevailing dank mist. After what seemed like an age in time and many miles in distance he passed a sign indicating the M6 and Newcastle Under Lyme. Eventually by-passing the town he drove onto the motorway heading south. The mist started to clear and a watery sun struggled through. He began to feel hungry and remembered he had eaten nothing since breakfast. West of Stafford he pulled into a motorway service station, filled up the Jensen with petrol and, parking it went into the café.

The meal was ugly, glutinous with fat, but his hunger overcame his repugnance and he ate ravenously. Finished, he went into the men's room and stared into a mirror above a hand-basin that reflected a drawn, tired image. With soap and water he attempted to make the image more recognisable.

It was nearly six o'clock when he came out of the thick glass doors of the cafeteria area into the car park. He came to a halt at once.

Two men, in heavy raincoats, were standing beside the Jensen staring at the numberplates. The car was some fifty yards from the glass doors and James stepped quickly back inside, still observing the men. One nodded to the other who pulled up the collar of his raincoat and, leaning against the bonnet of the car facing the Jensen, settled back obviously to wait. His companion joined him.

James strolled over to the newspaper kiosk and bought a paper. He stood, paper in hand, staring at the headlines. Vaguely he noted something about another strike at British Leyland. But his mind was not on the newspaper. The two men outside were obviously looking for him. They were strangers but with the manner and appearance of plain-clothed policemen. And waiting for him as they obviously were they had cut off his avenue of retreat. There was no way he could get to his car without being intercepted.

Then the thought came to him, why am I worried? The body was no longer in the boot, he was a private citizen driving towards his home in London. If they attempted to detain him they would have to inform him of their reasons for doing so. That might be enlightening.

He folded the newspaper under his arm and strode purposefully through the glass doors. He approached the Jensen, his eyes straight ahead but aware that he was being watched by the two men.

It was only when he reached for his key to unlock the car door that they came over to him.

'Excuse me, sir, but is this your car?' The taller of the two men spoke.

'If it isn't, I'm not a very good car thief.' The attempt at humour he knew was feeble but he seemed to carry it off with a lightness of manner which pleased him. Any sign of inner tension he reckoned he had effectively disguised.

'Why do you want to know?' he continued, forcing a smile.

'We're police officers and we'd like to have a look inside the car.'

James felt irritation rise within him. No explanations, just a forceful request.

He decided to be awkward. 'I think you've had a good look at it already.'

The tall man persisted. 'If you would let us have your key ... '

'But how do I know you are police officers?'

The two men looked at each other and the tall man reached into an inside pocket and produced a card.

'My warrant card.'

James peered at the card. Detective Sergeant Hazeldine. He looked up at Hazeldine who allowed his face momentarily to relax into what passed for a smile.

'Your key, sir?'

'All right, I accept you are police officers. But I would like to know why you wish to search my car. And shouldn't you have a search warrant?'

'We have had orders to search a Jensen with this registration number.'

So you don't intend to give any grounds, James thought. Well, I can be as determined as you.

'I think I'm entitled to know why.'

'Information received.'

'What information? Received from whom?'

'I don't have to tell you that, sir.'

It was James's turn to force a smile. 'Then I don't think I have to let you search my car.'

The smaller man stepped forward. 'You'd be well advised to do so. Otherwise . . . ' he shrugged.

'You'll arrest me? On what charge? I'm not accustomed to having the police stop me for no reason.'

The small man scowled at him. 'We are entitled to detain anyone we consider acting in suspicious circumstances.'

'Getting into my car to drive home hardly qualifies for the description, suspicious circumstances.'

The tall man took over again. He was obviously playing the sympathetic part.

'Look, sir, we haven't said you're acting suspiciously. But we do feel any honest law-abiding citizen might help us by co-operating.'

'I would co-operate. If I knew why and for what reason,' James replied, beginning to enjoy himself.

'Sir, we are given an order to carry out. We're not ourselves always party to the reasons for that order.'

James tried a different tack. 'Did Superintendent Beddoes send you?'

The men looked at each other and either they were genuinely puzzled or very good actors.

'Don't know a Superintendent Beddoes,' Hazeldine said.

'Chester CID.'

'We're not from Chester, sir. We're from Scotland Yard.'

James was surprised. 'A little out of your territory, aren't you?'

'We don't just operate in the Metropolitan area,' Hazeldine explained, a tone of exasperation creeping into his voice. 'Now, sir, we would like you to be helpful. We could ask you to come along to the local police station but at this stage, we'd rather not.'

'If you ask me to do that I should refuse,' James stated firmly. 'Unless you intend to arrest me?'

The smaller of the two spoke again. 'We could do that, sir.'

'And I would then instruct my solicitor to sue for false arrest.'

Hazeldine shuffled his feet. 'We can't tell you any more, sir, than that we have instructions to search this car. You're perfectly right that we might have to obtain a legal document. But if you insist on that and on driving off you will be stopped again by other officers who will have obtained the right to search your property, that is the car. Now if you have nothing to hide you'll save the police and yourself some considerable time by giving us your car keys just now.'

James was almost amused at Hazeldine's precise tone and his careful choice of words. He decided now was the time to capitulate. He threw the detective sergeant the keys. Hazeldine caught them expertly but could not conceal his expression of surprise at James giving in so abruptly.

He handed the keys to his companion who at once walked to the boot and unlocked it. He stared in and frowned. Hazeldine joined him and aped his frown. Hazeldine lifted the rubber mat, peered into the interior and then let the mat drop back into place.

'What did you expect to find?' James asked lightly. 'A body? Or a bag of heroin?'

Hazeldine looked up at him, a cold look. His companion closed the boot, walked around to the off-side door of the car and unlocked it. He peered inside, stared for a moment into the rear of the car and then withdrew, locking the door again. He looked across at Hazeldine and shrugged.

'I only smuggle heroin on Fridays and bodies on Wednesdays,' James continued flippantly.

The small man handed James back his keys.

'Thank you, sir,' said Hazeldine. 'That wasn't as bad as going to the dentist, was it?'

The man's attempt at humour reassured James. It was on a level with his own endeavours.

'Now will you tell me why?' he enquired.

'Told you. Information received.'

'Not very accurate information.'

'No, sir. Not unless you knew we were coming.' Hazeldine smiled without humour and nodded to the small man.

They walked away from the Jensen without looking back. They climbed into a rather dirty Ford Cortina and drove off, heading south. James let them go before starting up the Jensen and by the time he had reached the motorway there was no sign of the Cortina.

Why had they searched his car? Obviously they had been ordered to do so and equally obviously whoever had given the order had expected to find Skinner's body in the boot. Information received? From whom? Again too many unanswerable questions.

Two hours later James drove into the underground car park below the block of flats in which he lived. There was a porter who lived on the premises and was on duty during the day, a rotund little man called Aston, an ex-sergeant in the regular army. He was still in the foyer of the building when James walked up from the car park.

'Thought you were away for a fortnight, Mr Ryder?'

'A slight change of plan, Aston. I may go off later. Something came up.'

It was a classic understatement. He wondered how Aston would have reacted if he had told him of all that had happened. The small ex-soldier was a taciturn man. He would probably have shrugged and said, 'These things happen.'

James walked to the elevator. He lived in one of the larger flats on the third floor.

'Oh, by the way, Mr Ryder, two gentlemen called to see you this afternoon,' Aston said. 'Told them you were away.'

'Did they leave any message?'

'Nothing. Just shrugged and went out.' Aston's brow furrowed. 'They hung around, mind you. Sat in a car across the road for some time. If you don't mind me saying so I can always spot them. The busies, I mean. You haven't had any trouble, have you, Mr Ryder?'

'I'll tell you about it sometime, Aston,' James replied, stepping into the lift. Could it have been Hazeldine and his companion? They would possibly have had time to reach the motorway café. But no, he thought, they'd have no certainty that's where he'd be. Probably colleagues of theirs. Or the others. If there were others. And who where they?

The moment he unlocked the door of his flat he knew something had happened. There was nothing obvious he

64

could see as he surveyed the lounge. It was simply that everything was not quite as he had left it. A chair in front of his
desk had been moved fractionally. One drawer of the desk
was minutely open and he knew he had left it firmly shut.
Ornaments had been moved very slightly and furniture too
seemed not to be in the precise spot in which he had left it.

It was the same in the other rooms. A door ajar that he
knew he had shut, a cupboard again slightly open. Even his
bed although still neatly made up had been moved, the bed
linen disturbed, and remade.

His flat had been thoroughly and expertly searched, and a
careful attempt made to conceal the search.

4

He slept.

This time he slept without dreams. Exhaustion took over.
Without bothering to unpack, he undressed and crawled
between cold sheets. When next he opened his eyes it was
morning.

Beyond the windows of the flat it was a grey day, a low
unbroken cloud level dimming the city. He rang down to
Aston and asked if the porter would be good enough to buy
him several morning papers. Ten minutes later Aston
delivered them with a cheerful smile, the one bright spot in
the morning.

While making himself coffee James prowled the flat
assuring himself that the intruders of the previous day had
stolen nothing. Once reassured he could only presume they
were searching for some evidence of contact with Nora
Matheson. Obviously they didn't believe in the casual
meeting two days before.

Despite the fact that nothing had been stolen the knowledge that the flat had been searched now produced in James an unpleasant sensation, the kind most people experience after a burglary; as if there had been a violation of privacy, an assault on one's life that was almost obscene.

Putting the thought from him, James settled at the small kitchenette table with a large mug of coffee and went through the newspapers. There was no mention in any of them of the discovery of a body in a ditch in the Midlands. Not that he could presume that to be indicative of anything other than the fact that the body had not yet been discovered. He found himself reading the news stories in each paper, a deliberate evasion of his intention to follow up the disappearance of Nora.

The news stories themselves were bleak and depressing. The British Leyland strike was spreading, steel workers in Wales were threatening to walk out, and the government was not simply helpless to do anything but actually seemed to have little interest in taking any action. The Prime Minister seemed more concerned with agreeing with the President of the United States that the Red Menace was spreading. New developments in nuclear missiles were hailed as further sureties for peace. The great powers could now blow up the planet fifteen times over. James found himself filled with anger at the stupidities of those in power.

He was further inflamed by a feature in *The Times* which pointed out that in the event of nuclear holocaust the government had created for itself the most advanced deep shelters and would survive to emerge and benevolently put the world together again. It was, James thought, a new moral principle; the captain and crew of the ship saved themselves at the expense of the passengers. His anger increased. He cast the newspapers aside.

Action. This was necessary. Action to find Nora. The telephone book provided the number of *The Sunday Times* and after some moments of argument with an anonymous female voice he was finally put through to the features editor.

The voice was cold, hard-edged, with an Oxbridge arrogance. 'Miss Matheson is not in London at present.'

'I'm aware of that,' James replied. 'But I am a good friend and I'm trying to contact her urgently.'

'Of course you realise we don't give out private addresses of staff. But even if we did you'd find she's not at home. Actually she's in Paris.'

James paused before responding. It was necessary to utilise any kind of dramatic effect.

'But she's not in Paris. I last saw her in Chester the day before yesterday.'

This time the pause came from the other end of the line. James was sure he heard a distinct intake of breath immediately after he spoke. Then the silence.

Finally it was broken. 'Who am I speaking to?' demanded the features editor.

'I told you, I'm a friend of Miss Matheson.'

'And I've just told you she's in Paris.'

'And your information is incorrect.'

Another brief silence.

'Look, would you like to come in and see me, Mister . . . eh . . . ?'

'Possibly. Who do I ask for?'

'Grady. Richard Grady, features editor. I think we should have a talk. Now, your name is . . . ?'

James hesitated again. Should he trust the man who was Nora's boss, a man who should know what story she was working on? Grady after all was insisting Nora was in Paris and presumably had already done so to the police in Chester. Was he covering for the police, or was he covering for Nora? James decided it was better not to take chances.

'My name isn't important,' James finally replied. 'But I may call in and see you. I just may do that.'

James replaced the receiver. He felt pleased with himself. He had given away nothing and, by the nervous manner of Grady's request that he come in and see him, James sensed Grady had betrayed himself, perhaps revealed a crack in the facade. If Nora really had been in Paris, why should Grady feel the need to talk to James? Something was not as it should be. He smiled wearily to himself. God knows, nothing seemed to be as it should be, not for the last two days.

67

Again he turned to the telephone book. Mansfield, Ronald B. Mansfield. The address was in a small village in Kent about twenty miles south of London. He stared at the entry in the telephone book, trying to remember what he knew of Ronald Mansfield. An occasional feature writer in the more intelligent national newspapers, Mansfield was something of an expert on matters of international espionage; but he was more than that in the literary world. James had read at least two historical commentaries by Mansfield and knew from various critical articles the man had a reputation as a maverick historian. The first of his books James had bought claimed that certain international banking institutions in the City of London had financed Hitler's rise in the early thirties. Of course many elements in the United Kingdom had backed Hitler at the beginning, hoping the dictator would provide a bulwark against Russia. But Mansfield had named names and alleged that the support had continued up until 1939 and even beyond. He had incurred at least three libel suits out of that one book alone. A later book on international arms manufacturers had pointed out that even during the war these manufacturers had maintained contact with Germany through Switzerland and continued to aid the Nazi armaments drive well into the early forties. Again libel suits had ensued.

Mansfield's newest book had added to the libel suits by accusing and purporting to prove a famous general had lost a minor battle of the war through personal cowardice. The man was a literary swashbuckler, a distinct character.

James dialled his number. The voice at the other end of the line was brisk, businesslike, a gruff bass tone demanding to know the nature of the call.

'My name is Ryder, Mr Mansfield. James Ryder . . . '

'Never heard of you!'

'I appreciate that. I would like to see you.'

'So would a great many people. I am much in demand. But I will say right now that I have given up buying whatever you are presumably selling. Indeed I've given up buying everything. I am self-sufficient. I need no one and no thing. So good day – '

'Nora Matheson suggested I see you,' James ventured quickly, aware that Mansfield was about to hang up on him. There was a short silence. This was terminated by a sigh.

'You're a friend of Nora's?'

'I am.'

'She's a dear and lovely lady and will appreciate that I am very busy, Mister . . . what did you say your name was?'

'James Ryder. And Nora is missing.'

'What do you mean, missing?'

'She has disappeared. I'm trying to find her. You may be able to help me.'

Mansfield coughed, a deep hacking cough, that of a confirmed smoker. 'If you are one of Nora's boy friends, it may not have occurred to your ego that she may have thrown you over. She's a very independent lady and might well disappear should your personal appeal wane on her.'

James smiled to himself. 'My personal appeal has nothing to do with this. Nora was working on a story which seems to have turned ugly.'

'Don't they all? The sum of activities of the entire human race today adds up to a mountain of ordure. The readers of all newspapers seem to be inordinately interested in that very mountain.'

'You may be right. Anyway Nora left some notes with me and I'm going through them trying to find out what happened to her. In the notes she says she intended to consult you. Actually you and Chapman Pincher.'

Mansfield made a noise at the other end of the line. 'I trust my name was above Mr Pincher's?'

'Can I see you, Mr Mansfield?'

'I confess to being intrigued. And I am fond of Nora. She is a small light in the over-powering darkness. Are you a journalist Mr . . . Ryder?'

'I'm an antique dealer.'

'Really? How quaint. You may come and see me provided you don't attempt to sell me ancient artifacts. I have enough ancient artifacts of my own.'

'I could be with you in about an hour.'

'I shall expect you. The candle will be burning in the

69

window.'

It was nearly midday by the times James reached the pleasant Kentish village. Mansfield's cottage was at the edge of the village, set some way back from the road. It was a long, low building with a picturesque thatched roof and mullioned windows, a meticulously neat reconstruction of the ideal old English dwelling place. Its very quaintness concealed the central-heating devices and other mechanical attributes of modern living. A large notice was prominently disaplayed on the garden gate.

NO HAWKERS, NO SALESMEN. NO APPOINTMENT, GOD HELP YOU!

The front door was opened by a maid, a tiny girl dressed in what was considered the uniform of her service in the twenties and thirties; a white apron, stiffly starched, a white collar and a white cap. She ushered James into a comfortable, low-ceilinged room, ancient beams strapping the roof. The furnishings were expensive, deep armchairs drenched in chintz. Two walls of the room were lined with books and an open fire burned away in a large fireplace set deep in the third wall.

Mansfield rose from the depths of chintz, a large man, broad-shouldered, with a round, moonlike face and deep-set shining eyes, like two old sixpences. He was dressed in a thick pullover and expensive dark blue corduroy trousers. James estimated he was in his late fifties.

'Come in!' Mansfield said expansively. 'Welcome to my little nest. It may look like a scene from an Agatha Christie novel but I like it that way. I call it comfortable, old English camp. Do sit down. I hope the room isn't too warm for you but I love heat. The orchidacious temperament.'

James acknowledged the greeting with a firm handshake. The room was more than warm, it was excessively hot and he began to perspire freely.

'Do take off your jacket, my dear man,' Mansfield went on. 'Can I offer you a drink or would you prefer tea?'

'Tea would be fine.'

Mansfield pressed a bell and the maid flitted in, received her orders and flitted out again. James found himself sinking into the chintz-covered chair facing Mansfield.

70

'Tell me about it, then,' his host directed with a wave of a large hand.

James told him of everything but the discovery and the disposal of the body in the car. He didn't feel at this stage it would be wise to involve the large man in what might be considered a degree of criminal activity on his own part.

Mansfield was fascinated by the attitude of the Chester police. 'They seemed to think you were trying to hoax them in some way,' he said with a wry smile.

'They did. And I found that most frustrating.'

'Then why did you not produce Nora's briefcase?'

It was the obvious question. And James had no obvious answer.

'At first I had forgotten about it,' he explained. 'Then, in view of their attitude, I somehow felt I could help Nora by examining its contents myself. Perhaps it was foolish but – '

Mansfield cut in. 'No, no, I do understand. Officialdom can be so obtuse at times. Or appear to be. Yes, they may have assumed an obtuse stance to discourage you from going further. One would suspect that they were receiving orders from the man who followed you and attacked you.'

'They were certainly friendly with him.'

'Which would indicate he was in some sense able to instruct them. Or they, him. The police are so unimaginative considering their profession. I've always thought a really good policeman should have the imagination of a poet or novelist. The ability to conceive great mysteries and fantastic explanations for them. They might then arrive at the truth quicker. However let's turn to Nora's notes.'

James told him of the jottings in the notebook. Mansfield considered them one by one.

'Roy Skinner? Means nothing to me' Mansfield shrugged. 'From his age one would say a minor civil servant who seems to have uncovered something. Or then again it could simply be a personal grievance. Works for the Home Office? Nothing there.'

At that moment the maid re-entered with a large tea tray. Mansfield poured two cups in silence and handed one to James.

For some moments he sat sipping his tea and staring at James. When he did finally break the silence it was with a frown and a shaking of his head.

'It's Skinner's second phone call that brings us into an interesting if dangerous area.'

'Dangerous?' James sounded what he considered to be the right note of naivety. To himself he could say he was aware of dangerous areas. Skinner must have known briefly before he died exactly how dangerous these could be.

'He suggested that Nora should check on what happened to a man called Harrington,' Mansfield continue. 'That too means nothing to me. But one should check. Then you say Skinner told her it . . . whatever it is . . . started when the Rear Admiral died and Carteret retired. And he mentioned the *Section*. Now I am in an area with which I can claim a passing acquaintance. The Rear Admiral, for instance.'

'Nora named a Rear Admiral Sir Arthur Morris who did die.'

Mansfield again waved a plump hand. 'I know about Morris and the Section. And the other name, Carteret?'

'Carteret.'

'I knew him quite well at one time. Old Carteret. I wonder if he's still alive.'

Again a silence as if Mansfield, ruminating, were considering how much he could say to James.

'You *are* an antique dealer, Mr Ryder?' Mansfield suddenly asked.

'I've told you . . . '

Staring at James fixedly, Mansfield seemed to be reassuring himself of his visitor's veracity.

'You could be some kind of *agent provocateur*.'

'I assure you . . . '

'Oh, I don't believe you are.' Mansfield shifted awkwardly in his chair. 'But I have at times irritated what, for want of a better word, we sometimes call the Establishment. It exists, make no mistake. Not quite as cohesive a body as the Mafia. More a fragmented collection of individuals who possess power. I have at times in my career upset some of the fragments of our Establishment and I wouldn't put it past them to try and compromise me. However, in your case I believe you are genuine.'

James couldn't resist an edge of sarcasm in his response. 'Thank you for that. I should be more reassured by your confidence if I knew what you were talking about.'

Mansfield smiled crookedly. 'But that's why you've come to see me, isn't it? To learn what our friend Nora was investigating. And I can give you some help. Bring a little light into murky corners. But as regards the main story, the subject of Mr Skinner's concern, I haven't a clue about that. I only wish I had. And I'm tempted to join in your search. But I can tell you something of the area in which Nora seemed to have been involving herself. A rather fraught area. For the journalist, an area filled with D notices. For the civil servant, one bound by the Official Secrets Act.'

'Please go on.'

'Of course I've always thought the Official Secrets Act is quite idiotic. Our politicians and civil servants know all our secrets that are worth knowing and so does the KGB. So who are we hiding them from? That much abused mass, the British public. More tea?'

James refused impatiently. Mansfield was obviously enjoying himself but his enjoyment did not allay James's curiosity.

'Still, let's talk about details,' Mansfield went on as if sensing his guest's impatience. 'The Section! I believe the full title is Intelligence Co-ordination Section. ICS. It was formed comparatively recently ... in fact just after Burgess and MacLean defected. The old wartime SIS had been replaced by MI5 for counter-espionage activities in this country and by MI6 for our own overseas intelligence work. MI5 of course had the help of the Special Branch in seeking out the enemies in our midst. But of course they had not been very successful. Burgess and Maclean got to Moscow, followed in due course by Philby. And this was in the sixties – before Blunt was revealed ... and allowed to get away with his little treacheries. But before Burgess and Maclean there had been the shock of treason committed by Pontocorvo and Fuchs ... you will know what I'm talking about ... ?'

'Even antique dealers do read newspapers.'

Again a smile from Mansfield. 'Much of the news is so antique anyway. However the Prime Minister at the time ... that clever little mouse, Clem Attlee, decided that MI5 and MI6 needed keeping an eye on. So he formed the Intelligence Co-ordination Section ... which became known simply as the Section. A man called Carfrae, a rather outré Scot, formed the Section to keep a weather eye on the other intelligence branches. Carfrae was a middle-aged member of the Labour Party ... the type that is more conservative than the Tories and more patriotic. He was completely trustworthy ... hated Communists ... so he was ideal. But after some years Carfrae retired and his place was taken by a typical service type who was ideal for this kind of work. I think he came from Naval Intelligence. Rear Admiral Arthur Morris. Did rather well and after a few years got his K.'

'His K?'

'K.B.E. Sir Arthur. Undoubtedly the gentleman referred to in Nora's notes. Morris was good at his job. Very good. Trusted by Prime Ministers. Kept the Section's existence out of the Press. Oh, journalists got wind of the Section but they were never able to write much about it. Damn good security and D notices. But Morris did more than keep the Section out of the Press. He created out of what had been a body meant merely to keep an eye on the other services, his own intelligence service. The Section became, I believe, more powerful than the Military Intelligences. For example MI6 usually has one or two men attached to our embassies abroad. But the Section has one man attached to each embassy and he has authority over the MI6 men. It is also believed that the Section was responsible for the creation of GCHQ.'

James frowned. He was increasingly beginning to feel he was out of his depth. 'What is GCHQ?'

'Government Communications Headquarters. In Cheltenham. It is the heart of British communications intelligence. Listening stations all over the world. It employs probably around twenty thousand people,' Mansfield sighed. 'Imagine all these little people, bound by the Official Secrets Act, sitting in little cubicles in two large buildings in Cheltenham, listening to friends and enemies, decoding, analysing, translating. Like bees storing information on everything. They have a giant computer that stores a world of knowledge. All this encouraged as it was by Sir Arthur Morris. And all the information available to the Section and to the other intelligence services. Anyway that is the Section.'

'Nora would know it existed?' James asked.

'Oh, yes, but what stimulated Nora to go chasing her Mr Skinner? That is what we should know.'

'And Harrington's name means nothing to you?'

Mansfield shook his head. 'Nothing. Nora mentioned he was killed and he was a civil servant. He could have been working for the Section. They keep their operatives' names very secret. Apart from Morris . . . and . . . yes . . . another . . . ?'

'Nora says Skinner claimed to be a civil servant. So he could have been working for this . . . this Section?' James pressed on.

'Indeed he could. We'd have difficulty finding out. The Civil Service lists never specify that anyone is working for intelligence. They merely list them as part of the Home or Foreign offices or the Ministry of Defence. Another interesting fact. We know that MI5 has its headquarters in Curzon Street and has five or six other offices in London. We know too that the administrative centre of MI6 is Century House. But old Morris was very clever. We haven't the foggiest notion where the Section operates from.'

'You say Morris died some months ago. Who took his place?'

'My dear Ryder, I haven't the foggiest idea,' Mansfield replied with an expressive tremor of his shoulders. 'Oh, eventually a name will come out. But Morris's successor is lying very low just now. Of course a few years ago I could have told you at once. That would have been the other name on your list. Carteret.'

'Was he in the Section?'

'Carteret was the Rear Admiral's right-hand man.'

'What happened to him? Another sudden death?'

75

Mansfield shook his head. 'Retired, honourably. He was an old intelligence hand was Mr Carteret. Clever sod. Worked for SIS during the war. Then went over to MI6. When Morris took over the Section from Carfrae he asked for Carteret as his second in command. Carteret was bloody marvellous. They say he was the first man to spot Philby was working for Moscow Centre. And Philby was very afraid of him.'

'How do you know all this?'

'It was my job to know at one time,' Mansfield's smile broadened. 'I did a little work for the SIS during the war. Oh, I was very young and thought espionage was very romantic . . . '

Suddenly the smile disappeared and Mansfield was staring into the fire, his eyes cold. He lifted his right hand and brushed it over his brow. James noticed the hand trembled slightly.

'Yes, very romantic,' the older man went on. 'Until a good friend of mine was . . . discovered by the Gestapo. I had to identify the body. It was lying in a cellar in a certain building in Paris. In a filthy, ugly little cellar, the walls splashed with old dried blood. Of course the Gestapo had made my friend tell them what they wanted to know. After torture. Then they left him to die. Which he duly did. As I said, I was young and the shock unnerved me. Another intelligence officer came in just after my identification. He was a very kind man. He arranged for me to be taken out of that theatre. Theatre of war, you understand. More than that. He got me out of the service. You see, when the Gestapo did what they did to my friend, they got rid of two agents. I was useless after that. The other officer, the one who got me out, was Carteret.'

'Yes, I see.'

'Do you, Mr Ryder? I wonder if anyone can understand what happened to many people in the war.' Mansfield sighed, produced from a trouser pocket a gold cigarette case and offered James a cigarette. James took it and after they lit up, sat back waiting for Mansfield to continue.

'When I was out of the service, I became a scholar. I like the word, scholar. Better than student. Read history and did a bit of journalism while I wrote ... wrote my more popular works. Because the word leaked out that I'd done some intelligence work I became an *authority*. The press are always looking for authorities. Of course in recent years I've been fortunate enough to earn a comfortable living from the books.'

He stopped speaking for a moment, looked up at James with a vague expression on his face. 'What were we talking about? Not my dull life story?'

'Carteret. And how you know all about the Section.'

'Yes, of course. Well, after my wartime exploits I used to bump into old Carteret. And there were times I became quite useful to him. Sometimes it suits these intelligence boys to have something in the press. A small paragraph, a planned leakage of information. Carteret used me. Until a few years ago when he retired. I admired him even on his manner of going too. He must have been offered at least a CBE if not his "K". Turned it down. I asked him about it in the Garrick one night. Oh, he was very self-effacing. Said if he had been offered anything he wouldn't have taken it. Simply did a job which he got paid for. And it was a job in which people died now and then. He genuinely didn't feel he should accept honours for deaths. I liked him for that.'

'And is he still alive?' James asked.

'Haven't an idea. Never read the obituaries in *The Times*. Always afraid I'll read my own name,' Mansfield replied. 'Anyway that's all I can tell you about Nora's little jottings. But I tell you what I will do. I'll ask around. Discreetly. It'll have to be discreet. Because if she has disappeared then the matter could be serious. The Section doesn't play games and neither does Moscow. Whatever Skinner wanted to tell her Moscow will want to know. And the Section will want to know.'

He doesn't know about Skinner's death, James thought. I've avoided telling him and perhaps I was wrong to do so. Of course if Mansfield was told he might stay out of the affair. Or he might go in deeper. The latter course would naturally help. But if the writer was going to ask around it might be better that he did not know what had happened to Skinner.

James rose, feeling he had learned all he could learn. Mansfield stood up and they shook hands.

'As I said, I like Nora, and I'd hate to see the girl get into trouble. So I will make enquiries. But I think you, Mr Ryder, should keep out of it. This kind of thing is not a game for amateurs.'

James responded at once. 'I want to keep out of it. As long as Nora is all right.'

'Give me your phone number. I'll contact you this evening. A few well-chosen words in the right ears pointing out that the press cannot be trifled with. These people don't like the press and they don't like falling foul of the press. Normally they'll bend over backwards not to step on our toes. That is unless . . .'

Mansfield left the sentence hanging in the air for some seconds. Finally James asked the question he was waiting for.

'Unless what?'

'Well, of course if Nora has fallen foul of the other side . . . you understand . . . our red friends, then there may be problems. But it doesn't sound like their form. More likely Nora's stumbled on something our own people don't want publicised and they've taken rather extreme action to shut her up.'

How extreme, James asked himself, again thinking of Skinner's body.

'They're not above putting people quietly away for a few days' incarceration to convince them they shouldn't be so inquisitive. Oh, it happens,' Mansfield was going on with a show of reassurance. 'They forget a D notice might be just as effective.'

Not quite as effective as Skinner's dead eyes staring sightlessly out of the boot of the car.

Mansfield stood up, indicating the meeting had reached its natural termination. They shook hands and James found himself skilfully ushered to the door of the cottage.

'I wouldn't worry too much, Mr Ryder. I may not know very much about the Section but I have a fairly good relationship with its masters. And that reaches as high as the Home Secretary. I'll have a word in a few influential ears.'

78

James drove away from the cottage with a certain sense of relief. Despite the memory of Skinner's death and the placing of the body in his car, he felt he had off-loaded part of his concern on more knowledgeable shoulders. Mansfield knew the world of espionage or at least assumed an attitude of confidence regarding that world. And he knew people who mattered. Nevertheless James couldn't help feeling he should have told Mansfield about Skinner.

He had travelled about ten miles towards London when he became aware of the car following him. A nondescript Ford Cortina it kept up with the Jensen with surprising ease, keeping a steady hundred to a hundred and fifty yards behind him. When he accelerated, the Cortina accelerated. When he slowed down before coming onto the M20, the Cortina slowed down.

As he reached the outskirts of London James had a desire to see the faces of his followers. It would not have surprised him if the same two policemen who had searched his car the day before were in the Cortina. He turned off a main roadway and drove slowly up a side street. Then quickly he pulled the Jensen into the kerb and brought it to a halt.

The Cortina turned into the side street and slowed down momentarily as the driver realised he could no longer see the Jensen in the road in front of him. He crawled along the street and drew level with the parked Jensen.

James found himself staring into a strange face whose owner reacted on seeing him, turning away to speak to the driver. Then the Cortina speeded up and disappeared around the corner at the end of the street.

Lighting a cigarette, James relaxed for some minutes. Whoever they were, the people in the Cortina had been trailing him. Now they knew he had spotted them, would they continue to follow him? And who were they and what did they want?

James started up the engine of the Jensen and drove along the street. Turning at the intersection at the end of the street he speeded up, alert for the Cortina. There was no sign of it.

Taking a different route through South London James decided to call in at his shop. Off Bond Street, it was in a fashionable and expensive area. Nevertheless it had achieved a certain reputation among collectors and other dealers as being well run, honest in its dealings and expensive enough to attract a good clientèle. And Anthony Cromer, although he hadn't the finesse James prided himself on having, was a good assistant, trustworthy and well able to handle the business for two or three weeks. And the two girls who worked for him were well educated and as honest as Anthony.

Presently James found himself driving through Brixton. The back streets he cut through were carved out of poverty and frustration and he could only find himself surprised at the gleeming cheerfulness of black and white faces that lived in such urban desolation. He drove past a gutted public house, a blackened shell, a ragged reminder of recent riots in the district.

Nearing Westminster Bridge James glanced again in his rearview mirror. And again the black Cortina was not far behind him. Was it the same car? He decided to find out. Swinging away from the river he headed towards Battersea and south-west London. The Cortina stayed on his tail.

Forced to stop every now and then at traffic lights James lost sight of the Cortina. For some distance he thought he had shaken it off until it appeared from behind a large pantechnicon. A few moments later the road ahead cleared and James, ignoring the speed limit, pressed his foot down on the accelerator. The Cortina dutifully increased its speed. There was no longer any pretence at not following him.

Eventually a street sign indicated Hammersmith Bridge and James veered again towards the river. The Cortina was closer now, obviously intent on not losing him. Perhaps they were surprised he was not driving towards South Kensington and his flat; more than that, curious as to where he was heading. It occurred to him now that they must have followed him to Mansfield's cottage and would know whom he had been visiting. He had possibly put Mansfield in some jeopardy. The thought troubled him and he put it from his mind. Mansfield was almost certainly better able to cope in such circumstances than James Ryder.

He drove across Hammersmith Bridge. The traffic was light now, the mid-afternoon calm before the rush hour. Taking an access road James steered onto the flyover. The Cortina followed, close now. Indeed it seemed so close that in the mirror he imagined he could almost make out the faces of the driver and his companion. The companion looked like the man he had seen in the Brixton street. So it was the same Cortina.

Ahead of him now James saw a clear ribbon of motorway flyover heading away from Hammersmith, bisecting Chiswick. He increased speed with a slight, cool smile. Despite a possible risk to the rear of the Jensen he had determined to give his pursuers a small shock. The speedometer arm rose in front of him and behind he noted the Cortina increasing its speed to match his own.

Then gently he eased his foot up from the pedal and the Jensen almost imperceptibly lost speed. This brought the Cortina right onto his tail, only a few feet separating the speeding cars. They were now on a high section of the flyover, the first-floor windows of small red brick houses speeding by on the left.

It had started to rain as he came over Hammersmith Bridge and had settled now into a thin regular drizzle which laid a damp shiny mirror on the surface of the road.

Now, James decided, was the time to give the occupants of the Cortina their small sharp shock.

Taking his foot completely off the accelerator pedal, he slammed the gear lever from fourth down to second gear. The Jensen's engine shrieked its protest as the car's speed dropped rapidly.

James's intention was either to force the Cortina to cut its speed as drastically as he had done or force the driver to steer the car onto the outer lane and draw level with the Jensen. At this point James knew he could accelerate much faster than the Cortina and shoot ahead, taking the first access road off the motorway. There was, of course, a small chance that the Cortina would ram the back of the Jensen but he reckoned the driver should have enough experience to avert such a collision.

Too late James realised that both he and the Cortina's driver had made a miscalculation.

The man behind the wheel of the Cortina, realising James had slowed down violently, applied his brakes and at the same time swerved into the outer lane to avoid the threatened collision. What he did not see was the lorry coming up fast behind him on the outer lane.

The side of the Cortina just above the front wheel hit the offside wheel of the lorry mashing the metal bodywork into the wheel. Instantly the wheel locked and the Cortina skidded on the wet tarmac. The lorry, heavy and laden, took the blow with a shudder but by its sheer weight and the strength of the driver's hands on the steering wheel continued forward.

The impetus of the blow dealt to the Cortina and the locking of its front wheel caused the rear of the car to rise up as it went into the skid. It spun sideways towards the metal barrier at the edge of the flyover but before it actually came in contact, the rear of the car was over the barrier.

James glimped in his mirror only something of what had happened. The Jensen had maintained enough speed to keep ahead of the collision but, just as he shot ahead again he saw the Cortina rise and come down, its rear over the barrier.

The barrier concertinaed with the weight of the car and the impetus of the skid propelled the Cortina over the edge of the flyover. It fell backwards through space into the window and wall of a small detached two-storey villa. The wall shattered spraying red bricks into the air as the car crashed down, metalwork twisting and tearing, the underside of the car buckling inwards.

A sheet of flame, possibly from a fractured gasfire within the house, blistered the paintwork of the Cortina and ignited the petrol tank which blew the rear of the car apart with a loud explosion.

James drove on.

5

Driving off the flyover three quarters of a mile further on, James Ryder steered the Jensen into a quiet Chiswick street and brought it to a halt at the kerb. He sat gripping the wheel for some minutes, staring straight ahead. Across the street a woman scrubbing stone steps leading to a front door paused and stared over at him, suspicious of a stranger in a strange car. In front of him a black cat ambled lazily across the road and disappeared behind a hedge.

Slowly James loosed his hands from the steering wheel and gazed at them as they started to tremble. He realised then that he was drenched in perspiration and he tried to relax, sinking back into the soft leather of the Jensen's driving seat.

Was he responsible for the Cortina's disastrous crash? The thought made him feel ill. It seemed unlikely that the two men in the car could have survived the leap over the barrier and the great bubble of flame that had flared up from the side of the villa. He would not acknowledge there was intent in his action in slowing the Jensen to cause a crash, but the driver and his companion must almost certainly have been involved in Skinner's death which, after all, was deliberate murder. He must not allow himself to feel guilt for a situation which he had not created and did not even understand. In all his actions his only aim had been to find Nora Matheson.

Leaning forward he again started the Jensen and, under the quizzical eye of the stair-scrubbing lady, he drove off. Determined to avoid the flyover James was nevertheless compelled by what he could only define as morbid curiosity to move under the shadow of the flyover towards the section where the Cortina had crashed.

The police had already arrived and were erecting signs to divert the traffic. A thick plume of black smoke was rising and drifting above the rooftops and, in the distance, James could hear the sirens and clanging of bells announcing the imminent arrival of fire engines and ambulances.

Following the diversion signs he headed for Hammersmith and the West End. He decided to abandon for the time being his intention of visiting the antique shop. His only wish was to return home as if his flat offered the security of familiarity. He needed that security desperately now. His normal well-regulated life had turned into a nightmare of intrigue and death. He had been projected into this nightmare unknowingly, unwillingly. He had no knowledge of spies and counterspies, nor of the Section, whatever it stood for. And what had Nora Matheson to do with that world except to listen and report on some grievances held by a sad young man who was now dead? Should he, James Ryder, not abdicate his position, leave the search for Nora to Mansfield? The writer at least had the qualifications of past experience to assist him. And Mansfield, thank God, was concerned about Nora, knew her much better than he did. Leave it to Mansfield, that was the sensible course of action.

Yet, even if he wished to do this, how could he tell the protagonists, the people who were following him, who killed Skinner, how could he assure them he wanted out, was no longer concerned?

Parking the car in the underground park below the block of flats, he took the elevator to his floor and unlocked the door of his apartment with a sense of relief. But as he stepped into his sitting room, he became at once aware there was someone else in the flat.

She came out of the bathroom with a puzzled smile on her face.

'You were meant to be in Scotland!' The tones were light but contained a quality of accusation.

Sybil Graham had a slim, willowy figure under fine golden hair. It was the hair which had first attracted James with its soft flowing style. As divorcees they had both been wary of new relationships but their mutual attraction had been strong and their affair had been inevitable. It was only after the first months of enjoying the physical and mental exploration of each other that they had decided there was to be no commitment, no deep entanglement. They would enjoy each other yet maintain their freedom. James had at first doubted whether this understanding would work but six months later it seemed to have succeeded.

'How did you get in?' he asked, kissing her lightly on the cheek.

'Your porter downstairs is in love with me, darling. One look and he let me in with his pass-key. You look ghastly, James. What have you been up to?'

'What makes you think I've been up to anything?'

'You were going away for two weeks.'

James couldn't resist a rather grim smile. 'Things happened,' he said. It was the classic understatement culled from an old W. C. Fields movie. 'Anyway how did you know I was home?'

Sybil hesitated, frowning. She seemed concerned and sat on the edge of the sofa as if to gain time. Finally she spoke. 'Two men came to see me. They were looking for you.'

'Two men?'

'Very proper, very official. I told them you were on holiday. Away for two weeks. But ... but they seemed to think you had changed your plans.'

There was something else. She was edgy, nervous.

'Sybil, they must have told you who they were,' he insisted.

She bit her lip. 'Police officers. Why did they want you, James?'

'I don't know,' James responded a shade too quickly. 'Why didn't they simply come here?'

She shrugged. 'They obviously knew we were friends. They wanted to know all about you. Were you simply in antiques, did you have any other interests? Did you ever write for the newspapers? Of course I asked them what business it was of theirs.'

James poured two large gin and tonics from the bottles on a side table.

'And did they tell you?'

85

'They went very silent and serious,' Sybil pouted. 'Then one of them muttered something about investigating stolen antiques.'

'The bloody liars!'

'I thought so too. And I told them. I also told me if they wanted to know anything about you they should ask you themselves.'

'Good!' James handed her one of the gin and tonics.

'Thank you. I thought I was rather good, considering I didn't have an idea what they were on about.'

'What happened next?'

'Oh, they left. Almost at once. Minute they saw they weren't going to get very far with me. Have they seen you yet?'

'No,' James shrugged, the chilling thought coming to him that the two men in the Cortina might just have been Sybil's visitors. They wouldn't be coming to see him now, that was certain.

'So you must now sit down and tell me all about it,' Sybil demanded, assuming her maternal smile, the one he knew too well and one of the few things about her he found unattractive. He was only too well aware of how she used the smile whenever there was some doubt as to whether or not he would do what she wanted.

James sat down. He felt immeasurably weary.

'I don't think you should know about it,' he replied and then realised he was only increasing her curiosity.

She sighed, an affected sigh. 'Two policemen come to my house asking about you! You come back from a fortnight's holiday after only two days – '

'I changed my plans,' he cut in, trying to stop the flow.

'You look as if you haven't slept for a week – '

'You know that's not true. You slept with me five nights ago.'

'Don't be crude. You appear to be involved in some sordid police matter, and you tell me I shouldn't know about it! Really, James!'

'I'm not sure I know about it myself.'

'Don't start lying! For God's sake, James, we are . . . close.

And when these people come to see me asking stupid questions, I am involved every bit as much as you.'

If only you knew, he thought. Then we'd see how close we were.

'Well?' she demanded.

A long silence. Two people in a room staring at each other. James looked away, taking a sip of his drink. He had already told his story to Mansfield that day. Excluding, of course, the death of Skinner. And since then there had been the horror on the motorway. He couldn't go over it again, nor did he want to. Still less to Sybil. She would be practical, sensible, insist he go to the police. He was sure that was not the solution. It would be like walking into an enormous lion's den; they would be waiting for him, waiting to savage him. Oh, God was he losing his sanity? The thought made him shudder visibly.

She noticed this at once.

'James, you are not well. You must tell me everything!'

The telephone rang. With relief he lifted the receiver.

'James Ryder?'

'Speaking.'

'Mansfield here. I think you should come and see me.'

'You've found out something? What?'

'Not on the telephone. Come down. Something's going on.'

'Look!' James burst out. 'I should tell you – '

The receiver was replaced at the other end of the line. James had intended to tell him about being followed from his cottage back to London. And about the accident. The opportunity was lost for the time being. Just as well with Sybil sitting staring at him. And he could tell Mansfield when he reached the cottage.

'I have to go out,' he informed Sybil as he replaced his own receiver.

'You can't just walk out without telling me what's going on!' Her voice rose, indignation covering something else, a kind of desperation. Why, he asked himself.

'Sorry but I wouldn't take bets on that, Sybil,' he replied moving to the door.

'You have to tell me. Otherwise . . . otherwise I may not be here when you get back.'

What the hell was she so desperate about? He forced a smile. 'It could be better that way.'

She stood up, trembling slightly. 'James, what . . . what happened in Chester?'

He spun around on his heels to face her. Her desperation had caused the mistake.

'What did your visitors tell you, Sybil?'

She stammered now. 'Nothing . . . no, not really. They . . . they suggested I . . . I find out what you were up to. Something to do with Chester – '

'*They* told you! The police asked you to do their job?'

She nodded, dumbly, trembling.

'And you just agreed? No questions? You do what you're told?'

A silent shrug.

'Two strangers say they are policemen, walk in on you, ask you to find out what I am doing and you don't ask one question,' he went on. 'You must be joking. Or lying.'

She half turned away making an ineffectual gesture with her hands. 'I . . . I knew one of them.'

Now it might come out. He pressed on. 'Tell me about that.'

'He's . . . he's just a man I know. Knew him years ago. Before I ever met you.'

'I don't believe in coincidences!'

She looked from side to side, desperation increasing. 'It's true. After my marriage broke up I went out with . . . with this man for a time. Then I met you. By that time I . . . I wasn't seeing much of him.'

'That was a couple of years ago. Now he turns up wanting to know about me. This . . . policeman!'

'Not exactly a policeman. Something . . . something to do with intelligence. Yes.' A pause. 'James, he knows so much about so many people. He always did. Said he was checking on you and . . . and my name came up. He said that was a piece of luck. So . . . so he came to see me. Said I could be useful – '

'And you jumped at the chance?'

'No! He . . . he frightens me.'

'Nice boyfriend.'

'That was another reason I stopped seeing him.'

'Until he turned up?'

She nodded. 'Yesterday. He said your name had come up. A matter of security. Then he was checking your friends and my name was there.' Suddenly she became louder. 'Yes it was a coincidence! But he said he wanted me to find out what you were doing in Chester. He wanted me to bring you to him – '

'Where?'

'Simpson's in Piccadilly. It would be an accidental meeting. There! I'm telling you, James. He said he could clear it all up . . . whatever happened in Chester.'

'That was all he told you?'

'Yes.'

'And you were going to do it? Without telling me?'

'I was afraid. He threatened me. Said if I didn't do what he wanted I could be taken into custody. That's what he said. Custody. But the way he said it – '

'Did he mention a woman called Nora Matheson?'

She shook her head. 'No. No names. Nothing. But he frightens me, James. He was always . . . always a violent man.'

He crossed the room and gripped her by the shoulders. 'This man. His name. Tell me.'

She bit her lip again. 'I don't think – '

'His name, Sybil!'

'You're hurting my shoulder!'

He was aware of the strength of his grip. But he was angry and he had no intention of relaxing it. Her pain didn't trouble him. Skinner had died, two others in a Cortina had almost certainly died. These justified his anger and her pain. And James felt a sense of betrayal as he stared at the woman. Three unpleasant deaths and she was nervous and in discomfort. Didn't matter. Her attitude wasn't good enough. She should have told him about these men at once. She should have been someone he could trust.

'Tell me his name!'

'Buller.'

It didn't mean anything. 'Have I ever met him?'

'Not with me.'

'You say he's in intelligence. What department?'

She tried to pull away. 'I don't know.' the eyes flickered.

'You're a bad liar. I can always tell. Till now it's never been important. Now it is. Where does he work? MI5? MI6? The Section?'

She took a deep breath. 'I heard him . . . once . . . mention the Section. . . .'

He released his grip on her shoulders. She staggered back and started to massage them. She was shivering violently again.

'All right, Sybil, I believe you,' he said. 'Now I'm going. And I don't really expect you to be here when I get back.'

'But . . . what do I tell Buller?'

'Your problem, my dear. Perhaps you should tell him what you should have told him when he called on you yesterday. To go to hell.'

'If he arrests me . . . ?'

'I think he would only have arrested you if I had told you what had happened in Chester. Since you know nothing, you're probably in the clear.'

He turned and went back to the door.

'Please, James,' she said plaintively. 'Will I see you again?'

'Let's see how it all works out,' he replied. 'But I wouldn't count on it.'

He left her standing in the centre of his living room, staring after him.

As he drove out of London he felt a cold anger. Despite death and mysteries, now his personal life was being affected. Up until now, beneath his fears, beneath the horror that was happening to him, there had been the belief that some time it would finish and he would resume his normal life as before. But now fragments of that life were involved, were falling away and a return to normality seemed a remote prospect.

His eyes darted to the rearview mirror. This time there was no sign of any car following him. He tried to relax, lit a cigarette and switched on the car radio, tuning in to a news broadcast.

'Two men were killed this afternoon in an accident on the Chiswick flyover when their car was in collision with a heavy lorry and crashed over the safety barrier into the wall of a private house.' The news reader's voice was flat and unemotional. Of course, he should be, James reckoned. The emotion of horror belonged to him.

The news reader continued: 'The occupants of the house, Mr and Mrs Alexander Slocum narrowly escaped serious injury when both car and house caught fire. The names of the two men killed have not yet been released.' At least he did not have innocent victims nor the names of the two dead men to attach to his conscience. He changed channels until he came upon music.

Three quarters of an hour later he drew up at the kerb outside Mansfield's cottage. Mansfield appeared at the living-room window as James walked up the path. The writer acknowledged his arrival with a brief wave and disappeared from sight.

It happened as James waited in front of the door. At first he could hear Mansfield's footsteps approaching the other side of the door and then suddenly all sound was cut off as if James had been struck deaf, as if he had entered a dead zone. Then the door of the cottage seemed to move outwards in slow motion – brick, wood and mortar from the lintel moving with it. Behind the door a bubble of dust and flame burst forth and with it sound returned, a great rush of air followed by the roar of the explosion. James was thrown backwards, the door grazing his shoulder, and he landed on the trim grass of the lawn, stone and brickwork falling around him.

He lay for a moment, dazed but fully aware of what had happened. Then he struggled to his feet and faced the cottage.

The door and the walls at each side had been ripped apart by the explosion and the interior of the hall was wrecked, part of the dividing wall to the lounge having been blasted away. One of the beams which had strapped the roof was split and sagged downwards above a heap of plaster. And at the side of the plaster lay Mansfield, his head twisted, one side of his face scorched and streaked with blood. Unsteadily James picked his way through the debris and knelt beside Mansfield.

He gripped the older man's wrist. There was no pulse. Somewhere at the back of the house a woman screamed. The maid at least was alive. Backing out of the ruins of the hall James turned and staggered down the path. Climbing into the Jensen he found himself shivering again. Shock. Reaction. He should be hardened now to death. It seemed to be a constant companion. Perhaps in time it would cease to bother him; he would accept it as he accepted the postman on his round, traffic in the street.

In the road in front of him people were appearing, villagers coming from their houses, shaken by the explosion, James tensed himself, started the Jensen and drove slowly through the village as if he had been passing when the explosion had occurred. His driving window was down and he could hear fragments of sentences as he steered along the narrow street.

'Bloody great explosion!'

'Shook all my windows. . . . '

'Gas mains. Has to be gas mains . . . '

'Knew they'd blow . . . always said they would . . . the Mansfield cottage . . . hope nobody bought it.'

Mansfield had bought it. And James was sure it was no gas main.

On the road back to London he caught a glimpse of himself in the mirror. Face streaked with dust. A small cut on his left temple. Looking down at his clothes he saw that his suit was filthy, ripped at one shoulder. He increased speed, only slowing down when he reached the outer suburbs.

The flat was empty now, the only sign of Sybil's presence being the empty gin and tonic glass smudged with lipstick.

James lay on the sofa. Study the ceiling, a safe thing to do. Study the cracks and lie in the torn dirty suit, Skinner's dead eyes merging with Mansfield's scorched dead face. Outside the windows dusk settled on the city. Distant traffic sounds. The ticking of the carriage clock on the mantlepiece.

After a time he poured himself a brandy. Not that he wanted the brandy but it seemed the thing to do. Supposed to make you feel better, warm you. He needed warming. The chill was deep in the bones, in the marrow, at the nerve endings; a painful feeling of ice in his chest and in his head. Night outside now. He had never before worried about the night. It had been a time he enjoyed, anticipated its coming throughout the day. Now the darkness frightened him and the distant neon of the night city only emphasised his fear. And he knew that the return of the day would not change this.

He had omitted to switch on the lights and the room was filled with moving flickering shadows. God, he thought, would the good calm days come back?

Finally he roused himself and switched on the lights. He switched on every light in the house as if brightness would assuage his fear. Stripped of his dust drenched, torn clothes, he ran himself a bath. Surprisingly, as he lay soaking in the comforting warmth of the bath, he felt ravenously hungry. A man who normally had regular if modest eating habits, he realised that the last meal he had eaten had been the previous day. He had survived on coffee, tea and gin today. And now brandy. He felt light-headed as he dressed and the feeling lessened the tension of fear. Whatever happened he was going out for a decent meal. As he donned a pair of slacks, the telephone rang.

New disasters, he thought, further terrors. He lifted the receiver angrily.

'Yes?'

'Am I speaking to Mr James Ryder?' The voice was low, well-modulated, that of an educated man.

'Who's calling?'

'I'm afraid my name will mean nothing to you. Martindale. Derek Martindale. I called at your shop today. They told me you were out of town.'

'Then why are you phoning me?'

'It occurred to me that I might catch you before you left.' Catch him? The operative word. The voice went on: 'I simply took a chance. Apparently I'm lucky.'

James tried to keep the tremor out of his voice. 'I have been out of town,' he replied calmly. 'And will be again shortly. Just now I'm going out and I haven't much time – '

'I am a very keen collector, Mr Ryder. Porcelain. I gather you're an expert. Dresden. I'm interested.'

93

Too pat. The cool reply. 'If you contact my place of business in about two weeks I may be able to help you.' Be businesslike. He may be genuine and there would be a time he would have to get back to normality. Hopefully.

'I'm sorry.' The voice sounded genuinely regretful. 'But I shall be in America in two weeks. I have a fair amount of money to spend and I did want to talk to an expert. I gather too you have the best selection of Meissen in London for sale.'

Glib and calculated. Appeal to the businessman in him. Reply calmly again. 'I have a fair stock but I'm not the only one. You could try Alston's or Maccabees. They're both very good and reliable. Unfortunately I'm just going out for a meal.'

'I don't like to be persistent, Mr Ryder, but I am only in London for a couple of days. If we could meet – '

'My entire stock is in my shop – '

'I appreciate that. But a talk with an expert would be most valuable. You could describe what you have in stock and perhaps I could negotiate and see your assistant tomorrow.'

The man was certainly persistent. Too persistent. But then some collectors were like that. Selfishly absorbed in his collection. Or he could be something else. The memory of Mansfield's body came to him.

Martindale continued. 'Look, you're probably dining with someone but, if you weren't, why not have dinner with me? As my guest. I'm staying at the Savoy. You could bring along a catalogue if you have one handy. And ... and there is a piece I'd like your opinion on. Bought it in Germany last week. Rather special, I think. Of course if you have a previous engagement.... '

He left the sentence hanging in the air. And he had given James the way out. A previous engagement. So easy to plead. And throwing in the bit about the piece he'd bought in Germany. Intriguing. And for James the prospect of a return to sanity, to his work. If the man was genuine. And if he wasn't? If he was connected to the whole business, then he might provide another lead, a way to finding Nora Matheson, provided of course he, James Ryder, kept alert. After all,

94

what could happen to him in the Savoy? And it was time to take a chance.

'It's very good of you, Mr Martindale,' he said. 'I'll be happy to meet you for dinner.'

'Would the Savoy Grill be satisfactory?'

'Fine.'

'Splendid. Shall we say the Grill Room in an hour. Just ask for me.'

The acceptance of the invitation meant a change of clothes. He could not walk into the Savoy Grill in slacks and polo-necked sweater. He changed into a conservative grey suit and dark tie.

As he entered almost exactly an hour later, the Grill Room was quiet, probably because it was actually quite early. On the few previous occasions when he had dined at the Savoy, James had always felt a rather adolescent delight at the historic Grill. He told himself it was a mixture of snobbery and extravagance. Not that he had not dined in more exclusive and more expensive places. But there had been a charm about the Savoy, a slightly ostentatious elegance he had enjoyed. Yet now to James there was a tired faded garishness about the room, as though it were a relic of another time, another place. Certainly the room seemed still elegant, luxurious, impeccable in its small splendour, but it was somehow out of key. Under the surface luxury there was the same feeling of decay that pervaded London. It was all connected. Like that afternoon, when he had noticed the chipped, flawed stonework of the tenements. Under the surface of the entire city the worm was at work.

The *maître d'* was in front of him now, the dark Italian eyes noting with a minute twinge of disapproval the folder under James's arm containing the catalogue he had dug out from the depths of his desk. One should not bring the visible evidence of a business encounter into the Savoy Grill Room. Of course one could discuss business but documents cluttered the table and made the place look untidy.

'Mr Martindale?'

The Italian eyes moved downwards. The body did not bow but the eyes did the work. James was shown across the room and Martindale stood to receive him. A tall man in a beautifully cut Saville Row suit, he was almost certainly in his late forties but looked younger. The give away was the streaks of grey in the hair, the harrowed lines around the eyes and a tight wrinkling of the skin around the throat.

'Mr Ryder! I'm Derek Martindale. I can't thank you enough for coming and I trust the dinner will make up for any inconvenience.'

James muttered a polite reply and sat down, studying the few other occupants of the room as if he might spot someone out of place, another follower. There was no one recognisable as such. Martindale noticed his glance around the room.

'You might run into some friends here perhaps?'

'I don't think so.'

The business of the menus followed, Martindale making suggestions quietly. 'I have a weakness for escargots. But they assure me the smoked salmon is very fresh.'

Snails for Martindale accompanied by smoked salmon for James. Then both settled for filet steaks and Martindale suggested an expensive Burgundy to go with the steaks. James felt himself relaxing.

'I found this piece in a small shop in Bonn. I was there last week on business . . . ' Martindale hesitated feeling the need for further explanation. 'I'm in insurance. International insurance. Quite big stuff. Which is why I live in New York most of the time. The company is American. Of course, I'm a Londoner.'

James smiled. 'And a collector.'

'I have this thing about Dresden. Something so exquisite in a really fine piece. I have a general interest in antiques mostly as a form of investment. But with china, that's something else. I have quite a collection in New York.'

He was going on and on, the enthusiasm becoming tedious. Then as if realising this, he stopped, paused and changed the subject.

'Coming back to London is like coming home.' A nervous laugh. 'Well it is coming home, isn't it?'

At first James was required to say very little. The

occasional nod of assent, the polite acknowledgement of a statement.

'There's something about London, don't you agree? It never changes,' Martindale went on. 'The same charm, the same leisurely pace. At least compared to New York.'

James found then that he had to disagree. 'I'm sorry but I find London changing all the time. And not for the best. It's like a machine running down.'

Martindale stared at him in silence for a moment. 'You find that, do you? And, of course, you're living here all the time. Which I am not. Not now. You may be right though. I wouldn't just apply it to London though. The whole of Western Europe is like your machine running down.'

'I only pay occasional visits abroad.'

'Then you might not see it. But it's there. As if people no longer had any interest in their country. France, Germany, Italy . . . especially Italy. Something rotten happening. You read about it every day. Terrorism. Gangsterism. The young . . . turning to anarchy, to violence. Like a disease. Yes, I'm prepared to believe London is the same.'

'It is, I assure you,' James replied, appreciating his own irony.

'No discipline any more,' Martindale continued. 'As if democracy has gone wrong. The children of democracy becoming spoiled. First taking things for granted, then demanding them as a right. Without the need to work for them.'

James felt his first twinge of uneasiness. How had they got on to this subject? Was it leading somewhere? Or merely comment. Glib comment. Easy to condemn the malaise of dissatisfaction but the causes of it could not be ignored.

'I think the consumer society must bear some of the blame,' he heard himself reply. Perhaps he felt the need to assert himself.

'I'm not sure you can say that,' Martindale responded with a smiling shrug. 'After all the consumer society creates employment, makes life somewhat easier.'

'For those that can afford it.' Was he becoming too relaxed?

97

'But come now, Mr Ryder, you're in a luxury business. If you attack consumer capitalism you attack yourself, surely?' James was on the defensive. 'I'm in a very small way of business. And it is a business which seeks to preserve the best of the past. I don't just sell to private collectors, I sell to galleries. The public can enjoy the past perhaps even more than the private collector.'

'But do they appreciate what you give them? I doubt it. One could hope they might be educated to an enjoyment of the things of value in life. But that doesn't simply include artifacts. It includes morality. People have to be educated to behave decently. It's not happening . . .'.

Not with Mansfield and Skinner, James thought. He shifted uneasily.

'Oh, it could happen,' Martindale went on. 'With discipline. With strength. People have got to be taught harshly, even forcibly, that they must behave in society. They must learn to leave the structuring of society to those best fitted to do the job. Without interference.'

James felt warm. Hot. His hands trembled slightly. Something not right. He shouldn't have come. And he didn't like the trend of the conversation. Too relevant.

He was relieved when Martindale changed the subject. More than relieved. Slowly relaxing again. Martindale told a witty and irrelevant story about life in New York. He found himself responding with an effortless laugh. After all the man seemed harmless enough despite the fascist tendencies in his opinions. And he could tell a good story turning it against himself.

Over coffee Martindale glanced through James's catalogue, nodding with approval. And with the meal, the horror and the tension of the day seemed to dissipate, a memory becoming a dream, unreal. Here, now, was the reality of his life.

'I would like to see that, yes . . . ' Martindale pointed to an item in the catalogue. 'And that piece of course. I shall enjoy tomorrow morning in your establishment, Mr Ryder.'

James noted, with a slight stirring of surprise, the items that Martindale picked upon. He usually found that, depending on their financial status, the pieces that interested an individual were usually around the same price range. The wealthy collector went for the more expensive items, the more modest collector, the more modestly priced pieces. Martindale was not following the pattern. His interests were utterly diverse. Deciding to steer the man to rarer items he indicated an exquisite figurine, one he was almost loathe to sell.

'It is something of which I'm rather proud. Hence the price,' he said. 'A beautiful piece. Around 1725, I believe. It has the crossed swords and the K.P.M. markings.'

Later, much later he would wonder if he was subconsciously testing Martindale. No reason so far why he should and yet there was a feeling growing within him.

'Ah, yes, K.P.M.,' Martindale echoed the initials uncertainly. Two large brandies were placed in front of them.

'Of course others did imitate the crossed swords. But these are genuine. From the arms of the Bavarian state.'

Martindale nodded without reacting. James swallowed his brandy too quickly. The man should have reacted. The crossed swords were from the arms of Saxony. A collector should have known. The old chill from the earlier part of the day crept back into his spine despite the brandy. Yet perhaps Martindale had merely not heard him.

'Have you made a study of Meissen, Mr Martindale, or do you simply buy what you like?' He had to give Martindale the benefit of some doubt. Martindale sipped his brandy and beckoned the waiter over to refill James's glass.

'Bit of both really. Don't like to think I can be fooled ... '

No conclusion. The uncertainty still within James. The second brandy seemed stronger. Martindale insisted they have yet a third. James demurred unsuccessfully. Then, the brandy finished, Martindale signed the bill with a flourish.

'Come to my room. I must show you the piece I bought in Germany. At first I thought ... typical ... the pretty shepherdess ... but then it has something more.'

The Grill Room lights seemed inordinately bright to James. The room seemed to tremble. Weariness, the horrors of the day, and the brandy, that had to be the cause. The invitation to Martindale's room should have put James on his guard and yet he was beginning to believe in Martindale. Curiosity overcame caution. He rose none too steadily. After all they were in the Savoy, in the heart of London. And the man was amiable. And James had been through enough. What more could happen?

Three minutes later they were on the second floor of the hotel and Martindale was unlocking the door of his room. As he pushed it open he stood aside to let James enter. James stepped forward. No alarm signals now. A kind of weary acceptance. Despite mistakes, the man had to be genuine.

The room was in comparative darkness, the curtains open to give James a view of the glittering lights on the other side of the Thames. The lights sparkled, moved, were uneven, moving again, starting to spin around. Martindale stepped in behind James but made no move to switch on the room light. Instead he made a sudden move to the left and James, puzzled, half turned.

Instant realisation came now. They were not alone in the room. All the suspicion and fear came back in one particle of a second. Then the pain shot down from the side of his head to his neck and along the length of his spine, a jarring, screaming jolt of agony. The force of the blow threw James forward and as he did so the lights through the windows flared and merged into one bright white glare. The confirmation of all suspicion was brief. Then the light was cut off and he fell further into a dark sea, blackness embracing him.

PART TWO

1

There were dreams.

In his own personal darkness they were abstractions, those dreams, form without content, shape without direction. He would have no memory of them later but in the dreaming of them there was fear. Could shapes and colours changing, melding and separating produce the emotion of fear in the sleeper? There was no argument; they could and did. And while there was no remembrance of the forms, there was a lingering aftertaste of fear.

He came awake, aware of being afraid and yet moments later he could relax into the pleasing mixture of warmth and coolness in the bed. He opened his eyes and blinked.

There was a light above his head, bright and glaring, and it was reflected in the white walls of the room. Clinically white, they surrounded him at a distance of several feet. The room was a perfect square. The wall facing him was bisected by a high wooden door. The wood was painted a glossy white and was so spotless that it seemed to hold within it a reflection of the room. On one side of the bed was a small white table on which stood a glass, a carafe of water and lying at the foot of the carafe his wrist watch. On the other side of the bed was a white chair. To the right of the chair was a wash basin of white porcelain.

He sat up. Or rather he eased himself up slowly, aware of a shooting pain at the side of his head. He brought his right arm from underneath the white sheet to clutch at the area of pain in his head, and as he did so he became aware of a series of red dots in the crook of the elbow. He counted them. Five in all. Injection marks.

He thought, now I should ask where I am. He asked himself the question aloud, expecting only a reply from his own memory. None came. He could not know or he could not remember.

Second question. Who am I? Not said aloud. It was unnecessary to do so. No one in the room to reply. The answer came automatically from memory. James Ryder. I am James Ryder.

Third question. Who is James Ryder? Here some confusion of thought occurred. He could not seem to give himself the answer direct. The confusion grew into a multitude of images. The eyes of a dead man staring at him. A shepherdess, a china ornament that seemed to reproduce itself into a succession of china ornaments.

He shook his head in an attempt to clarify the images. He succeeded in causing a recurrence of pain at the side of his head.

He lay back trying to concentrate but without success. The images remained jumbled. Attempts at clarification set his teeth on edge. The feeling spread through his body, an unpleasant pricking sensation, as if every pore in his skin was opening and closing. He squirmed under the sheet and gradually after a time the feeling eased and passed away. After a time.

Time. No sense of time. How long had he been lying in this bed? How much time had passed since he had awakened? He sat up again, reached out and clumsily poured himself a glass of water from the carafe. As he poured he spilt some of it on the table top where it lay in small pools. As he drank it, he spilt some on the white sheet and on the white garment he was wearing. It became damp in patches against his skin. Frowning at the garment he swung his legs from the bed and looked down. He was wearing some kind of nightshirt, a kind he had seen before. In hospitals. Yes, in hospitals. Places he had visited but had never stayed. Until now.

He was in some kind of hospital.

He stood up, swayed unsteadily and righted himself by holding on to the bed. After a moment he propelled himself forward, regained a kind of equilibrium and crossed to the wash basin. There he turned on a tap and put his hands beneath it. Warm water flooded across the hands. He bathed his face in it. Then he turned and again surveyed the room.

There was nothing to help him in his attempt to gain recognition of himself or his position. He went back to the bed and lay on top of it.

I am James Ryder. Say it over and over. It gave him an anchor to reality. Whatever that was. Now, he told himself, think basic thoughts. One step at a time. James Ryder. Self. Living in ... living in a city. London. Concentrate now on London. He lived there. That was his life. Large city on a river. Beauty, familiarity and decay. Count the memories.

He closed his eyes and then opened them quickly. Colours, lights, shapes crowded under the closed eyelids and they were frightening. They held terror. He must keep his eyes open and not sleep.

Time passed. Few thoughts. James Ryder, London. A room that pleased him. His room. Then back to James Ryder, London. Minutes passed like hours or hours passed like minutes.

A key turned in the lock of the door. Remember that. The door had been locked. He had been locked in this white room. The door opened and a man came in. He knew the man, the memory of the man was close to him. But he could not name the man.

'How are you?' The voice held some concern.

'I don't know.' A stupid answer. One must know. I must know how I am.

'It's difficult at first,' the man said.

'Yes.'

'Do you remember me?'

'I remember your face.'

'My name?'

James Ryder shook his head.

'My name is Derek Martindale. Does that mean anything to you?'

James stared at him. 'Derek Martindale?'

'That's it.'

Should know the name. Should know it. Can't remember.

103

'I think I should remember it. Derek Martindale.'
'It'll come back to you.'
'Where am I?' James giggled as he asked the question. It was so expected.
'You're not well, James. We're treating you for your illness.'
'What is my illness?'
'I'm not a doctor. You must ask him. Of course I could say you are suffering from the twentieth-century disease.'
'What . . . what's that?'
'Oh, it has many symptoms. A kind of paranoia. The belief that you are important, that you should have some say in the affairs of nations.'
James closed and then opened his eyes. What was being said to him? What did it mean?
'But don't we have some say? Don't we have a voice . . . a vote . . . ?'
'Do we?' the reply came smoothly, without hesitation. 'A man shouts, protests, does anybody listen? Oh, he votes, but what does it mean? A granule of sand in the Sahara. And he votes for people, not for morality, not for ideas.'
A pause. Seconds ticking by. 'But why am I here?' James finally asked.
'Talk to the doctor. Or, if it helps, call it a nervous breakdown.'
'Induced by a blow on the head?' James surprised himself by the question. It was uttered with no conscious awareness but came from somewhere of its own volition.
A small frown, a tiny cloud in a clear sky. 'You could say the blow on the head was part of the treatment. But, you know, there are many names for a nervous breakdown, many reasons for its occurrence. Yours may be only too common.'
'What is mine. Tell me.'
'Paranoiac obsession, perhaps.' A slight shrug from the speaker. 'A series of events which seem to have occurred but may actually have no basis in reality.'
James frowned. A word came to him. 'Brainwashing?'
Derek Martindale smile. 'Does your brain need washing? Is it so soiled? Anyway brainwashing is such an emotive

word. Implying the need to be cleansed, implying methods like hypnosis, interrogation, sensory deprivation. We haven't done that to you, James. We've merely let you rest. Helped you to rest. A little sedation when needed, stimulation when necessary. Against what ails you, shall we say? Against what ails you.'

Martindale straightened up. He had been leaning over James and now he moved away. James wanted to pull him back, have him close to provide reassurance.

'So you see, you must rest now,' Martindale went on. 'The doctor will look in. But you must not worry. This is your home for the time being. Everything you need will be provided. Will be brought to you.'

'Everything I want?'

'I said everything you need. Trust us. We will know what you want. We will know what is correct for you to want. It is an enviable position. Without concern.'

Martindale walked to the door and with his back to James hesitated then spoke. 'I shall see you occasionally. When it is useful. Meanwhile, good night, Mr Ryder.'

As he went through the doorway James called out, again without thought. 'Is it night?'

Turning, Martindale smiled across at him.

'After all, what is night, Mr Ryder?'

The door closed. Martindale was gone. A lock clicked in the door.

Martindale? The name again. He knew the name certainly now. Perhaps the face too. But from where, from what long corridor of memory and event? James lay back on the bed and slowly slipped into a soothing sleep. Soothing because it took away all questions, faded the traces of memory at the edge of brain and corner of eye.

Some time later, the stirring from the warmth of sleep, the clinging to the foetal position. Then a slow movement of legs, enjoying the coolness at the sides of the bed and then withdrawing into the warmth.

And then awake again. Thoughts while lying awake alone in the white room. Trace images of people getting killed. Violent death. James Ryder does not kill them. He is not responsible.

105

Anyway killing people is wrong. Why should he think it? Why should he dwell on violent death?

The white room is calm, almost silent. Only a drop of water escaping from the faucet occasionally disturbs the silence. Everything is serene in the white room. But, outside . . . ?

Outside something is wrong. Outside in the city, if the city is outside. There is no reason to believe it is. No windows. But wherever it is the city is dying. The signs and symbols of decay come to memory. And something is wrong within the white room. Its very stillness, its very calm is wrong. Realisation of that is the beginning of remembering.

Time passed. No indication of how long, no knowing whether a minute was an hour, an hour was a day.

The sound of a key in the lock. Martindale came in again.

'How are you?'

James shook his head. 'Not how am I! Where am I?'

'Where?'

'Outside. The city. Is it London?'

Martindale smiled. He was such a suave, well-groomed man, youthfully distinguished. And James did not trust him.

'London?' said Martindale. 'What is London? A place. When you are unwell, Ryder, it doesn't matter where you are. As long as you are in the right place. And we are making sure you are in the right place.'

James looked away from him. There were never any real answers, only evasions.

'Is there anything you wish?' Martindale enquired politely, benevolently, concern and goodness written on his face.

'Anything . . . ?'

'Anything?'

'I have nothing to do. I just lie here – '

'Part of the treatment.'

'But I want something to do!' James insisted, sounding querulous to himself. 'Books, newspapers, something to pass the time.'

'No newspapers. None. The printed word is dangerous. You may find it would pull you back into your depression.'

'For God's sake, books surely . . . ?'

'I'll see. Something light perhaps. I'll see to it. Something to occupy your time. Puzzles, maybe.' His own suggestion seemed to amuse Martindale. 'Yes. Puzzles,' he went on. 'You should be good at puzzles. Jigsaws. I shall bring you a jigsaw.'

He went out smiling. And after an indeterminate time a man in a white suit with a blank nondescript face came in pushing a table that fitted over the bed. On the table were two books and a large box containing a jigsaw puzzle. The man manoeuvred the table in front of James, propped up the pillows and left without speaking.

James picked up the first of the books. It was a translation of *Gargantua and Pantagruel* by Rabelais. The second book was *The Pilgrim's Progress*. James asked himself the question, was Martindale amusing himself with his book selection?

He then looked at the box containing the jigsaw. It announced in large letters it contained over a thousand pieces. Below the announcement was a picture of the jigsaw. It was a strange black and white drawing by Escher, showing staircases mounting to other staircases and turning back upon themselves. It was full of false perspectives, insane, unreal projections.

He opened the box and tipped the myriad pieces onto the table. He started on the task of assembling them. The puzzle was complicated and he became for a time engrossed. He completed one corner and was trying to link the outer edges when he began to feel heavy and his eyelids started to droop. He slept.

For how long he slept again he had no idea. He awoke this time to find a round black face staring down at him.

'And how are you keeping now?' the black face enquired grinning and revealing a row of uneven but gleaming teeth.

James forced himself to sit up. The black man was wearing a white coat over a pair of striped trousers.

'I am your doctor,' the black man informed him anticipating the question. 'Doctor Sebastien Higgins.'

James, not yet fully awake, shook his head. 'My doctor is Joe Glasser. Surgery in South Kensington.'

'Indeed. I don't think I know him,' Dr Higgins went on.

'But then you have been referred to me.'

'By who . . . whom?'

'The gentlemen.'

'What gentlemen?'

'I was told you were a great man for the questions. The gentlemen who are in charge here.'

'Where the hell is here? And what are they in charge of?' James felt himself getting angry.

'Here?' Higgins replied. 'This place. This room. Other rooms. As to who they are, they must tell you that themselves.'

James sighed, a long tired exhalation of breath. The game was getting boring. If it had ever been anything else. If only he knew what the game was. If only he knew who he was. If only . . . too many if onlys.

'All right,' he said. 'Then tell me what's the matter with me. They told me you would. They told me, ask the doctor.'

Higgins was taking his pulse. 'Running a little fast, Mr Ryder. That is not good. You excite yourself, the pulse runs fast. Like a clock telling the time of the body to itself.'

'To hell with the time of the body? Why am I here?'

Higgins let go of his wrist.

'Because you are not well.'

'Okay. What's the matter with me? Once and for all.'

The black doctor stared at him thoughtfully.

'You have to be treated!'

'For what?'

'Drug addiction.'

It was James's turn to stare.

'Drug addiction! I've never been a drug addict in my entire life!'

'You remember your entire life then?'

He couldn't reply. He couldn't admit he only remembered his name.

'You see, Mr Ryder, you do not answer,' Higgins went on. 'It is possible that drug addiction creates a fugue. A period of nothingness in the mind. Aphasia of the memory. It is all there.'

Higgins reached towards the table which held now not

108

only the debris of the jigsaw puzzle but an elegant metal case about nine inches long. The case was open and a hypodermic syringe lay inside. Higgins lifted the syringe, held it needle upwards and squeezed the top. A tiny bubble of liquid appeared. He then pulled James's sleeve up.

'You're not going to inject me?'

'Indeed I am. This will sedate you and lessen the effects of the withdrawal of the drug.'

'But I haven't . . . I'm not on . . . any drug . . . Don't you sterilise the spot where you're going to inject.'

Another black and white grin. 'This room is so sterile even a professional lady would be considered a complete practising virgin.'

James tried to pull his arm away but Higgins moved with speed, gripping his forearm in a pincer grip. The pressure of the large black hand caused a vein to stand out, a bluish ridge against pale skin.

The prick of the needle caused a numbness to spread along the arm. Since childhood James had feared needles and injections and now as the needle had broken the flesh he had winced and turned his head away. As he did so a flash of perception ran through his brain. Ryder. Himself. Antique dealer. Flat in Kensington. Shop in the West End. That was all. But it was something. Another step forward. Just as he realised he'd mentioned Joe Glasser, his doctor, without thinking. Joe Glasser, old friend, Jewish doctor from Belfast. Funny a Jew with a Belfast accent. Good old Joe. Remembered you without thinking. More to come. Please. Please come soon. So many things were trying to get into his head. Or were they trying to get out?

'There you are,' Higgins said withdrawing the syringe and placing it in its case on the table. 'Another day nearer your cure.'

James began to feel weary again, his body weak, as the contents of the syringe coursed through his system. He lay back against the pillows as the room went into a pendulum motion swinging from side to side, Higgins, in front of him, swung with the rest of the room. James was the only stable entity or so it seemed.

'You will go to sleep in a moment,' Higgins assured him. 'You must not concern yourself with silly questions to which you undoubtedly know the answers.'

Yes, I know the answers, James told himself. The only trouble is not being able to remember them. Not even being able to remember the questions.

Higgins, still swinging in and out of focus, was fiddling with the syringe, ejecting from it the spent capsule of whatever he had used on James. Then something distracted him and he put syringe and case down as the male nurse who served James with meals came in.

'Spot of bother, Dr Higgins,' the man said tentatively, with a look at James.

'Well?'

The nurse still stared at James.

'Tell me!' Higgins insisted, exasperation in his voice. 'You don't need to worry about Mr Ryder. He is almost unconscious.'

'The woman in number three. No reaction to her injection. Making a lot of noise.'

Higgins hissed. 'They develop an immunity. I will come now.'

Through a mist James saw him leave. Then the mist became thicker and James slid back into sleep.

Some time later he woke and lay gazing at the white ceiling. Some time later? But no idea how much later. Awake anyway he let his mind roam. The idea was to stumble onto a memory. One might lead to another and fill in the blanks; like doing a great mental jigsaw.

There was a body somewhere in all of it, that he was sure of. He kept seeing it. He kept seeing dead eyes then a figure lying on a stone step. Also dead. Patterns of blood surround the body. And the mist again.

Was it mist? Or was it dust? Or was it false? Was he simply preoccupied with murder? He could think of no definite connection with murder. Except for the eyes staring up at him and a pattern of blood on concrete and on flesh. But nothing more could come from that line of thinking. Not now.

He twisted on his side, luxuriating on the comfort of the

bed. There should be no worries here, no concerns. Just sleep and rest. Food would be brought when he was hungry. He would wash at the sink when he found it necessary. It was a closed cocooned world without problems. Enjoy it, relax in it. No creation of terrors.

Yet the terrors kept creeping back. There was an explosion, he suddenly remembered that. It made him afraid. You should not be here, he decided. It was an easy escape from the terrors outside. A lack of responsibility, that's what it was.

He swung his legs over the bed and, reaching out, pulled the table nearer him. The two books were still there, the two lent to him by the man who called himself Martindale. The tiny section of the jigsaw he had completed remained untouched.

Section?

Familiar. Something . . . the section.

The section . . . the Section . . . THE SECTION. Like a boomerang in his head, the sound bounding from one side of the brain cavity to the other. He shook his head violently to wake himself up. Not to be thought about now, he decided. Creates problems. Throw it away. Don't try to remember.

He pulled the table to the side of the bed and, climbing into the bed again, he lay back studying the pieces in front of him. Then something caught his eye on the table: the case, open, containing the empty syringe. Higgins, called away in a hurry, had abandoned it. He reached over and grasped syringe and case. Closing the case he placed it carefully under the pillow. It could be useful, of value. As a weapon if necessary. Considerable damage could be wreaked on the human body by the long needle of the syringe.

Why should he think he might need to wreak damage on a human body? He frowned. Perhaps he was confined in this room because of such thoughts.

No. He knew that under normal circumstances he was not a violent being. But what then were normal circumstances? *A car crashing over a barrier?*

The image intruded. It was clear in his mind, a nightmare coming alive. To find out if that was normality he had to get out of this place.

111

Sleep again. A deep sleep punctuated by noises off. Then the twilight between waking and sleeping. And still the voices. White sound in darkness. Whispering.

'How long?' Martindale's voice.

'How long can he be kept like that?'

'No limit of time.'

'After effects?'

A silence.

'Possibly. Coming out. Might have an effect.'

'Damage?'

'Always possible.'

Then he was sliding back into sleep again.

Twilight again. Voices.

A strange voice. 'Why not just kill him?'

He was warm and comfortable and the voice was far away.

'We have scruples.' Martindale speaking distinctly.

'Do we?'

'Alteration of state of health should be used only when necessary.'

'. . . Christ sake, Derek, it's already been necessary twice.' The other voice was harsh, uncompromising.

'Exactly. It was necessary. This one is not. If it became so, then we would do it. But it isn't.' Martindale in command. 'Leave him here until it's over. Then let him go. No problems.'

So you say, damn you. I will be a problem.

'He may never come out of it. Not after your black quack has pumped him so full, he's not capable. You could end up with a vegetable.'

I will not end up as a vegetable. I am James Ryder, antique dealer. I should be on holiday.

The last thought brought him to a kind of alertness. On holiday? Going on holiday? Driving on the M1. Meeting Nora. Nora? Who was Nora?

Time passed.

'You'd better be on alert tonight, Dr Higgins.' Martindale again.

'Tonight?' Higgins now, face black and round. Another injection.

'Civil disturbances. There will be casualties.'

Higgins' voice now strained. 'Never liked that part of it. Using my people.'

'We are your people, Dr Higgins. Irrespective of colour. We have complete tolerance. We only ask that the job be done.'

Another pause. Then Martindale saying, 'His eyelids, they were flickering.'

'Of course. He's not dead.'

'Can he hear?'

'Possibly. Depends how deeply he is under. Different metabolisms, different results.'

Without opening his eyes, James was aware that Martindale is leaning over him.

'Mr Ryder? Mr Ryder?' A sibilant whisper.

'I'm here,' he wanted to say but he didn't. Why bother?

'We are looking after you, Mr. Ryder. You understand, we are looking after you.'

Now they're the Salvation Army. All things bright and beautiful. You are a liar, Mr Martindale. And I still have to get out of this place. But first I must remember.

Martindale's shadow drew away.

'Just keep him here. For his own good.'

'I don't think he will try to leave,' said Higgins.

'You don't think? You don't think? You must be sure.'

'No one can be sure, Mr Martindale. As I said, different metabolism. He may achieve a toleration for the drug.'

'He can't be allowed to leave. Make sure. Now, if you'll excuse me, I have a great many other things to do.'

'The civil disturbances, Mr Martindale?'

'Our part in that is over. Goodnight, doctor.'

The door opening and closing. Alone now. Knowing they were drugging him. Knowing he had to get out. But there was the drug and there was the locked door.

On your feet, James Ryder. On your feet and over to the wash basin. Get to the basin. Get there. Hands on porcelain. Balancing. The cold tap running now. Cold water on your head, on your face. Dripping and running under the gown. Ice cold but the head still swimming in water. More and more cold water poured over the head and face. But not enough. Other things to be done. Make yourself sick. A finger down the throat. A retching gagging sound and nothing. Try again.

Then there was a degree of clarity but not enough. It came after he vomited into the basin. He had to do something else. Exercise. Keep moving. Work the drugs through the system. To the bed, tottering, then forcing himself erect and stumbling back to the basin. Back and forward, swaying, yawning, exhausted.

After what seemed like hours he sat on the bed gulping air, hands trembling. He wanted to lie down and sleep. It would be so easy just to stretch out and close his eyes. The thought kept recurring and he kept thrusting it away. Must not relax, must not fall asleep.

He began to concentrate on the problem of getting out of the room and out of the building. First of all there was the locked door. Could he smash the lock? Find something to use as leverage. But there was nothing. The bed and the washbasin? He examined the table over the bed, the kind that moved up and down. Wood and metal. It was on wheels but the screws on the underside of the table were firmly embedded in the sockets. Perhaps he could ram the door with the table? It would make a great deal of noise and he doubted it would do more than dent the door.

He found the syringe case under the pillow. The case was of smooth metal, useless as far as the door lock was concerned. He considered the syringe with its long, thin needle. Perhaps an expert lockpicker could use the needle to open the lock, but it was a thin hollow needle and he was sure, in his own hands, it would break.

Staring at the syringe he found himself sagging forward, eyes blinking. He forced himself to his feet and started walking again, to and fro across the room. The pain in his head increased but his body began to respond, the agony in his muscles ebbing away. He told himself he was winning.

More time passing. Now he felt he could sit on the bed without falling asleep. There were more problems to consider. If he could get out of the room, there was the problem of clothes. To appear in the street, if indeed the house was on a street and not somewhere isolated in the countryside, he needed his clothes. In a long, damp, hospital gown he was sure he must look like a fugitive from an asylum.

Involuntarily he lay back on the bed. He had been right, he did not feel like sleeping. All he had done had had its effect. The drugs had been successfully combated. Now there was time to remember. It was still like a jigsaw, still fragmented. But the mind seemed to be clearer. He was James Ryder, antique dealer and he had been going on holiday. No questions there. And he had been driving out of London. He was going to Scotland. And then there was Nora Matheson.

A key rattled in the lock of the door. James shut his eyes and lay perfectly still.

Higgins came into the room, dark skin shining in the light. He approached the bed. James had one hand half under the pillow gripping the syringe case. Higgins peered down at him.

'On top of the bed, Mr Ryder. You have been trying to get up. But the drug soon sent you to sleep.' Higgins was talking aloud to himself, a small smile on his face. 'Better not to fight it. Better to be in here, safe and secure. Outside is not so pleasant tonight.'

Leaning over he studied James's face and then felt for his pulse. As he dropped his eyes to James's right wrist, James tightened his grasp on the metal case with his left hand. The syringe, now lying under the pillow beside the case, he ignored.

'Your pulse is racing, my friend,' Higgins said frowning.

James moved at speed, bringing his left arm from under the pillow, coming to a sitting position and striking the doctor as hard as he could behind the coloured man's right ear. He'd read somewhere you could knock someone unconscious very easily if you hit them behind the ear. It was not as simple as he'd been led to believe. Higgins' head fell forward and he yelped. It was the only way the sound he uttered could be described. A yelp, like an animal that had been kicked. Then he shook his head violently as if to shake off the pain he must have felt. But he was still obviously conscious.

James struck him again behind the ear with the metal case. This time he made no sound but reeled backwards, his eyes rolling up until only the whites were visible. But still he was on his feet. A third time James struck out at his head. But now Higgins was a few feet from the bed and the blow connected on the front of his forehead gashing the skin. At last however he sank to the floor, on his knees at first and then slowly toppling forward, face down. The gashed forehead hit the stone floor with a loud thump.

On his feet now James looked down at his erstwhile medical supervisor. A thin trickle of blood stained the stone, oozing from the black man's forehead. James turned and staggered to the basin where he promptly vomited. After a moment he cupped his right hand and, switching on the tap, took a gulp of cold water.

Turning back he went over and knelt beside Higgins. The doctor's body shivered, a series of shuddering twitches and then, except, thank God, for the movement of breathing, was still. James turned him over and checked his pulse. Higgins was alive, and though blood smudged his forehead the cut was not deep. Certainly now he was unconscious. It was James's turn to shiver. It had always looked so easy in films, so safe. The quick blow to the head and the villain was out of action. No yelping, no shuddering, no sinister flow of blood.

He told himself he had only done what he had to do. Higgins was unconscious and the door of the room was open. The next problem was to find clothes and a way out of the building. He studied Higgins' body for a further few seconds. The man was too small, his clothes under his white coat would never fit James's lean frame. But where had they put his own clothes? Normally, in a hospital room there would be a wardrobe or a cupboard for the patient's belongings. But this was not a normal hospital room. Yet they would have had to put his clothes somewhere.

The solution was actually simpler than he imagined. Straightening up James walked to the door, suddenly aware of how incongruous he must look, a tall unkempt figure in a crushed white nightgown now damp and stained. Higgins had closed the door behind him but had not bothered to lock it. James opened it with infinite care. A corridor outside, James's room at the end. A dead end. The corridor ended in a blank wall to his right. To his left it joined another corridor. But now facing James on the wall opposite the door was a cupboard. James stepped into the corridor and, gripping a small handle pulled it open.

His clothes were inside, lying crushed at the food of the cupboard. He withdrew each item, placing them over his left arm. Underwear, socks, shirt, jacket and trousers, all were there. At the foot were his shoes and tie, crushed into one of the shoes. Untidy bastards, he thought. His best suit, selected for dinner at the Savoy Grill. He remembered the Savoy Grill now. Dinner with Martindale. And then up to his room on some pretext, to value a piece of china and then . . . nothing.

Stepping back into the room he dressed quickly. As he did so, Higgins stirred and gave a low moan. Loathe to hit him again, James stripped a sheet from the bed, tore it into several strips, tied his hands and feet and fixed a gag across his mouth. The black doctor, still semi-conscious, offered no resistance. Searching his pockets James found the key of the room. Good. He could lock the doctor in. A further search of the pockets revealed some small change and a wallet containing two pound notes.

The wallet brought to mind his own possessions and he searched his jacket. His wallet was intact as were the keys to his flat and car. And his money, several pounds, was still in his wallet. At least his captors drew the line at thieving.

Depositing Higgins on the bed in what seemed a reasonably comfortable position, James looked around for some kind of weapon. The metal syringe case lay on the floor where it had fallen when he had hit Higgins. The metal was dented now where he had struck the doctor. Hardly a weapon, it had at least served to stun the doctor. He picked it up and slipped it into his pocket. On the bed, he found the empty syringe and this he held in his right hand. The needle was sharp and might be useful.

He went out into the corridor and locked the bedroom door behind him. The corridor was ill-lit, one bare bulb hanging from the ceiling. But the passage into which it led seemed better illuminated, bulkhead light fittings spaced out at intervals.

Reaching the corner James had to make a decision. Left or right. At each end were firedoors and on each side a number of what appeared to be doors leading to other bedrooms. A thin draught of cool air seemed to be coming from his left. He decided to follow this.

Beyond the fire doors the passage turned to the right. With the cool air on his face James approached the turning. As he did so his head started to swim, his vision momentarily blurring. He stopped, steadying himself against the wall. The drug was still having an effect. After a moment, his eyes cleared and, though his head still throbbed, the passage in front of him settled down and he was able to continue.

The spasm had however made him careless. He came around the corner without hesitation. The man was sitting behind a small desk, legs stretched under it across the corridor. He was a large man in a dark suit, his eyes alert. As James appeared he pushed the desk forward and was at once on his feet. They faced each other.

'How the hell did you . . ? '

James stood, uncertain as to what he should do. His head throbbed even more violently than before.

The large man smiled without humour. 'Thought you were the little black quack. But you're not, are you? What have you done to him?'

'He's . . . he's sleeping,' James said, stammering.

'That's not right. You're the one who's supposed to be having a long nod.' A questioning look came into the large man's face. 'How did you do it? Get out? Thought they'd given you a shot of dreamland.'

'I'm an insomniac.' God, how could he be flip at a time like this?

The large man reached under his jacket and produced a large revolver. 'You've had your little walk then,' he said cheerfully. 'But now it's time to go back.'

James shook his head but he knew his denial was futile. The revolver loomed large in the other's hand.

'You've no right to keep me here.'

'I have, you know,' the large man replied, the smile still fixed. 'This gives me the right.' He indicated the revolver.

'I . . . I intend to leave . . . '

'Sorry. No way. Against orders.' The cockney accent was getting stronger. 'You just let me take you back to your nice comfortable kip. Because, if you don't, my orders are to stop you, even if I had to do you in.'

'You may have to do just that,' James found himself replying. It was a brave attempt but he didn't feel brave. He felt sick again.

The large man frowned. He gesticulated with the gun, taking a step towards James. 'I know how you feel, chum. But it's no go,' he said. 'Anyway you wouldn't want to be out there tonight.' He inclined his head back indicating the way out. At least it gave James the general direction for his escape.

'It's going to be a hot time on the town tonight. White faces not welcome in the street,' the man went on.

'In London?' James ventured.

'We're not talking about Timbucktoo!'

So he was still in London, that was something. Within reach of friends, within reach of the police. Or was he already within reach of the police? Were these people in some kind of authority?

'Now let's go back quietly,' the large man repeated. 'After all, what's the point? We're in charge and it's for your own good.'

'The police! I want to see the police,' James was putting it into words now, testing the man with the gun.

'No good. The police are on our side. I think Mr Martindale told you. We're the bright blue Harolds. Anybody against us, they're the bad guys.'

The large man's smile broadened. He was now close to James and he pushed his arm forward, prodding James with the revolver.

'Come on now. You look a right mess anyway. Be a good boy and turn back.'

James stood his ground motionless. He was curious to see what the large man would do if he stood still. He found out.

The heavy revolver suddenly smashed forward into his solar plexus. James doubled up, gasping for air, pain spreading from the centre of his body. He staggered against the wall retching, flashes before his eyes. The large man stood patiently over him still smiling. He enjoyed his work.

'Don't want to have to carry you. But if I have to I'll drag you. So be a good lad, get your breath and walk.'

James took time regaining his breath. He took longer than he had to deliberately. He was gathering his strength and it seemed to him that the blow in the solar plexus had, as the pain eased, brought him to a greater alertness, seemingly dispelling any last vestiges of the effects of the drug. Then, very slowly he eased himself erect. As he did so he held on to the wall with his left hand and reached forward with his right as if to balance himself by grasping the large man's shoulder. The large man took a step backwards, then, gun in his right hand, he held out his left to assist James in standing.

It was then that James propelled himself forward from the wall and brought his right hand down onto the side of the large man's neck, the syringe gripped in it like a knife. As he did so he twisted himself to his right out of the line of the revolver.

The needle of the syringe sank into the side of the large man's neck. He gave a dull moan and brought his left hand up ineffectively in an attempt to pluck the needle from his neck. At the same time he tried to bring the revolver around towards James. James slammed his left hand out bringing the side of it down onto the gun hand with all the force he could muster. The gun fell from the large man's grip onto the floor with a loud clatter.

Still clawing at his neck the man staggered back across the corridor. James picked up the gun and turning quickly brought the muzzle down on the man's forehead. The man fell backwards, eyes rolling upwards, a thin trickle of blood running down his neck.

Steadying himself James leant down and drew the syringe needle from the man's neck. Throwing it across the corridor, he checked the man's pulse. It seemed strong. The needle's damage had been minimal, he judged, the shock achieving the effect of surprise. And now James had no need of the needle. He had the large revolver.

Past the desk at the far end of the corridor James went through another door. Through this he found himself at the top of a stairway leading down to a large hall at one side of which was another desk. Behind this desk was a middle-aged man in the black uniform and gold crowns that denoted a civil-service commissionaire. Above him facing the door was a small television camera which obviously monitored all arrivals. It was, James noted, in a fixed position so that it would not monitor prospective departures at least until they were going through the door.

His footsteps echoing around the hallway, James descended the stairs. His hand in his jacket gripped the large man's revolver. As he moved towards the desk and the front doors he smoothed his hair back trusting his appearance would not be too dishevelled to arouse suspicion.

The middle-aged commissionaire seemed accustomed to such visions. He glanced up as James approached.

'Off duty?'

'Eh, yes.'

'You're new, aren't you? You look rough. New men always look rough,' the commissionaire said with a smile. 'Still I expect they pay you that much more to look rough. Some of those mental cases take some handling.'

So that's what the middle-aged man thought they were. Mental cases, upstairs in their safe little boxes protected for some reason by government employees.

'They do indeed,' James responded, assuming what he considered an authoritative attitude.

The attitude passed muster. The commissionaire nodded and pressed a switch. The double doors sprung apart with a small jerk, and automatically unlocked.

'You'd better be careful out there,' the commissionaire went on. 'Hope you've got transport. Either way keep clear of the Park Drive road. That's where the trouble is. Still I expect the police'll have it cordoned off by now.'

The trouble? What the hell was going on? The large man had told him he was lucky not to be outside and now the commissionaire was warning him. Against what?

James stepped through the double door and down some steps. He was in some kind of garden with a path leading to a metal gate between high stone walls. All this he could make out dimly as it was night. And yet the night sky was lit with the reflection of nearby neon lights and the reflection of something else. Ahead of him above the roof tops but only some blocks away the sky was red and streaked with sparks flying upwards.

'They've really gone off now,' a voice said from the darkness ahead.

James peered forward and out of the blackness came the figure of a large uniformed policeman.

'Evening, sir,' the policeman nodded affably, his face a white patch in the reflected light.

'Evening,' James replied affecting an affability he did not feel.

'George tell you to avoid Park Drive?'

'He told me.'

'Got your own transport, sir?'

'Eh, no. I thought I'd get a cab or a tube.' The moment he spoke he regretted it. He had no idea of the time, of whether the tubes would still be running. He felt the shape of his watch in the pocket of his jacket and cursed himself for not putting it on, not finding out the time.

The police constable was unfazed. 'Better off without a car, sir. Run into any of those black bastards and they wouldn't hesitate to turn it over, set it on fire and turn you into a piece of toast.'

Reassuring sod, James thought. And a prejudiced one.

'What's it all about anyway?' he asked.

'What are they all about, sir? Gangsters, if you ask me.

122

Hooligan gangsters. Call it a race riot, I just call it hooliganism. Another Brixton. But not as bad. I think we got the boot in, in time.'

James took a deep breath, drawing the cool night air into his lungs. His face was hot, starting to burn now once he was out of the central heating of the building behind him.

'Better get along then,' he said, moving towards the gate. The constable took a step in front of him, and he felt the chill of the fear that had been with him inside the building. Having got this far, he was to be stopped now by a policeman? His fears were unfounded. The policeman merely unlocked a padlock and opened the gates for him.

'I'd keep an eye open if I were you, sir,' the policeman went on. 'Trouble is no matter how much we contain them there's always a gang of kids sneaks through. And those kids are a lot more dangerous than the adults.'

Having portentously donated his advice to James, the policeman stepped aside and ushered James into the street. Suppressing his sense of excitement and relief, James gave the officer a brief nod and strolled off along the pavement. He was out, free, on his own. Now the problem was what to do? Where exactly was he? And if he was within reach of his flat should he go there? Questions, questions.

The sound of a police siren rang out nearby as it whined its way through night streets. In the distance James could hear shouting, the occasional dull sound of what might be a small explosion. Riots, probably race riots, that was something he could do without.

He crossed a road, turned a corner and walked quicker and quicker away from the walled building which had been his own personal prison. A battered street sign hung crookedly from the wall of a large grey tenement. Below the street he read 'Borough of Paddington'. He sighed, expelling air from his mouth and throat, a kind of relief. He was in London and not too far from his home.

They came charging round a corner, both of them, running breathless, their eyes wide. They struck James by accident of speed and propulsion. They were about fifteen, two thin coloured youths, their faces gleaming with perspiration and panic.

'Fuck!' one of them said as James's body brought them both to an abrupt halt.

'What's the panic?, James said, staring at them curiously. They were dressed in grubby tee-shirts, and crushed blue jeans and they were afraid.

'You a pig, mister?' the taller of the two boys asked aggressively.

'No. Are you?'

His reply disarmed them.

'Us? Pigs. Go on . . . !'

James looked around. The street was wide, with tall tenements, once elegant Victorian houses, now delapidated, on either side. The sky in the direction of the presumed riot, was even brighter, clouds of smoke turned to orange by the light beneath them climbing towards the sky.

'What's happening then?' he asked the two boys. They, in their turn, were studying him now.

'If you ain't a pig, mister, did the pigs do you up as well?'

'As well as who?'

'Anybody with black skin. And maybe a few honkies too. That's what they're doing on Park Drive – '

The second boy cut in, 'Anybody they can get hold of.'

'Who started the riot?' James asked.

'What's it worth to tell you?' the first boy demanded.

'I want to know,' James insisted.

'The pigs started it. And a couple of white mothers! Big blokes – '

'Looked like SPG pigs.'

'But you'd expect us to say that.'

'Are you one of them investigative journalists?'

It seemed to James as good a pose as any. 'Something like that,' he said.

'Give us some money then!' the first boy demanded aggressively.

The second boy chimed in. 'Right enough! You pay people for them news stories. We're people. Pay us!'

James felt in his inside pocket. He pulled out his wallet.

'Don't bother to count it,' the first boy said. 'Just hand it over.'

'You're joking!'

The boy looked down at his boots. 'See them boots, mister. Steel tipped. Your lot started this so you can pay for it. I kick you. I break your leg.'

'He'd do it too,' the second boy assured James with a grin.

'You ... you just lost a couple of quid,' James replied stepping back, wallet in one hand and the revolver now in the other.

'Christ, he's got a shooter,' the second boy exclaimed.

They were both eyeing him warily now as if considering whether or not he would use the weapon.

'He was just kidding you, mister,' the first boy insisted. 'We don't want no trouble.'

James found himself smiling. The black faces, the cockney accents, the touch of criminal opportunism, they struck him suddenly as amusing. God knows why. Perhaps it was the contrast between the people who had held him in the white room, drugged and helpless, trying somehow to destroy his memory and these two openly criminal youngsters.

'We wouldn't have broken your leg, mister,' the first boy went on. 'Ain't only done it a couple of times and they was skinheads from up Kilburn way. I mean, we wouldn't mind settling for a couple of quid, would we, Jerry?'

Jerry nodded his head in violent agreement. 'I think he's gone off us, Pete. He won't give us no two quid now. Probably just shoot us.'

'You wouldn't shoot us, mister. Couple of kids. Still at school. Fucking waste of bullets that would be.'

James laughed, actually admitting to himself he was amused for the first time in ... how long?

'Tell me,' he asked. 'What day is it?'

'Eh?' said the first boy, Pete.

'Wants to know what day it is,' said Jerry with a look of superiority. 'It's Saturday.'

It had been Wednesday when he had gone to meet Martindale at the Savoy. They'd held him for three days. Or a week and three days. Or a month and three days. His head swam momentarily and he swayed on the edge of the pavement.

'You okay, mister?' Peter the opportunist was wondering

perhaps whether his wallet was not out of their reach after all.

'I'm okay!' James insisted, waving the revolver towards them. They backed away cautiously.

'Just asking, just asking – '

'What date is it?'

Pete told him. Three days only since the Savoy.

'Can you get me a taxi?' he asked Jerry sensing more sympathy in the second boy.

'No way taxis'll come to Notting Hill tonight. Asking for trouble, that would be.'

James thought quickly. 'All right. Get me to the nearest tube. And not by way of the riots. Get me there and I'll see you two are all right.'

'Get you across London for a fiver, mister.' This from Jerry. 'And nobody'll touch you, shooter or no shooter.'

'I only want to get to . . . to South Kensington.'

'You're on,' Jerry assured him cheerfully.

They passed a street at the edge of the riot. The tarmac was littered with rubbish, stones, bricks, broken glass. A few youths, black and white, were hauling crates from a public house, the door of which had been smashed in. There was a sad viciousness about the wreckage.

Another street, nearer the heart of the riot. Faces, again black and white, shouting, screaming, beyond sense, bordering on a kind of lust for violence, a freedom to destroy. A van lay on its side aflame. The petrol tank exploded with a loud thumping sound and liquid fire flowed around the metal skeleton. At the far end of the street James could make out the figures of policemen, dancing dervishes in the flickering light moving backwards and forwards behind riot shields. In the distance, the clanging bells of fire engines could be heard, the sound mingling with that of police sirens.

Pete and Jerry, true to their agreement, arraigned themselves on each side of James and any strange looks cast in their direction by passing young blacks were countered with brief warning curses or the simple explanation, 'He's with us.'

They reached a tube station out of the riot area and the two boys insisted they would take him to South Kensington.

James was too tired to argue. And he knew they respected, if not him, the revolver in his pocket.

It was as they sat in the tube, rattling through the tunnels of the Circle Line that James realised why he had been so curious as to who had started the riot. It was something he had heard as he lay semi-conscious in the white room. Martindale talking. Martindale aware the riot was about to happen. 'You'd better be on the alert tonight, Dr Higgins . . . civil disturbances . . . there will be injured . . . ' How could Martindale know? It must have been hours before. How? Unless they had started the riots. But for what reason?

Pete dug him in the ribs. 'South Ken, mister.'

At the entrance to his apartment building James found a fiver in his wallet and gave it to the two youths.

'Thanks, mister,' said Jerry. 'Anytime you need a bit of muscle, call for Jerry MacCrow. 5 Lansbury Block.'

James smiled. Muscles seemed the last thing these two skinny youths could provide. Yet he knew they meant what they said.

Ten minutes later, he was pouring a brandy and falling with relief in the soft comfort of his own sofa. The front door of the flat was double locked and the revolver was on the arm of the sofa. If anyone tried to get in there'd be a miniature riot in South Kensington.

The brandy mixing with the traces of the drug had a soporific effect. He felt heavy, his body screaming for sleep. Shouldn't have taken the brandy but . . . what the hell . . he'd got away from them . . on his own . . . no help . . . who were they anyway? People killed . . . drugged . . . race riots . . . London Bridge falling down . . shattered glass on the streets gleaming under the light from the flames of a burning van . . . riots in the street . . . riots created by them . . .

He slept.

3

Waking with a start, fear coursed through his body, as if he were still in the hospital room. And then the sense of relief flooded into his consciousness. He was in his own sitting room, on his own sofa, daylight lighting the room. He sat up, trying to remember. Like a dream, a long continuous nightmare it lay at the back of his mind, fragmented, hazy but there. Was it a dream?

Then he saw the revolver lying on the arm of the sofa and he knew he had lived the nightmare. But there were so many things he seemed to have forgotten. He lay back, concentrating. They had wanted him to forget, filled him with some drug, a method of destroying memory. And even now it was still misty, a jigsaw with blank unfilled spaces. Like the jigsaw in the white room.

Shakily he rose and went into the small kitchen. He made himself a pot of strong black coffee and drank two mugs of it, now intent only on the warm and slightly acrid flavour of the liquid. He filled the mug a third time and went back into the lounge and sat erect on the edge of the sofa.

And then he remembered. He remembered it all. From the meeting with Nora Matheson to the meal in the Savoy Grill with Martindale. And the events in between.

He started to tremble. Coffee spilt over the edge of the mug and stained the sofa. Bubbles of perspiration broke out on his forehead. He sat staring at the carpet, his mind racing.

Very rarely in peacetime does a man feel real fear. James had, over the last few days, lived several lifetimes of fear. Now it seemed as if those lifetimes had all come together with the complete realisation of all that had happened to him.

Normally, he thought, if something criminal occurred in his life ... there had been a break-in at his shop some years before ... he went at once to the police. But now it seemed the police were on the other side. The police and the authorities were, to echo Martindale, the bad guys.

There had been the police at Chester discussing amiably the situation with the man who had, less than an hour before, beaten him up. There was, too, the Section, of which Mansfield had talked within hours of his death. There was Martindale who obviously held some position of authority at the same time as he was instrumental in ensuring James was drugged and out of the way. What way? And there was even a policeman on guard outside the house in Notting Hill in which he had been detained.

But what way? Out of whose way? To prevent him finding Nora? To prevent him even searching for Nora? And now what could he do? Sit in his own living room, shaking with fear, unable to seek official help, waiting for them to find him, perhaps decide this time it was not worth keeping him drugged. Simpler to kill him. Even though Martindale didn't like killing people. People didn't like being killed but it was for the greater good in Martindale's eyes. Skinner had died for the greater good, Mansfield blown up for the ultimate necessity; better he should die than the authorities be incommoded. People who didn't like being killed had no say in the matter. He, James Ryder, would have no say, no argument in their eyes for going on living.

He rose and went to the window. He stared down into the dull South Kensington Street. There should, he told himself, be someone down there watching the flat. Sitting in a car smoking a cigarette, waiting for him. Or leaning against a lamppost acting casually, a man waiting. There was no one in sight. He turned away. Perhaps they were too busy with their race riot. He crossed the room and switched on the stylish and expensive radio cassette recorder. The voice of the newscaster boomed out filling the room.

'The Notting Hill riots are believed to have started when the police attempted to arrest a West Indian social worker, well known in the district, who is to face a charge of assault.

129

His fellow workers, denying the charge, insisted that John Benjamin Harrod, the social worker, had been nowhere near the scene of the assault the previous night when a middle-aged London estate agent was allegedly accused by Harrod of profiteering in the letting of certain properties in Notting Hill. It is alleged that Harrod became so incensed with the estate agent that he attacked him with a knife wounding him in the arm and neck. When the police, one CID man and two constables arrived last night at Harrod's home and effected the arrest members of the black community gathered and attacked the police car, setting it alight. The riot then spread throughout the district despite calls for calm from many local leaders including Mr Harrod himself. Statements are expected to be made this morning by the Home Secretary and the Commissioner of the Metropolitan police. . . .'

James switched the radio to another station and lowered the sound. A surprisingly gentle piece of pop music filled the room.

So that's how it could be done, he thought. Pick on some popular local figure, ensure he was treated callously in front of his fellows and the fuse is lit. But why should they bother? Why should they wish to start a riot?

He put it from his mind. It was another question in a forest of growing question marks. He now must be concerned for himself, for the next move he must make. He couldn't sit and wait for them to come for him. He couldn't wait for his own projected death without taking action even out of fear. But what could he do?

Leave the country. Pack, draw money from the bank and go abroad? If they would let him. Then his fear turned to anger. Why should he run? Why should he be made to run? He had committed no crime; indeed they were the criminals. And again the question, who were they? He wanted an answer! And he wanted to find Nora Matheson. He was sure that if he found her and she was alive he would find the answer, the many answers to the forest of questions. He had tried Mansfield. And they had killed Mansfield. But there was another name in Nora's notes, another who had been mentioned by Mansfield. Carteret.

Lived somewhere in Hampstead, Mansfield had said. A retired member of the Section. Perhaps he would still be one of them, this Carteret. There had been a first name too, Mansfield had mentioned the first name. What was it? Damn his memory. He'd remembered everything else clearly but Carteret's first name. He was sure Mansfield had mentioned it. The telephone directory, the simple solution. In one minute he found it. The one Carteret in Hampstead. 'Carteret, T. H. 27 Hampstead High Street.' He was lifting the telephone when the thought struck him. His line could be tapped, bugged, whatever they called it. That's how they would have known he was in touch with Mansfield. And now if he phoned Carteret he could be setting him up. That was the expression, setting him up. Placing him where he could be killed, murdered, assassinated, eliminated, his health status altered. Christ, the euphemisms of the trade, they were all so God damned alien outside the pages of spy fiction. But this wasn't fiction.

He went into the bathroom to wash and shave. A stranger stared at him from the shaving mirror; a hollow-eyed, ashen-faced caricature of himself. The drugs and his treatment had made their effect obvious. He reckoned he was at least half a stone lighter. That was possibly beneficial. He dressed quickly. A clean black polo necked sweater over light jeans and a comfortable, if old, sports jacket which accommodated the revolver he had taken from the large man with a not too prominent bulge. He felt better now; the exhaustion had gone and, apart from occasional twinges in muscles and joints, the residual effects of the drugs had gone. In the mirror he now looked reasonably presentable.

Leaving the flat he took the elevator down to the parking area in the basement. When he had gone to the Savoy to meet Martindale he had taken a taxi rather than use his own car and spend hours trying to find a parking place. The Jensen should be where he had left it. And it was, begrimed with dust and dried mud. Its condition parallelled his own. He drove out into the street, eyes alert for any conveniently parked automobile that would inevitably start up and follow him. There was nothing in the street. If they had wanted to hold him so badly, where were they? No one had come to the flat in the night, no one was waiting for him outside.

Two streets away a large American car pulled out behind him, a gleaming grey Cadillac with American number plates. It followed him as far as Hyde Park Corner and just as he was convinced they had picked up his trail the Cadillac veered away heading towards Piccadilly as he drove through the edge of the park. He was in a stream of traffic now and if anyone was following him it would be impossible to pick them out. Behind him was a laundry van now and, as he drove into Marylebone Road, it disappeared, its place taken by a Citroen.

The streets of London seemed unnaturally quiet and it was only when he noticed most shops were closed that he remembered it must be Sunday. As he drove finally into Hampstead High Street he saw the congregation of a church debouching onto the kerb, best Sunday clothes in evidence.

Parking the car across the road from number twenty-seven he studied the building. An Edwardian edifice above shops, red sandstone rather ornate in its decoration; a door set between a dry-cleaning establishment and a newsagent, the side of the door lined with bell pushes for the various flats.

James bought a Sunday paper in the newsagent's. The previous night's rioting was headlined, and in the centre pages a leading article called for 'stronger measures' and a firm, ruthless hand to uphold law and order. The tone of the article struck a chord in James's mind. It might have been written by Martindale. It was in fact written by some obscure Conservative MP., adding to his parliamentary salary by some occasional journalism of the type referred to as trenchant and outspoken.

It did provide James with another thought. If men like Martindale wanted to establish a stronger government control of the country then race riots were beneficial to their aims. A newly lit fire needed fuel. Notting Hill, Brixton and Bristol provided fuel. He dismissed the thought. Too complex, too *outré*. Anyway there had been other reasons for Brixton and Bristol. Official enquiries had shown that. But Notting Hill could have been different. No. Couldn't have been sanctioned by the present government. It didn't make sense.

He rang the bell of number twenty-seven under the small brass nameplate, 'T. H. Carteret'. Below the row of buttons was a microphone grill. After a moment a voice came through. 'Carteret here. Who is that?'

James took a deep breath. 'You don't know me, Mr Carteret, but my name is James Ryder. I'd like to speak to you. It's rather serious.'

The reply came back without hesitation. 'I've been expecting you, Mr Ryder. Please come up.'

Expecting him? How could Carteret be expecting him? They had never met, had never had any contact. All he knew of Carteret was what Mansfield had told him and the scribbled name in Nora's notebook. According to Mansfield, Carteret had held a high position in the Section. James shivered. Perhaps Martindale had already been in touch with Carteret.

There was a buzzing sound from the street door and James pushed it open. He entered cautiously. If Martindale had been in touch with Carteret he could be walking into the proverbial trap. But, as he climbed the narrow stairway, James realised he had no place else to go. Carteret was his last hope of tracing Nora.

On the second landing a door was open.

'Come in, Mr. Ryder,' said the old man standing in shadow in the doorway.

He was in his seventies, a thin elderly man leaning on a stick, a shining black ebony stick. His face was a network of lines, wrinkles and, as he stepped into the light of the hallway behind him, a number of small scars. He was dressed in a rather baggy pair of tweed trousers and a jumper over a light blue shirt which was open at the thin neck. Hair, grey to white, was combed backwards and thick over the shirt collar.

'You must excuse my not wearing a tie, Ryder,' the old man said apologetically. 'But it is Sunday and being casual is a small relaxation for me. You see I never had a casual life so I'm apt to indulge now.'

The sitting room James was shown into was small and

133

untidily comfortable. Two walls were lined from ceiling to floor with books, some, leather bound, expensive editions of some antiquity; others, recent publications, were well thumbed but still in their paper jackets. The furniture was serviceable with a pleasing elegance. Two deep leather armchairs faced a large coloured television set, the only item in the room which somehow jarred.

Carteret followed his eyes. 'You must excuse the television. A retirement gift from the ... the Section in which I worked.' He sighed. 'Still it is a way of keeping one's eye on the events of the day. A blessing at my age. But come, do sit down. You have something to say to me?'

'It's ... it's a long story,' James hesitated. 'But you said you were expecting me ... ?'

'Mansfield. He telephoned me a few days ago. On the day he was killed, actually.'

An expression of pain crossed Carteret's face, a fleeting haunting look of sadness. He turned away quickly and went on. 'But before we talk may I offer you a sherry? ... I have some rather good Amontillado.'

'Thank you.'

The old man poured the drinks in silence and then, handing one of the glasses to him, sat facing him. 'I was sad about Ronald Mansfield's death,' he went on. 'He was a prickly character but his heart was sound. He told me something of your story.'

'I was going back to see him again when he was killed,' James interrupted. 'He phoned me and asked me to come urgently.'

'That may have been my doing. It seemed to me that you had stumbled on something rather unhealthy. My advice then was for you to get out. Hand the whole matter over to the proper authorities.'

'Didn't he tell you I went to the police in Chester?'

'Yes, but this is not an ordinary police matter. I told Mansfield you must go to a man called Martindale.'

Carteret stopped as he saw the expression on James's face change.

'You know the name?'

134

James nodded. 'I met Mr Martindale. If it hadn't been for him I might have come to see you sooner.'

Carteret pursed his lips. 'I see. Or rather I may not have been seeing.'

James was on his feet. 'I'm afraid I must go.'

His head was throbbing again as he turned away from the old man. This was to have been the last chance, the final note in Nora Matheson's book. And now it had come around in a circle leaving him with nowhere to go. But he knew he had to leave this flat, had to start running again.

Rising, Carteret spoke. 'Don't go, Mr Ryder. I think we may have been talking at cross purposes. I want you to tell me the whole story from beginning to end. I want you to leave nothing out – '

'If your advice is that I see Martindale, then we have nothing to talk about.'

'I think we have. Forget what I said about Martindale. Remember I only heard your story second hand on the telephone from a man now dead. And that was several days ago. Things have obviously happened in those days. They may alter my advice to you. Please sit down and tell me.' He could see James was still uncertain, unconvinced. 'It may be incidental,' he added, 'but I recruited young Skinner and I liked him. If he has defected, become involved in trouble I would like to know.'

James remembered. He hadn't told Mansfield of Skinner's fate. He had deliberately omitted the body in the boot of his car.

'Skinner is dead.'

There was no change of expression in Carteret's face. He simply stared at James, willing him to continue. After a long moment he said, 'Please go on.'

'You were shocked by Mansfield's death,' James said, suddenly irritated by the lack of reaction. 'But not Skinner's?'

'In my business, Mr Ryder, I long ago became accustomed to the deaths of people close to me. I think my reaction to Mansfield's death was one of bafflement. He was long out of the game. But Skinner was not. Please, do as I ask. Tell me everything.'

James did so. When he had finished Carteret said nothing at first but poured them both another sherry.

'This must have been quite traumatic for you. Apart from the drugs and that place in Notting Hill,' he said almost kindly. 'I know the place. One of our safe houses. The medical facilities were there in the event of one of our people coming in from abroad injured. It was never meant to be used in the way it has been towards you.'

James drank the second glass of sherry in one gulp. Not the thing to do, he thought, not at all. Should be sipped, savoured.

'Look, Mansfield had some respect for you,' he spoke quickly now. 'Told me you were some kind of agent in this ... this section, whatever it is before you retired. I want to know what to do.'

'Yes, I expect you do. And it presents us with a problem ... what to do?'

'All I wanted to do was find out what had happened to Nora Matheson. Since then two people have been killed and I've been – '

'I appreciate what you've been through.'

'Do you? Mr Carteret, I'm an ordinary man. I'm no hero, I'm in business and reasonably successful. Up till this I was a contented man. Now I feel hunted, afraid for my life and without the slightest understanding of what is going on.'

'You accidentally kicked over a stone, Ryder, and some unpleasant things crawled out.'

James rose and paced the small room. 'Too easy. It's as if I'm standing outside myself watching he who ... who is me, wondering how anyone can be so afraid, wondering whether the character I'm watching can be so foolish. And yet ... yet I see no alternative for him ... for me to act otherwise.'

'Believe me, I've been through it. Living in occupied France during the war, one developed a split personality. I was ostensibly a French citizen, a businessman in a small way. And yet I could stand away from this character I adopted, look at him from the distance, knowing he was an agent of British Intelligence – '

'That was during the war! There is no war just now!'

The old man raised an eyebrow. 'You think not? There's always a war going on under the surface.'

'You mean between the West and the East?'

'Sometimes. Sometimes it's between us and the French. Or the Americans. Or one of the emergent nations. A battle of manoeuvre for position, a battle for information. And it has its casualties.'

'Skinner? Mansfield?'

Carteret shrugged expressively. 'Certainly casualties. But we have to identify the war. Who is fighting whom.'

'Tell me,' James said, the tone of desperation creeping into his voice. 'I'm in the middle and I don't like it. I don't want anything to do with spies, espionage, whatever you call it.'

'It may not be to do with the conventional intelligence scenario. In fact I doubt it is. I think this is something else.' Carteret ran his thin hand across his brow. 'Yes, something else. Did Mansfield tell you much about the Section?'

'He told me it was a kind of super intelligence organisation founded to keep an eye on the others. MI5, MI6 and so on.'

'Founded by Clement Attlee when he was Prime Minister,' Carteret said. 'Rear Admiral Sir Arthur Morris was Director. I was his second in command. Deputy-Director to be exact. A man called Harrington was in charge of communications. In time the Section grew rather important. Had a good reputation too. Never was infiltrated by the Reds like MI5. Not that Moscow Centre didn't try. My God, they tried. At least three possible recruits over the years were identified as Russian Agents.' He smiled smugly. 'They never got into the Section.'

'Somebody's got in now!' James said coldly.

'Not the Russians.'

'Then who the hell is Martindale?'

Carteret took a deep breath before replying. 'Derek Martindale is the present Director of the Section.'

There was a pause as Carteret allowed his words to sink in. James stopped pacing and stared at the old man.

Finally Carteret went on. 'That's why when I heard you say Skinner had problems, I referred you to Martindale. It seemed logical.'

'But it isn't now.'

'As you say. Of course if you have stumbled upon something top secret then Martindale would be correct in taking steps to stop you passing on that secret.'

James flushed. 'But I'm not an enemy. I'm no flag-waving patriot but I can shut up when security's involved. They don't have to drug me, they don't have to kill people I go to for help. Martindale could have talked to me – '

'Possibly,' Carteret replied. 'If he could be sure of trusting you. But I certainly think he could be mishandling the situation, whatever it is. Unless . . . unless – '

'What?'

'Unless it is something he is sure you would react against. For example if you stumbled upon the fact that Martindale was working for the other side. If he was another celebrated mole working for Moscow.'

'You think he is?'

Carteret shrugged. 'No, I don't. Martindale was checked out by me years ago. He's no Russian agent. But I am interested in how he knew there was going to be a race riot in Notting Hill before it happened. And of course I would like to know why Skinner and Mansfield were killed. And why Harrington was killed.'

'Harrington? But if he's the man in Nora's notes surely he died accidentally?'

'Fell under a tube train? Oh, I doubt that was an accident.' He stared hard at James. 'May I tell you a little story, Mr Ryder? Some months ago, when the Rear Admiral died, I went to his funeral. Mark of respect for an old colleague. Mind you I was retired. Anyway I went. They were all there, his colleagues. Martindale, who was Deputy Director, my old job. And, of course, he was the natural choice to take over as Director. Buller was there too. Not a man I like. He's in charge of . . . shall we say . . . the strong arm department of the Section. Known as Buller's bully boys. Oh, someone has to be in charge of that kind of work, but Buller actually seems to enjoy it. And Harrington was there. He was communications chief. In charge of everything going in and out from all the agents abroad. And the others.'

138

'They would be there, wouldn't they?'

'Oh, yes, all perfectly normal. I got a smile and a nod from Martindale. But the only one I actually spoke to was Harrington. He and I had been the veterans. Both served under the Rear Admiral from the beginning. Oh, it was a very conventional exchange. How was he, how was I, how was his family? Just before we parted he did say one thing though that stuck with me. Changes, he said, now that the Rear Admiral was dead, changes and not for the better. He was worried. That was all. Then we went to the graveside.'

'Not very much to go on,' James responded weakly.

'True, true. But when I left the cemetery I was followed. Two of Buller's men. Not very effective against an old hand like me. Anyway I faced them with it in the street. Why were they following me? What did they think I was up to? They told me. They told me they wanted to know what Harrington had said to me. I didn't enlighten them. Why should I? They became rather annoying. . . . ' He became silent for a moment staring into space. Under his left eye a nerve twitched. He was reliving the time in the street. At once he squared his shoulders and went on. 'Actually they beat me up.'

'For God's sake, why?'

'I don't know. A warning. Keep off. Stay retired, something like that. I think, too, they were wondering whether I would attempt to bring charges.'

'Didn't you?'

'Officially? Through the police? Dear me, no. Not a police matter. If I did that they might believe Harrington had said something to me. No, as far as the police were concerned I was just another old gentleman who had been mugged. I spent a week in hospital – '

'They could have killed you!'

'No, they're quite expert. They know just how far to go. Training, you see. But I wanted to know why they were so interested in whether or not Harrington had said anything to me. But if I contacted Harrington immediately I felt they would know. So I decided to leave it for a time. Oh, except that I did phone Martindale.'

'What did he say?'

'He was quite distressed. Couldn't understand it at all, he assured me. Would have a word with Buller.'

'That was all?'

Carteret pursed his lips. 'No. He phoned me the next day. Buller knew nothing about it. Knew of no reason why they should do this. Of course I hadn't mentioned Harrington to them. Didn't want to create more trouble. I think that was a mistake. Within weeks, before I could contact Harrington he'd had his "accident". I think had I mentioned Harrington had spoken to me, had said that he was worried I might have had an "accident" too. That was the end of it.'

He was an elderly man, James thought, what could he do? And yet he had the expertise, the experience to know his way around that kind of world. Surely he should have done something.

Carteret seemed to read his thoughts. 'Of course I could have gone higher. Above Martindale. But what could I tell anybody? That Harrington was worried and I got myself mugged? No, I determined to keep my nose to the ground. Listen and perhaps gain some indication of what was happening. If anything was happening.'

'But you were retired. How could you – ?'

'I still had a few contacts. We all do. Polish refugees, Russian emigrés, a few informers on the edge of that kind of world. Mansfield, too, he was a source. As a historian of modern history he knew people, he would keep his eyes and ears open.'

James was leaning forward now. 'You found something?'

'Only in the negative sense,' Carteret replied. 'Nothing was happening abroad. Europe was calm, quiet, the Russians seemed to be behaving themselves as regards the West. Oh, there was trouble in the Middle East as always. A few operations going on. Nothing else. And then Mansfield phoned me about you.'

'So you're no wiser than I am?'

Carteret gave a dry little chuckle. 'Wisdom is relative. It teaches caution and patience. If nothing is happening, then that is suspicious. And everything is calm. Until you arrive with your story. And now you tell me Skinner is dead. So

140

something is happening. You see, Roy Skinner worked for Harrington. He was one of Harrington's men. Oh, a small job. I recruited Skinner some years ago because he had an aptitude for languages. Originally he was going to be a field man after training. But during training he smashed up his right arm. An awkward parachute exercise. Rendered him unfit for field work. So he went into communications. Working for Harrington. And Harrington was unhappy after the death of the Rear Admiral. So he died. Then Skinner had to run. Why?'

'Can you tell me?'

'My boy, I don't know. But something is rotten in the Section and that worries me.' He paused then, rose and poured a third sherry for both of them. When he sat down again he was frowning, the lines deep on his forehead.

'Have you ever thought, Mr Ryder, where the power really lies in this country?'

'House of Commons?'

'Oh, sir, don't delude yourself.'

'Well . . . the . . . the Cabinet, then?'

Carteret nodded. He looked at once like an aging owl. 'Certainly, the Cabinet. But the Cabinet and the Prime Minister rely on the departments under them both for information and for implementation of action. You would agree?'

'Yes, of course.' James sipped the third sherry, calmer now, fascinated by the old man.

'But of all the departments and ministries, where does the most power lie? I shall tell you. Between the intelligence services and the security services. Between the Special Branch of the police, MI5 and MI6 and General Communications Headquarters at Cheltenham. They receive all overseas intelligence information and they compile all information regarding internal subversion. And more than simple subversion. Do you know that between these agencies they hold records on over forty million people? More than two thirds of the entire population is on file, on computer tape.'

'I thought it was illegal to keep records of people other than those who commit crimes.'

'What is legality? James Ryder, an antique dealer is on

141

record somewhere. The Inland Revenue know what you earn, or claim to earn. The police will have a record of any minor infringements of the law, parking offences and so on. You are divorced. That is on the court records. Put these together, feed them into a computer and there's the beginning of a file on James Ryder. If you need to enlarge that file put a team of investigators onto Mr Ryder and they'll find out who you sleep with, who your friends are, and what secrets you have. Anything disreputable, they'll find it and it'll go into the computer. Very useful when you become a problem.'

James stirred uneasily. 'And I've become a problem,' he said.

Carteret took a sip of sherry. 'Your file, Mr Ryder, will have expanded considerably in the last week or so. It will have been extracted from the computer and will be lying on someone's desk, probably Derek Martindale's, marked "Action Now". Your concern should be in what that action is going to be.'

'They haven't done anything since I got out of that place at Notting Hill.'

'Exactly. And that worries me. You went home. You were easily accessible. You fell asleep. I'm quite surprised you woke up.'

'That cheers me considerably,' James responded, his voice heavy with irony.

'Why have they not come for you? That is another question. Still, you must be thankful for that small reprieve. The question now is what can we do? Here we have the intelligence agencies of our country behaving in an aberrant manner for no reason we know of. We have to take some action.'

'If we could find Nora Matheson . . . ?'

'She could be dead,' Carteret said mournfully. 'Or she could be held in any number of houses. Too long a shot. But there is something else.'

'Say it, for God's sake.'

'The Section in theory is answerable to the Prime Minister.' the old man explained. 'But the person in Downing Street cannot be concerned with its day-to-day activities. Therefore

142

there had to be a liaison. Someone above the director.'

'Who?'

'One of the assistants to the Permanent Secretary to the Cabinet. For some years a man called Maurice Withenshaw. Official designation, Deputy Under Secretary, Cabinet Office.'

'He controls the Section?'

'Not exactly. Officially he is the go-between, the man between the PM and the director, Martindale. But through the PM he can control the Section's activities.'

James shook his head doubtfully. 'Supposing he's involved with Martindale in whatever is going on?'

'I doubt it,' Carteret replied. 'I know Maurice very well. He's an establishment man. Goes by the rules. Wouldn't stand for the deaths of innocent bystanders like Mansfield. Unless there was some overpowering reason of national security. And then he would refer it to the PM.'

'So what do we do?'

Carteret rose with surprising agility for his age. 'We contact Withenshaw! We put your story to him. We do it now!'

Crossing to a telephone on a table beside the window he stood, brow furrowed again, looking down at it. 'The number,' he murmured. 'I know the Cabinet Secretariat number. Have known it for a long time. Still I always have to think of it . . . remember it.'

'Why don't you try and get through to the Prime Minister?' James enquired still with a trace of residual irony in his voice. He was not quite sure in his mind whether or not he believed the old man. Whether he dared believe.

'Yes, yes, I have it now,' Carteret said and then looked owlishly across at James. 'I remember. What did you say? Why don't I phone the Prime Minister? Good. A good point. Except that one doesn't get through so easily there. One is after all aiming rather high. This way is possible. Through channels, as they say. Channels surrounded by official reefs.'

He lifted the receiver and dialled a number. After a moment James could hear the number ringing out across the room. Then Carteret was connected. 'I wish to speak to Maurice

Withenshaw.' A pause. 'You may tell him Reindeer is calling.'

James smiled. The old man returned the smile covering the receiver with his hand.

'An old code name. We still have our little games, Mr Ryder. The trouble is most of us engaged in espionage were brought up with the spy films of the cinema. They taught us how we ought to behave as spies and we learnt the lesson rather well.'

A voice at the end of the line called him back to his phone call.

'Yes, yes, I see. Very well, put me through to Mr Gray.' Another pause. A number of distinct clicks on the line. Then Carteret was speaking again. 'John? This is Reindeer. Yes, yes, I'm fine. Enjoying being put out to grass I suppose. No more day-to-day pressures. But something has come up. I have to speak to Maurice. Yes, so I've been told. Where then? My dear man, whether you are supposed to give it out or not, you know if you don't and I have something important Maurice will have your guts strung out across the garden of Number Ten.'

Another pause. Frantic rapid noises from the other end of the line. 'John, you know who you are speaking to. Would I bother if it wasn't important? Now come on and don't be foolish. Yes, hold on for a moment.'

Carteret gesticulated to James, indicating a pencil and pad on a rather ancient desk in the far corner of the room. James brought them to him.

'Right. Proceed!' The noises recommenced at the end of the line and Carteret scribbled on the pad. 'Thanks!' he finally terminated the conversation gruffly and hung up. He tore the top sheet from the pad and turned to James.

'He's on sick leave. I persuaded his assistant to tell me where.' He handed the sheet to James. 'You'd better take it.'

'What do I do?'

Carteret went into a paroxysm of coughing. When it was over he wiped his mouth with a large white handkerchief extracted from his breast pocket. Then he took a deep breath. 'Excuse me. Lungs aren't what they used to be. Fifty cigarettes a day for fifty years. That's 912,500 cigarettes approximately. Not counting leap years. You see I have little to do now so I work out such obtuse calculations. Of course it'll kill me in the end. Oh, not lung cancer. Emphysema. Lungs distend. Not a bad way to go. What were you saying?'

'What do I do with this?' James held up the sheet of paper.

'You go and see him!'

James glanced at the address. 'He's in Scotland.'

'Yes. Always goes to Scotland on vacation. This time, sick leave. You go to him and you tell him everything. Then he takes action.'

'You're sure he'll take action?'

Carteret nodded with some vigour. 'He has to. He has to investigate all you've told him. Martindale will be answerable to him.'

'Supposing he's involved with Martindale?'

'Then at least you'll receive civilised treatment. And some kind of explanation.'

'That will make everything all right? An explanation why two men died.'

Carteret coughed again. 'Only course of action. Until we know what's going on.'

'You want me to go to Scotland?'

'I understand you were heading there to start with. When you met Miss Matheson. So go now. Get out of London, away from ... from them. I don't think they'll let up on you, Ryder. As I said I don't understand why they haven't already come after you.'

James was on his feet again. 'You'll come with me to Scotland?'

'No. Apart from anything else I don't feel fit to travel. Ever since the little beating they gave me after the funeral ... ' His face reddened with anger. 'Haven't been the same. When I was younger I could have ... could have taken them. Both of them, imagine that. Both of them. I was very good then. But not now. I shall stay here. Anyway I have certain avenues of enquiry. Old connections. I'll follow them up.'

He hesitated, staring into space for a moment. Then he

straightened up, cleared his throat and stared at James. 'Have you money with you?'

'Yes,' James replied, puzzled. 'I still have most of the cash I was taking to Scotland. And my credit cards. Actually I'm surprised your Section people didn't lift them when I was drugged.'

Carteret smiled a humourless smile. 'Oh, they wouldn't do that, Mr Ryder. You see they're scrupulously honest people. They'll kill you if the scenario calls for it but they'll never steal. I mean, that would be theft. Unless, of couse, they were ordered to do so. It's a strange morality, sir. Highly selective. Right and wrong exist but only outside the scenario. So ... go to Scotland. Directly. Don't go back to your flat. They could be waiting. Straight to Scotland. Inverkeil House, Inverness-shire. Just north of Fort William. You'll find it. And speak to Withenshaw.'

'I have to pack a bag.'

'No, Ryder. Buy what you need on the way. You have my telephone number. I will give you another number too.' He scribbled briefly on a piece of paper and handed it to James. 'If any voice but mine answers this number, hang up and try that one. It's an old friend's, a police inspector, but on our side. Whoever you phone give your number, hang up and wait until I phone back. In case our friends are listening in. Understand?'

'Yes, I think so.'

Carteret suddenly smiled. 'Quite like old times for me, briefing an agent. Pity you have so little experience. You've been lucky until now though. Luck is important for a good operative. Keep being lucky, Ryder. And do what I tell you. That way we might find out what the Section is up to.'

What were they up to? Old fears arose in the old man's mind. Too much power in the wrong hands. If they were the wrong hands.

The two men shook hands at the door to the landing. Carteret had another fit of coughing but managed a small wave, a gentle gesture as James went down the narrow stairway.

The old man went back into his sitting room, closing and

locking the front door behind him. The bout of coughing had subsided and he lit another cigarette with a small, cold smile. He savoured the cigarette as he sat down, enjoying the soothing feeling as he inhaled. At his age what did it matter if he didn't stop smoking? One of the few pleasures left to him even if it dilated and hardened his lungs. God, how pitiable the thought. The old man in the dry month with few pleasures and a hell of a lot of self pity. Damn it, no time for self pity. Something was happening, something which frightened him. Mansfield and young Skinner both dead; Ryder would be next. Unless he could get to Withenshaw. Unless Withenshaw believed. But would he?

He certainly would believe if, after he'd seen Ryder, they got to the antique dealer. But that meant it would take a death to convince Maurice Withenshaw. Another death? Another example of wastage. Carteret had seen it happen before. He had seen it happen too often. He started to cough again as the cigarette smoke filled his lungs.

They would kill James Ryder now. It was the only course of action left to the Section to protect whatever scenario concerned them. In their position he would do the same thing. But what was the scenario that it required the death of James Ryder?

He started to cough again and as he did so he felt a great sadness envelop him.

4

James came into the street, the soured taste of sherry in his mouth. He walked across to his car, head down, deep in thought. Leave London at once, Carteret's advice, go to Scotland, find Withenshaw; a clear course of action. And over it all the threat that the Section would be looking for him and now would not hesitate to kill him. If only he could understand why. The little he knew obviously presented a threat to them. Yet he knew so little. All he had wanted to do was find Nora Matheson. Therefore it seemed logical that the knowledge of her disappearance was the one fact they feared. So it came down to find Nora, if she was still alive. Nora was the one who knew what the Section was about. What was the word Carteret had used – Scenario. She must know what the scenario was, what it implied.

He unlocked the door of the Jensen. The perfume, a particularly subtle aroma assailed him at once. He looked up, across at the passenger seat. It was occupied.

She was a lean attractive woman, faultlessly made up, dressed in a beautifully tailored, grey trouser suit. Long, honey-blonde hair was pulled back into a faultess bun, not a hair out of place.

James instinctively recoiled from the car door, a startled stab of fear showing in his face.

'Don't worry, Mr Ryder,' the woman said quietly, her voice low with the slight trace of an American accent. She had at once recognised his fear. 'I'm not here to do you any harm.'

'Who . . . who the devil are you?' he stammered. 'And how did you get into my car?'

A smile underlined the laughter lines around her eyes. 'Getting into your car was pretty easy. It's not hard to pick a lock when you know how.'

'What do you want?'

'To talk, Mr Ryder. You owe me that.'

James, despite his fears found himself relaxing. There was something plausible about the woman. More than that he felt an obvious attraction. He estimated she was in her early thirties, and he could see she was poised, assured.

'How do I owe you anything?'

The smile again. The Gioconda. 'You would have been dead if it hadn't been for me and my people. How do you think you were able to stay alive in your apartment last night?'

James frowned, uncomprehending. She went on talking quietly.

'Oh, Mr Martindale sent a couple of Buller's boys along. We took care of them. Now would you please get into your car. This is a kind of public place to be talking.'

'What do you mean, you took care of them?'

She motioned that he climb into the car. He did so cautiously. 'Don't worry, Mr Ryder, we didn't kill them. We don't do that to our cousins – '

'Cousins?'

'Close friends most of the time. Mr Buller's boys will wake up some time tomorrow morning in a cottage down near Brighton. I think they came to kill you last night but we stopped them.' She smiled showing a line of unblemished white teeth.

'Who are you?' James demanded impatiently. He was tired of mysteries, irritated by this woman presenting him with yet another mystery.

'My name is Jean. . . . Jean Thurman,' she replied. 'Don't look so baffled. We haven't met before but I know quite a bit about you, Mr Ryder. Look, why don't you drive me to your apartment and I'll tell you what I can over a drink.'

Again she seemed to read James's mind because the smile widened as she went on. 'Don't worry. It's quite safe to go to your place. My people are looking after it. Of course, I gather Mr Carteret would have warned you to stay clear . . . and he would have been right. But then he didn't know we were in the picture.'

'You know Carteret?'

'I never met him. He was before my time but I know of him. The best man the British had in his day. But his day's past. You going to drive to your place now?'

James drove.

There was a chill about the flat and, despite the fact that he had spent the night there, it had an unlived in feeling. James switched on the gas fire and when he turned to face the woman she was comfortably ensconced in one of his armchairs.

'A scotch, if you have it,' she said before he could ask.

He poured her a scotch and himself a brandy. Then he sat facing her. 'All right, Miss Thurman, tell me.'

A teasing smile. 'Where shall I start?'

'Who are you?'

'I told you. Jean – '

'Not the name. The occupation?'

She took a sip of her whisky. 'Okay, I'll give you all of it. Jean Thurman, official assistant attaché at the US Embassy concerned with trade. You can check that with the Embassy. That's all they'll tell you.'

'But there's more?'

'Trade attaché is a cover. I am actually assistant head of station for the CIA in the United Kingdom. That you can't check. You'll have to take my word for it.'

James must have registered surprise as she came back instantly. 'Sure, there are women in the CIA. No heads of stations yet who're women but I guess as deputy head I'm as far as a woman has got to date.'

'All right. I accept that for now. But what has this business to do with the CIA?'

'If I knew what the business was, Mr Ryder . . . hell, I'm going to call you James. . . . if I knew what it was, James, I'd be able to tell you exactly how interested we are. That's why I have to speak to you. We want to know what's going on.'

'How did you get on to me?'

Jean Thurman shrugged. 'Look, I'll level with you, James, and I'll hope you'll level with me. But all I say is off the record. Throw it back at me and I'll deny every word.'

'Agreed.'

She took a deep breath. 'Whether you know it or not the CIA have had a pretty close relationship with your MI5 and MI6. We've exchanged information, worked pretty closely for years. We helped build up your communications complex at Cheltenham, Gloucestershire. We even use the facilities. And we've liaised for a long time with the Section under Admiral Morris and under Mr Martindale. That is, until recently.'

'What happened recently?'

'Although we work closely with the British we have our own people placed around your intelligence groups just to keep an eye on things. A time after the Admiral died one of

150

our people tells us something is going on. Well most covert operations we're informed about so they don't clash with our activities. This one we get nothing. Not a whisper. So we get curious. We keep our eyes open. And what do we learn?'

James was hunched forward now, hoping for answers to some of his own questions. 'What did you learn, Miss Thurman?'

'For Chrissake,' she said easily. 'Call me Jean. What did we learn, you want to know? Nothing. We know something's going on, we don't know what. From our point of view Martindale and his people could have all gone pinko. After Philby and the others we've always reckoned it could happen. So we get keen. Then we get a break a few days ago. The word comes from our man that the Section wants one James Ryder who is asking questions about a woman journalist who disappeared and she's linked with Roy Skinner, a Section communications guy who has also disappeared. This is all our man can learn, he's not high enough to be told everything. We had contacts with Buller who's in charge of the Section's hit men but he's clammed up. Nothing's going on according to him, Skinner's on leave and he's never heard of James Ryder or Nora Matheson.'

'He's lying!'

'We figured either he's lying or his left hand doesn't know what his right hand's up to. Then we hear they've got Mr James Ryder tucked away in one of their safe houses at your Notting Hill. So we have a man keeping his eye on the house. Then you escape in the middle of a Goddam race riot and our man is close behind. He figures you're crazy when you come home here but you've been showing all the signs of an unwilling amateur so we forgive you. But we protect you last night so we can talk. We want to know what you're up to and where you're going. Which is why I'm here now. Oh, and one other thing. We got a copy of a new file that the Section have opened on you.'

'What does that tell you?' James enquired dubiously.

'That you're an accident, James. Confirms you're not a professional. But you have stumbled on something they want to keep quiet.'

151

'I wish to hell I knew what it was. If I did I'd be glad to tell you.'

Jean Thurman smiled again, her eyes seemingly assessing him. She crossed her legs and he noticed her shoes. Very high, pointed heels. Elegant. She reached into her handbag, fumbling briefly. The handbag was a work of art. Gucci, obviously. She produced a packet of cigarettes and offered him one.

'I keep saying I'll give it up but what the hell . . .' she said.

He accepted a cigarette, lit hers and then his own.

'Okay, James. Now tell me all about it.'

He hadn't at first intended to tell her. He had been highly suspicious both of her and the CIA. He'd always had the impression that the CIA was much more suspect than even British Intelligence. But somehow her presence made him feel at ease, comfortable. She appeared to have the quality of frankness that many Americans possessed. Of course it might be deliberately assumed but now he found it refreshing after the subterfuges he had experienced in the past week.

'You see, James,' she went on, pressing her advantage. 'We like to know what our friends are up to. You might think we don't trust them and you'd be right. We don't. But especially we don't trust them when they're supposed to let us know what they're up to and they don't.'

James told her everything. It was the second time in one day he had related all that had befallen him and he found it came easily. As if he had learnt it by rota. This time there was the addition of the visit to Carteret and what Carteret had advised.

'That sounds like the truth.'

'It is the truth!' he flushed indignantly.

'Okay, okay. But all I've got is your word. I'm accepting it. The point is it doesn't take us much further forward. It just shows that whatever Martindale is up to he's willing to kill to keep it quiet.'

She drew on her cigarette in silence for a moment. Thinking. Considering the next move in the game. They were all like damn chess players, James thought, working their brains out on alternative moves, varied possibilities.

She broke the silence. 'What are you going to do now?'

'I have no choice. I stay here and seemingly I'm to be killed. Presuming your people can't adopt me for ever. I intend to take Carteret's advice. Go to see Withenshaw.'

She considered this briefly and then nodded. 'Yes, only thing you can do. How about Nora Matheson's paper? You never followed that up.'

'They'd tell me she's still in Paris.'

'I wonder what they'd tell me. I could call.'

It was James's turn to nod. 'You could.'

She stood up briskly. 'I'll do that. Give you a chance to pack for Scotland. And then you wait here. Or no, meet me. Grosvenor Square. Our Embassy in two hours. Give me time to pack.'

'Where are you going?'

'To Scotland with you. I've never seen Scotland. They tell me it's beautiful. And I think I should see Withenshaw with you.'

James frowned. Was it a good idea?

She tried to allay his doubts. 'I know Maurice Withenshaw. He plays it straight down the line with us. Anyway I might just be able to help get you out of trouble.'

'Yes. All right,' James said uncertainly. 'But while you're away – '

'You'll be okay, James. My people are keeping an eye on you.'

He tried to return her smile and found he wasn't very successful. He was sure it came out more like a grimace.

'It's not that I'm afraid,' he tried to explain lightly. 'It's just that I'm frankly terrified.'

She ignored the levity. She walked to the door of the room and turned. 'One thing I have to say. If whatever Martindale is doing meets with our approval, then we're in a different ball game.'

'That means you take up where they left off and try to kill me?'

'Don't worry too much, James,' she replied. 'We'll try and get you out of it in one piece. Believe it or not none of us likes to be involved in having to terminate anyone.'

'Another hospital room? More drugs? And you'll charge me for it. At least Martindale drugged me on the National Health Service.'

She wasn't smiling now. 'We'll arrange something and charge it to the CIA.'

She went out. He heard the front door shut behind her. He poured himself another drink and then proceeded to pack a small case. This was the second time in the last week he had packed to go to Scotland. But this trip would not be a holiday. He packed only basic necessities. And one other item. In a drawer in his bedroom he found a small antique African club, an ancient weapon belonging to some forgotten tribe that had wandered the Kalahari centuries ago. Might come in handy. Though if he did hit anybody with it they'd be fortunate if their skull was still intact afterwards.

He sat for an hour then watching television without being aware of the images on the screen. He was reassured by the thought that CIA people were looking after him. Or so she had said. If she was lying he could have problems. He dismissed the thought. It was too unpleasant to dwell on.

Finally he decided it was time to leave. He switched off the television, picked up his bag and left the flat. He spent some minutes fumbling outside the door with his keys before he finally secured the locks. He then took the elevator to the ground floor and going to the front door he peered into the street. Cars were parked along the kerb and from what he could see they were all empty. Everything seemed clear to go.

He crossed back to the elevator to descend to the basement car park. As he did so he realised there was no porter in attendance behind the desk. Aston should be around somewhere. In the middle of the day, even Sunday, he was never far away. James crossed to the desk and looked around. A book was open on the desk, the ledger in which Aston entered the names of visitors. The book was blank for the day. Not usual, James thought. Beside the book was a small bell push. Below it a notice.

PRESS FOR PORTER

James pressed the bell and waited. Beside the bell was the

154

internal telephone switchboard with lines to every flat. Beside this was the receiver. The telephone bell rang. James lifted the receiver.

'Yes?' A woman's voice.

'This is James Ryder. Is Mr Aston on duty?'

'Oh, Mr Ryder. This is Mrs Aston. James was called away early this morning. A telegram saying his sister was ill. He went off to Birmingham.'

'Sorry to hear that. I just wondered who was on duty.'

The woman sounded apologetic. 'Of course I'm standing in for him. Anyone rings the bell it's routed to me in our flat.'

'That's fine then, Mrs Aston.'

'The only thing is, Mr Ryder, someone's been playing a joke on Aston. When he got to his sister's she was fine. He phoned me an hour ago to tell me. He thinks someone's been playing some kind of nasty practical joke on him.'

'There's a lot of it around.'

'But who would do a stupid thing like that?'

'Sorry I can't help you,' James replied. 'Just as long as he's all right. 'Bye, Mrs Aston.'

He hung up. Sorry, I can't help you; that was a lie to start with. Either Martindale's people had got Aston out of the way or the CIA was responsible. Probably Martindale. Giving his men a clear run to James. Only the CIA had frustrated that. Thank God and Jean Thurman.

He took the elevator down to the basement. It was cold in the concrete car park, and the lights, bulkhead fittings in the concrete, illuminated the place only dimly. Some of them were out, the bulbs obviously done. He must tell Aston about that.

His footsteps echoed against the walls as he crossed to the Jensen. But as he neared the car he became aware of another sound. At first it sounded like somebody snoring, a loud snorting noise. Then as James reached the car the sound became clearer as of someone gasping desperately for breath. It was coming from the space between the bonnet of the car and the concrete wall of the basement.

James moved slowly with a caution born of his experiences in the last few days. He edged between the Jensen and a parked Rover alert to the possibility of movement around him. The body of the man was lying against the wall, a livid bruise on his right temple. His mouth was open and he was uttering choking sounds as he struggled to breathe. James knelt beside him and felt for a pulse in the neck. It was strong. The man had obviously been struck hard on the temple and was semi-conscious but, as far as James could judge, in no danger. The eyes were shut but the eyelids flickered. James stood uncertainly and surveyed the man. He was dressed in a grey flannel suit, well cut and obviously expensive. But there was something about the cut of the suit that was different. It had not been tailored in this country. James knelt again and studied the face. About thirty, he estimated, well groomed, fairish hair fringing the bruise of the forehead.

'Are you all right?' James said. 'Can you hear me?'

The left eyelid flickered again.

'Can you hear me?' James repeated, leaning forward.

The left eyelid opened. The man stared up at James with a frightened, puzzled look.

'C . . . car . . . Bon . . . car . . . bon . . . !'

The eyelid closed again, the head slumped backwards. James felt again for the pulse in the neck. It was still beating. Quite regular. And the breathing had become quieter, deeper, more natural. The man had lapsed into unconsciousness.

Who the hell was he?

Reaching for the inner pocket of the jacket James brought out a slim leather wallet and flicked it open. A plastic identity card was the first thing he saw.

RICHMOND PACKARD

UNITED STATES OF AMERICA

DEPARTMENT OF STATE

UNITED STATES EMBASSY, GROSVENOR SQUARE, LONDON.

One of her people. CIA. On duty looking after James Ryder. And not doing it very successfully.

James stood up. Someone had put Richmond Packard out of action. Obviously that cleared the way to James Ryder. The problem was the next move. On his part? On their part?

And what was Packard trying to say to him? Something about carbon. Carbon monoxide? A way to kill. No, not in a basement this big. So what was he trying to say? Leave it until later, James told himself. Now he had to get out of the basement and take Packard with him. The guarded looking after the guardians; that wasn't the way it was supposed to work. Now he had to get out and take the unconscious American with him. Just get into the car and drive fast, it seemed easy enough. Once in the street they might follow him but they would hardly try and kill him in the streets of Central London. So he had to take the car and drive.

Car. The American's phrase, what was it? 'Car . . . bon . . .' James stared at the Jensen. The car? The bonnet of the car. He stared at the paintwork covered in a deep film of dust. Except for fingermarks around the edge, where the bonnet was opened! Someone had opened the bonnet!

Gently, tentatively, fingertips easing up the metal, James opened the bonnet. Despite the surface dust on the outside of the car the engine was still remarkably clean, the acrid smell of engine oil and petrol assailing his nostrils. He had little mechanical knowledge but machinery had a wayward fascination for James. He liked it clean, shining, its intricacies appearing efficient in their complexity. Everything seemed as it should be. The wires broke from their neat bunches over the carburettor – was it the carburettor? – dividing and running into the back of the dashboard. Except that there were two wires he hadn't seen before running from ignition to battery and down from the battery under the engine. They were new, green insulated wires and he was sure he had never seen them before.

It wasn't possible surely; something that only happened in films. Step into the car, switch on the ignition and . . . oh, for God's sake, it was a cliché of the cinema thriller. Yet what were clichés but simple, obvious examples of the method direct?

He lay flat on the concrete floor and pulled himself under the car.

They were there, exactly as he expected them to be; looking exactly like they were supposed to look. Like a bunch of dirty brownish candles held together by insulating tape and attached by the same tape to the underside of the engine. The two wires ran down from the car battery to a small shining silver phial attached to the bunch of candles. Only they weren't candles and the phial wasn't a phial, it was a detonator.

Time to get out. Without the car. Outside they'd be waiting but not for James Ryder to appear. They'd be waiting for the sound of the explosion. If he left now by the back entrance into the small mews he might just be able to get away. At the end of the mews there was a chance of picking up a taxi. But he couldn't take Packard with him. That would lessen his chances, hold him back. And the Jensen was safe as long as it was locked and he held the key.

James lifted the American with both hands, his shoulders trembling with the exertion. Out of training or rather, had he ever been in training? Dragging the CIA man across the car park he deposited him beside the elevator. If by some ghastly mischance the explosive in the car went off then Packard would be well out of range.

Two minutes later James came out of the building into the mews. It was a grey London Sunday. The mews, little more than a narrow lane, was bordered on the opposite side from the apartment building by a series of what had once been stables and were now converted cottages, picturesque, and expensive, marred only by the wire grids over the ground-floor windows. There had been an increasing incidence of burglaries in the neighbourhood.

A fat man in a pullover and stained flannels was washing down an ancient but lovingly preserved Bentley, scrubbing energetically at the metalwork with the fanaticism of the true enthusiast. His stomach added a second dimension to the work of the chamois in his hand as it pressed against the side of the vehicle. There was no one else in sight.

James walked slowly towards the main street troubled by having to leave the injured CIA man behind him. Of course Miss Thurman would know what to do about him. And she would provide an expert to remove the explosive from his car. The thought of those brown sticks of dynamite induced a

158

shudder in him. They really were out to obliterate him. And, as he walked past the fat man and the Bentley he was aware that there might be more of them. Certainly Jean Thurman had said her people were keeping an eye on him and people implied plurality. Packard should have companions. He could only hope they were watching over him.

He was approaching the exit from the mews when it happened. A sound, like the cracking of a whip, was followed immediately by chips of paving flying up from the ground in front of him. It wasn't a loud noise, not enough to detract the fat man from his carwash. Yet it took James some seconds to register that he was the target for a marksman's bullet.

A second cracking sound, louder this time, and he threw himself sideways into the doorway of the last of the mews cottages. There was no time for fear, simply the awareness of danger. Since there was no third shot he must now be sheltered from the marksman's sight. Time to breathe but how to get out? He was pinned down in the doorway. Where the hell were the CIA? He looked around. A potted plant stood at the side of the door. Above it a bell push. He pushed.

The woman who answered the door wore an out-of-date dirndl skirt and a peasant blouse. A mass of dark hair streaked throughout with grey tumbled over her forehead. In her fifties she was dressed as one thirty years younger and thirty years out of date.

'Yes?' she said, eyeing him up and down with some relish.

'I wonder if I might go through your house?' he inquired, amazed at the inanity of his request.

'Certainly,' she replied without batting an eyelid as if the request were commonplace. She stood aside and he entered a narrow hallway.

'Some trouble?' she asked pleasantly.

'Yes. A little.'

'Someone else's wife, I presume?' It was said casually, as if strangers walking through her house was an everyday occurrence.

'Eh, something like that.'

The woman smiled, delighted at the prospect of intrigue on a dull Sunday.

'May I offer you a glass of wine?' The smile had developed a seductive quality.

'I'm afraid I have another engagement.'

'You men do keep active. Just as long as you don't overdo it. My late husband did. Finished him. Heart attack fifteen years ago.'

A boy of about twelve appeared ahead of James in the hallway. He was carrying a number of milk bottles.

'My youngest son,' the woman said by way of explanation. 'A late-in-life consolation prize. Arrived three years after my husband died. Quite astonishing really. Willie, if you drop those milk bottles I'll break both your arms. Now put them down carefully and show the gentleman through to the basement of the big house. Tell them a friend of Mummy's wants to get through to Cromwell Road.'

'Thank you,' James stammered awkwardly.

'No bother. The lady in the basement of the main house and I are good friends. She knows my little ways. If you haven't got too many other engagements call again some time.'

At the rear of the mews cottage James found he had to cross a small yard to the basement of one of what had once been a block of large and rather elegant residences now converted into flats. The woman in the basement flat, a soulmate of the woman in the mews showed no surprise as the boy led James through her home with a muttered explanation about another friend of Mummy's.

Without further incident James flagged down a taxi on the Cromwell Road. The streets were Sunday quiet. The city was at rest. Fifteen minutes later the taxi deposited him outside the massive bulk of the embassy in Grosvenor Square.

A marine guard in spotless white gloves and hat saluted him and directed him to a long enquiry desk where he asked for Miss Thurman. Minutes later he was seated in a pleasantly large office overlooking the Square, a brandy in hand relating to Jean Thurman the events of the past hour.

'They can be efficient bastards, your intelligence people, when they're roused,' she responded, scowling. 'I got word half an hour ago that the two guys we dumped on the South

160

Coast got away a little earlier than we expected. Probably phoned Martindale and he put his little car bomb enterprise into operation. Since they put Packard out of action they must know now we're in it.'

'You can arrange for your Mr Packard to be looked after. He took a nasty crack on the head. And my car is rather a menace sitting there with all that high explosive attached.'

Jean Thurman nodded. A terse phone call seemed to take care of his fears.

'My little troubleshooting squad'll tidy everything up,' she explained as she replaced the telephone. 'And that'll include your car. Meanwhile I think it's time you and I took off for Scotland. We use my car and leave at once.'

The replaced phone rang. She lifted the receiver.

'Yes?' A pause. 'Tell him I'm out of town and the station head is on leave. No, I don't want anyone to see him. Tell him I'll be in touch in a couple of days.' She hung up. 'Your friend, Mr Martindale, wants to talk to me. As you heard I put him off. I think he wants to explain to me what's going on.'

James looked puzzled. 'Why not see him? You can tuck me away somewhere and listen to him.'

She shook her head. 'If they've kept it from us until now I don't think they're going to be too forthcoming. And lies bore me. No, we have to talk to Withenshaw. Better to go above Martindale's head. Later when I know the truth it'll be interesting to hear how Martindale distorts it. You ready to go?'

'Ready. And I'll feel safer out of London.'

'Don't worry. You're with me. The marines have landed. You play the game with the professionals now. We'll have to use one of the Firm's cars. Something unostentatious and not registered to the embassy.'

An hour later James was driving a blue Ford Granada north from London, Jean Thurman at his side. The memory of his previous journey north with a female companion produced in him a strong feeling of déjà vu. He'd been there before and the memory soured his outlook.

PART THREE

1

The corridors of power are long, cold and rather grubby. Each corridor is a clone of the last, suggesting an infinite multitude stretching back through time and space, and at the same moment moving forward towards more space and time. Somewhere in the past some unimaginative architect had created the prototype, possibly simply evolved some past corridor and it had proliferated. The predominant colour was a dullish light green suggesting a superfluity of government green paint or some corrupt civil servant of a long gone era who had a relative in the business of manufacturing green paint.

The old man waited, studying the walls of this particular corridor. Somewhere there were of course exceptions, he thought, corridors of grandeur in buildings of character. They were, of course, the inherited edifices of an older administration, perhaps an acknowledgement of rank. The old man reflected that he had spent most of his working life surrounded by civil service green. Rarely for him the grandeur of high and ancient office.

The Messenger at Arms returned. 'Sir Kenneth will see you, Mr Carteret. If you will follow me . . . ?'

Carteret followed. More green corridors. They reflected in the faces of those in the corridors. He thought, we are ruled by green-faced civil servants. Perhaps there was a secret subversive Irish influence. What was it about hanging lads for the wearing of the green? One way of combating the iron hand of officialdom.

The green corridor ended in a brown door, a relief devoutly to be grateful for; solid, heavy brown panelling. Of course the only civil-service alternative to green paint was brown varnish. Behind the brown door a female secretary and another two doors. The principal of the two opened into the Permanent Under Secretary's office. Here was the old Whitehall elegance. The marble fireplace, the wooden panelling again, the heavy tidy desk, even the portrait of the Monarch on the wall.

The Permanent Under Secretary was a tall thin man with surprisingly craggy features considering his height. He was dressed as one would expect, in dark jacket, striped trousers and dark, discreet tie. His knighthood had come early, some rather special services to do with Rhodesia. He rose with some show of cordiality as Carteret entered.

'My dear Tom, how nice to see you.' The first name, Carteret expected. They had worked together years before and developed if not a degree of intimacy, a kind of relationship. 'Enjoying your retirement?'

'I was until recently.'

'Well . . . take a pew. I can, unfortunately, only spare a short while. I have a conference with the minister . . . '

'I was surprised you could spare any time at all,' Carteret responded with some candour.

'Your message intrigued me. What was it? Dear Ken, I have information which leads me to believe the Section is running wild. I had to see you after that.' A nervous laugh followed, lacking humour.

Carteret thought it's really Withenshaw's job to look after the Section, not Sir Kenneth Ames. Ames was a channel to the minister and to the PM. But Withenshaw was on leave and one had to try the next section of the channel. He knew how Ames felt too. Carteret had, in his day, acted as part of the channel . . . one of the long tunnels of official procession. The whole fabric of Whitehall was made up of tunnels and channels.

'So tell me about it,' Ames commanded with the assurance only found in the higher reaches of the civil service, a benevolent condescension to the lesser mortals of the state.

Carteret told him. Carteret told him all that he had learned from James Ryder but omitted Ryder's name. It had all happened to an unidentified acquaintance.

When he had finished Ames pursed his lips. 'I have to say, Tom, I find it all hard to believe.'

'The facts are there.'

'What facts? Take Mansfield's death. A leaking gas main, a freak accident.'

'Ask for the forensic people's report.'

Ames nodded. 'Oh, I will. But really what are you saying? That the Section are engaged in an illegal or unauthorised operation?'

'The killing of civilians is rarely authorised,' Carteret insisted.

'If it is we don't know about it,' Ames responded. 'You know, too, that as far as the public are concerned; more, as far as the Government is concerned, officially the Section does not exist.'

'You and your minister act for the PM as regards the Section, don't you?'

'You know how it works, Tom. Through Withenshaw – '

'Who is on sick leave – '

'So I'm handling his brief,' the civil servant admitted almost reluctantly. He gave the impression it was a distasteful chore. 'And I get the daily situation reports from Mr Martindale. I assure you there is no such enterprise as you postulate going on.'

'Unless omitted from the situation reports.'

Sir Kenneth Ames was scowling now. He rose from his seat and prowled an area behind the desk. 'You're asking me to believe that Martindale is committing something close to high treason. I don't believe that. Not in situation reports, not in operations schedules.'

Carteret had a brief fit of coughing. Phlegm briefly clogged the back of his throat. Eventually he cleared his throat with a crushed grey handkerchief.

'Nevertheless you will carry out an investigation?'

Ames ran his tongue across his upper lip. 'I don't know.'

'Three deaths already, Kenneth. And you don't know – '

His face flushed, Ames retorted angrily, 'What have you given me? Nothing. Some incidents. Some events. No reasons, no motives. Why, for instance, should a department of British Intelligence stimulate a race riot in Notting Hill?'

'It happened!'

'The riot, yes! The proof that Martindale or ... or Buller or anyone was behind it is non existent. Tell me why they should do this. For what reason?'

'If I knew that I would not be coming to you to ask for an investigation. I would be demanding it. And if I didn't get it I'd go directly to the PM. And if I couldn't get there I'd blow the whole thing to the press – '

'Careful, Tom Carteret. The Official Secrets Act you signed a long time ago doesn't cease to operate after retirement,' Ames said.

'And what the hell does that mean? Tell it to Martindale and his people. They seem to be the ones engaged in covert and illegal activity.'

'We don't know that what they are doing, even if they are doing it, is illegal.'

Carteret rose now to face the Under Secretary. 'Damn it, Ken, if it's not on your operations schedule it's unauthorised and therefore illegal!'

Ames hesitated then spoke tentatively. 'If something had arisen, something unexpected, Martindale would be entitled to use his initiative.'

'And report to you immediately. This has been going on for over a week. Nora Matheson disappeared days ago. Martindale has been in London. Don't tell me you haven't seen him in that time.'

Another pause.

'I've seen him.'

'And he has said nothing?'

Ames nodded. 'He has said nothing.'

'Your question and suggestion answered.'

'If you're right. If it is true – ' Ames was still wriggling.

'You don't have to believe me. Inquire. Privately, officially, who cares as long as you do it!' Carteret was leaning forward, insistent.

'I shall need the name of your principal informant,' Ames said with a touch of formality.

'No! I'm not putting any of my sources in danger.' It sounded right, as if there were several sources. Better to keep it that way, create his own small smoke screen.

'I could hand it all to Withenshaw when he comes back,' Ames ventured.

'And when will that be? Too much of a delay and you know it,' Carteret came back at him.

'You believe I should disrupt everything with an enquiry now?' Ames asked, floundering. 'You're serious?'

'I'm grim.'

Yet another pause was broken by Ames. 'The Minister should know – '

'Tell him then. If he doesn't panic. Three months to the election, he may do. On the other hand if he opens this up he might gain votes. But you have no such problems. You're in until retirement. You're civil service. Do it!'

'Very well, I shall make enquiries. But if you are wrong – '

Carteret smiled. 'What can you do? Cut off my old age pension?'

Ames shook his head wearily. Carteret went to the door. At the door he hesitated.

'One other point. If my name is mentioned to Martindale tell him that should I have an accident in the next days, weeks or months, as Harrington did, all the information I hold and the story I've told you have been put on paper and are in the hands of a respectable solicitor. In the event that I should succumb to the consequences of any such accident then all my papers will be forwarded to the Prime Minister's office and to several rather radical newspapers.'

Ames expressed astonishment. 'What the devil are you implying, Tom?'

'Merely taken out an insurance policy. Did I mention I was attacked after speaking to Harrington at the Rear-Admiral's funeral? Of course I did. You might ask Martindale or Buller about that.'

'And I might ask that you be examined for advanced senility if this proves a figment of your imagination,' Ames retorted.

Carteret shrugged. 'You'd be justified. If. But I'm correct,

I'm sure of it. Think of the whole thing. Such an interesting situation. The servants take over from the masters. And who would be in a better position to do so than the Security and Intelligence services. Thank you for seeing me, Ken. I shall expect to hear from you.'

Carteret closed the door quietly behind him.

Sir Kenneth Ames, Permanent Under Secretary to Her Majesty's Ministry for the Defence of the Realm stood staring at the door for a long moment. Then he sighed and reached for the telephone.

Twenty minutes later in the saloon bar across the road from the Whitehall Theatre Carteret sat over a glass of Amontillado. One step taken. Something or nothing would happen. Depends on how weak a sister was Ames. Would he go to the Minister? Only if he had assured himself that the Section was involved in a covert operation, unsung, unauthorised. Martindale, of course, would deny it all convincingly. And if Ames was convinced, nothing would happen.

Different with Maurice Withenshaw. He would take action. It would therefore be up to James Ryder. Carteret shivered. Was it right to have placed everything in the hands of a novice, an amateur, a man who had fallen into it all accidentally? But he'd had no alternative, Ryder it had to be. Now he would put his ear to the ground. There were other contacts in the country, other voices to be heard. And they must have heard something, noticed something out of the ordinary. If only he knew what to look for, knew what it was all about. Aims, motives, objectives, the first rule of an operation. To establish them clearly. There was something at the back of his mind, something he had said. If he could only remember. He took another sip of sherry.

Then he remembered. The last thing he had said to Ames. The servants take over from the masters. Who would be in a better position to do so than – he didn't like the thought. But he had to face it. He'd said something similar to Ryder. But why? What would be the point? What would be the reason? And it couldn't be done alone. He glanced at a newspaper lying on the bar table beside him, abandoned by another customer.

168

Headline: 'More cuts in Armed Forces.'

Headline: 'Unemployment figures rise.'

Headline: 'Government faces bleak election prospect. Nine months more. When will the government call for a General Election?'

Headline: 'Crime rate rises!'

Christ, he told himself, I'm glad I'm old. To have to live much longer in a country that seemed to be falling apart, flaking away at the seams, was not a prospect to relish. It also made his life's work seem pointless. A grey depression threatened him. He used it as an excuse to order a second sherry.

Perhaps it wasn't so bad. He'd lived through worse prospects, like Dunkirk, when Hitler should have won the bloody war. Maybe it was simply that he was an old man living out of his time. Whatever was happening should no longer concern him. Ignore it, forget it, hide it away from thought. If only he could. The second sherry was too dry. It left a bitter acidity in his throat.

Some time later that afternoon Sir Kenneth Ames faced his minister. Charles Ewart Alexander, PC, MP, Her Majesty's Minister for the Defence of the Realm, was tall, thin, hair streaked with grey and piercing blue, blue eyes. A reassuring figure, a man who exuded strength and confidence, he listened in silence while his Permanent Secretary related all that Carteret had said. When Ames had finished, the Minister was silent for some moments. He pursed his lips, the high forehead wrinkled but the eyes remained fixed upon Ames. Finally he broke the silence.

'Opinion?' he demanded.

Ames twisted awkwardly in his seat. 'Some of the statements are borne out by the facts.'

'But not all of them,' Alexander interposed concisely. 'The man, Skinner. Nothing there. No published report of his body being found?'

'No, Minister. But he is on the civil-service establishment.'

'And where do they think he is?'

'On sick leave. I did follow it up.'

'Of course you did. And Miss Matheson?'

'According to information from her editor, she is in France.'

The blue eyes flickered. 'Well, then – '

'Doesn't have to be true – '

'Nonetheless more reliable than Carteret's information. A greater degree of probability. No, the whole thing seems like the dreams of an old man. Retired, wishful thinking, out of the scene and wanting to get back. Concocts a story of plot, counter-plot, conspiracy. Without foundation.'

'No action to be taken then?' questioned Ames. In front of his minister, he was a different personality. Not servile, indeed tending to be quite the opposite with elected ministers of government, he was, however, when faced with the personality of Alexander, inclined to be tentative. It was something that surprised and shocked him. Permanent civil servants should always be in control of their emotions and their ministers. It was standard practice, imprinted deep in his mind. But with Alexander all such practices went by the board when faced with those piercing blue eyes.

'I didn't say that,' Alexander replied. 'It ill behoves us to ignore danger signals, even fragile ones seemingly devoid of reality. No, I will speak to the relevant department chief.'

'Martindale?'

'Since Withenshaw is *hors de combat,* it will have to be Mr Martindale. Thank you for informing me. Good day.' The dismissal was terse and direct. Sir Kenneth Ames rose and made for the door. 'One other thing, Sir Kenneth,' Alexander said quietly when Ames had reached the door. 'We will have to protect Tom Carteret. Against himself, certainly. Perhaps against others. Keep that in mind.'

'Yes, Minister.'

When Ames had gone, Charles Alexander reached for the telephone. As he did so he smiled to himself. Ames phoned him, now he took the next step. Human life and contact was becoming an endless series of telephone calls. God knows how it had worked before the telephone was invented. The receiver at the other end of the line was lifted.

Alexander spoke. 'Mr Martindale? Minister here. I think you have some explaining to do . . . '

170

PART FOUR

1

They drove into a yellow neon-lit Glasgow in the darkness of night. The city seemed barely inhabited. An occasional shadow on a damp pavement. It was approaching midnight when they drew up at a small hotel at the residential west end of Sauchiehall Street. They were attracted by the anonymity of the place and a cracked electric sign, 'Ascol Hotel'. They registered as man and wife, a decision taken by Jean Thurman much to James's astonishment. She had laughed.

'God, you English! How you ever managed to colonise the goddam world I'll never know. Such narrow minds.'

'Constricted, not narrow,' he replied. 'Anyway we're male chauvinists. We're used to making the immoral suggestions.'

'Anyway I don't usually go to bed with a guy the first time we're being pursued.'

'You mean, if we have to go on the run again, things might be different?'

'Don't count on it.'

The hotel room consisted of a large double bed, an ancient wardrobe, one overstuffed armchair of ancient lineage, and a cupboard which opened to reveal an adequate, if primitive shower. James eyed the armchair with reluctant horror. Meanwhile Jean Thurman unbuttoned her skirt and a moment later, clad only in her slip, disappeared into the shower cupboard.

James stretched out on the bed while she showered, easing his back and arm muscles which were stiff with the hours spent at the wheel of her car. He luxuriated on the counterpane and despite his physical weariness a sense of contentment came over him. For long minutes he could forget his position as a man hunted for no reason he could understand by his own country's Intelligence service. He could substitute, in its place, the vision of Jean Thurman in her silk slip, the deep cleavage and the shape under the silk of large but firm breasts. Eyes shut, he stirred, ruffling the counterpane, savouring the first stirrings of a sexual excitement he had not felt for weeks.

'You asleep?' she asked coming out of the shower. She was wrapped in a large towel.

'Sorry,' he said, rising from the bed. 'Just easing the muscles.'

'Which ones, James?' she grinned impishly. She had started to call him Jimmy on the drive north but he had insisted on James.

He sat awkwardly on the armchair, unable to conceal his discomfort. She smiled at him, amused at the graphic illustration of his martyrdom on the armchair.

'Okay. We share the bed.'

'Not necessary,' he assured her without conviction.

'Don't argue. I won't make the offer twice. Come over.'

Realising she meant it, he capitulated at once and settled beside her. They lay together, the room lit only by a small bedlight. After a long moment he became aware that her left breast had spilt from under her slip. The nipple, he noted with excitement, was erect.

Later, he thought, the hell with it. He put his arms around her and drew her body towards him. He expected resistance but found none. They stripped each other with mock solemnity and some laughter. Then they made love, he almost frantically, she with a cooler but no less wild pleasure, an equal partner in every movement. He wanted to lose himself in her body, explore it, discover it and share with it his pleasure and his relief. She responded, hands, lips, flesh active and reactive. As they came to a surprising, simultaneous climax she cried out, a brief, moaning obscenity that served to increase his excitement. Then, when it was over, she lay back, trembling. It was then that he felt, despite her enthusiasm, her reciprocation to his every movement, she had still somehow strangely held back. As if she would not, or

172

could not, yield to him a part of her being.

'You've broken one of your resolutions,' he said eventually. 'Never let a man make love the first time.'

'Resolutions are made to be broken. But judiciously.'

A long silence. James sat up, lit two cigarettes and handed her one. 'How did you get into the CIA?' he asked. 'I thought the CIA were all clean-cut American gentlemen in Brooks Brothers suits.'

'Token acknowledgement to Women's Lib. I suppose I am rather exceptional. My father was in the OSS during the war. He was in at the start of the CIA. Then he went into business. When you have contacts as he had, when you know where the bodies are buried, you do well in business. He made five million dollars in two years.'

'A busy two years.'

'I was brought up not just with a silver spoon but a knife and fork to match. Vassar girl, deb of the year on the Washington scene. Hated it. Rich cattle market for rich husbands. Princesses learning to be queens. And I don't just mean the females. I finally convinced my father I had other ideas. He put a little pressure on and I went to work at Langley, Virginia, home of the CIA. At first I was a decoration ... typist secretary, a pleasant smile and fielding the occasional fumbles from the boys. After a couple of years I started to find out where the bodies were buried. And I pointed out women could be as good, in some cases better, operatives than men. They saw the point and here I am.'

She hesitated before going on, then turned to stare at him. Her eyes were suddenly cold. 'I've killed three men and one woman, James. For my country. You have to tell yourself it's for your country, for the greater good. You have to tell yourself something ... '

He said nothing. He felt chilled.

'I talk too much,' she said, leaning over and kissing him. 'And it's not always true.'

'I was listening but I wasn't hearing,' he replied, lying easily.

'Good. Let's get some sleep.'

James switched off the bedlight and they slept.

He knew he was dreaming but later he had no memory of the dream. It became a nightmare and he was conscious of dragging himself to wakefulness. He was drenched in perspiration and tense with fear. He forced himself to open his eyes. The room was in greyish darkness, a little light from some street lamp filtering around the edges of the curtain. Rain splattered on the window. Then he became aware that he was alone in the bed. The voice came from the direction of the shower room.

'Out, James, out of bed now!'

The cry was incisive, an order to be obeyed. He rolled from the bed, and as he landed heavily on the threadbare carpeting he heard three sounds, one after another thumping into the bed above him. Then the lights of the room were switched on.

The man was large, a bulky figure in a thick overcoat, the material glinting with dampness. He was standing in the doorway of the room, an automatic weapon in his hand, the barrel elongated by the silencer fitting. Behind him, in the open doorway of the shower cupboard stood Jean Thurman, her naked body shining in the light from the electric light bulb. In her hand, too, was a gun, pointing unwaveringly at the intruder.

'More carefully,' she addressed the large man. 'Lay down your weapon on the carpet and kick it towards Mr Ryder.'

The large man stood frozen, a bulky mammoth in a glacial quandry. He was staring at the empty bed, at sheets ripped across by the bullets from his weapon. The knowledge of failure was on his face.

'Now!' Jean said again. The man did not move.

Calmly Jean Thurman shot him through the wrist. The sound of her small automatic was like the cracking of wood. The man dropped his weapon, twisting aside, face contorted with pain.

'Fuck!' he muttered from between clenched teeth. Blood soaked into the sleeve of his coat.

James tentatively lifted his gun from the floor. The butt of the weapon was damp and unpleasantly warm.

'Sit on the bed!' Jean gesticulated to the man with her automatic.

'Bitch!' the man growled in a thick Glasgow accent. 'By Goad, I'll kick your bloody face in fur this!'

Jean stepped forward and, with cool deliberation, pistol-whipped him across the face twice. He fell back upon the torn sheets with a low moan.

'Keep an eye on him while I get dressed,' she said to James.

She dressed quickly and James followed. Then she once again turned her attention to the man on the bed.

'You! Sit up.'

The man ignored her.

'Sit up or it'll be your kneecap next.'

He sat up, his face marked by two livid weals where she had struck him. He was in his early forties, thinning hair, scalp shining through, heavy features scowling up at them.

'Who sent you here?'

'Away and bugger yersel'.'

The gun came up in her hand pointing at him. 'Who sent you?''

'London. Folk in London. We dae jobs fur them. Government, I think.'

'The Section?'

'I've heard them cried that.'

'How did they know we were here?'

'They'd a tail on yer man's car. Picked him up after he left London. Didnae say anything about a bird being with him.'

Jean looked across at James. 'He won't be alone. They come in twos.' She turned back to the intruder. 'You work for Buller every now and then? Right?'

The man nodded.

'Where's the other one then?'

The reply was grudging. 'Waiting outside. He's one of Buller's. Always wait outside while we dae the dirty work.'

'And the idea was to kill him?' Jean indicated James.

'Aye. Nae word about you, damn them!'

'So you just fired blindly at the bed?'

'Whit did you expect me to dae? Ask him to move over? As long as I got him, they wouldnae care.'

James said, 'What do we do now?'

'Leave him here. Take care of the one outside and move on.'

'Do we tie him up or what?'

She smiled grimly, turning back to face the man on the bed. 'We put him out of action for some time.'

The man cowered, sensing what was in her mind. 'Wait a minute . . . don't try anything, you bitch. I've got plenty of lads'll take care of you.'

Jean stepped around the side of the bed, lifted one of the pillows and pressed it down on the man's face. Then, to James's horror she lifted her automatic and fired twice, once into each kneecap. From under the pillow came a muffled howl. When it had subsided, she removed the pillow. The man was moaning in agony, eyes rolling back in his head as he subsided into semi-consciousness.

'For God's sake!' James exclaimed. 'Did you have to . . . ?'

'Yes! We need him out of action. Don't waste your pity. I've just done society a favour. And anyway he would have blown your head off.'

The stairway of the hotel was a dim tunnel stretching down to a small foyer lit by one unshaded electric light bulb. There was no sign of a night porter.

'They'd pay him to make himself scarce,' Jean muttered as she opened the front door. 'The other one'll be out there. Waiting for our ugly friend. You wait. I go out. All I need to do is get close enough. And he won't be expecting a woman.'

She slipped through the door and walked down the few steps to the pavement. The sky was streaked with black clouds, the horizon fringed with approaching daylight. James stood peering around the door, waiting.

He was sitting in a Rover some ten yards along the pavement. He was in the driving seat with the window rolled down, a white patch of face. He stared directly at Jean as she sauntered along towards him, trying to assess whether or not she was relevant to the business at hand.

Jean drew level with the Rover and addressed the occupant with a slow drawl. 'You're a late one. Looking for a little fun, honey?'

176

'Move on, lady.'

Ignoring this, she leaned towards the car window.

'I told you, move – ' The man repeated himself and then Jean's body obscured him from James's view. There was a dull thumping sound and a low groan. Jean straightened up and turned, waving towards him.

When he joined her the man was slumped forward, head resting on the steering wheel.

'He's okay,' Jean said. 'I just put him out for a few hours.'

'I know him,' James said.

'So who is he?'

'The man who followed me in Chester. Tried to beat me up.'

Jean reached into the car and drew a slim wallet from the man's inside pocket. She flipped the wallet open. 'See that?' She indicated a plastic identification card. 'Looks like a police warrant but it's not. He's Section all right. One of Buller's bully boys.'

She studied the rest of the contents of the wallet. There were three twenty pound notes and four fives. She extracted the notes and the identity card. Then, looking around, she walked to a drain in the gutter nearby and dropped the card into it. She then tore the notes in pieces and threw them after the card.

'The CIA are not thieves, James. But it will hold him up. No money, no identity.'

'Bit of a waste, isn't it? Throwing the money away?'

'If we got caught with that money the police could hold us. Never give anyone a chance to get a holding charge on you. Come on. I'm driving. First time outside of Glasgow we hire another car and dump this one.'

They reached Oban three hours later. They abandoned the car in a side street and using an American Express card made out in another name and a raucous mid-western accent, Jean Thurman hired a powerful yellow Volvo. Minutes later they were heading north again.

Carteret sat in an alcove in the public bar of the Wheatsheaf, head bowed over a crumpled copy of the *Guardian*. The economic crisis loomed large in the headlines. Three million unemployed, heading for four million. And no Royal Wedding or Falklands War to distract the populace. The Home Secretary had replied to a question about the latest Notting Hill Riots suggesting they might have been fomented by agents of a foreign power.

'Tom, how are you?' The voice was deep, tinged with the accent of North Yorkshire.

Carteret looked up. The speaker was a tall, squarely built man in a raincoat. He was in his fifties but looked younger.

'Sit down, my dear Walter. The usual?'

The usual was a pint of bitter and Chief Inspector Walter Harkness applied himself to it diligently.

'Sorry I was late. The Aldgate mob trying to imitate the Mafia. But we'll have them away this time.'

The two men were old friends whose work occasionally brought them together. There were times when Carteret had preferred to use the CID rather than the Special Branch with its in-built jealousies towards the Section. This had cemented his friendship with Harkness.

'What's the emergency?' Harkness went on. 'Thought you were retired. Wallowing in an income-related pension.'

'Something's come up.' A mild spasm of coughing came up and was subdued. 'The Notting Hill riots, who started them?'

Harkness's face clouded. 'Subject of an inquiry. Still to be determined. You're asking awkward questions.'

'It is awkward then?'

'Did I say that? Slip of the tongue. Still there are rumours. Somebody misbehaved.'

'Meaning?'

'Some narrow-minded bastards out of uniform but with warrant cards were prodding the local black gentry. Touch of provocation. Can't prove it though.'

Carteret pursed his lips. 'Who and why?'

'Aw, Tom, I can't – '

'Who and why, Walter?'

The detective rubbed his forehead. 'Word is the local super, Jack Greenlees, was spoiling for trouble.'

'I remember him. Friend of Buller's.'

178

'All you Section boys had your pet coppers. I was yours.'
Carteret smiled. 'You were straight, Walter.'
'Greenlees always seemed straight enough.'
'That's why he incites race riots?'
Harkness scowled. 'I never said that. There's been an increased rate of muggings by black kids around there. Maybe he got fed up . . . '
A pause. Then Carteret said, 'I took time to get here. Came a rather complicated route. Walked a lot.'
'So you like walking. Or you're being tailed.'
'If I am whoever's doing it is good. But I should have shaken him off. To keep you out of trouble, Walter.'
'Tom, I'm the police. The straight lot. I'm not on the take. I owe nobody favours. So I don't get into trouble.'
Carteret grimaced. 'A friend of mine thought that. Antique dealer called James Ryder. Honest as the day. Went looking for a friend and now everybody's looking for him.'
Harkness ordered another pint and a dry sherry for his old friend. 'James Ryder. I've heard the name. Countrywide. Keep a look out for. Request of the Section.'
Carteret nodded smugly. 'There you are. No crime listed. They just want to talk to him?'
He went on to tell Harkness something of what had happened to Ryder. He was careful to omit the death and disposal of Skinner's body. After all, he thought, Harkness is still a policeman.
When he had finished, the Chief Inspector looked at him shrewdly. 'That's it all?'
'All you need to know. But let me say this. Ryder's committed no crime.'
Harkness sipped his beer. 'So what does it mean?'
'I don't know. That's why I'm asking around. I spoke to Ames at the Ministry. Nothing. He'd looked into it. Storm in a teacup. Have a word with his master.'
Harkness nodded. 'That would be the Right Honourable Charles Ewart Alexander, Minister of – '
'Himself. I've heard nothing yet. Don't expect to.'
'What about Withenshaw?'
'On sick leave in Scotland. I . . . I am making arrangements

179

for someone to contact him.' Better not to tell Harkness Ryder was driving north, Carteret thought. Harkness was sympathetic but he was still a police officer.

Harkness shrugged expressively. 'Maybe Ames is right. Maybe it is all a storm in a teacup.'

'Walter, people don't get killed in stormy teacups.'

'Okay. What can I do?'

Carteret leaned forward. 'Two things. Let me know if you hear that Ryder's been picked up. Second, is anything happening out of the norm. In the police, at the Yard, in the SB – '

'Tom, I'll do my best. But I'm a crime man. CID. I don't know what the Special Branch are up to.'

'Appreciated. But there is scuttlebutt. Rumour. Also in government.'

Harkness shook his head, grinning. 'I've no connections in Whitehall. I don't get invited to Number Ten for tea. I wouldn't go if I did. My old man voted Labour all his life and under this reactionary policeman kit I'm still a good old social democrat. But, if I hear anything – ' The policeman suddenly stopped, brow creased, eyes suddenly cautious. 'There is one thing that's struck me as funny.'

'What?'

'Probably got damn all to do with your business but I thought it was strange. Your Minister, Charlie Alexander has just announced a big army and territorial exercise ... full scale manoeuvres on Salisbury Plain next week.'

Carteret was puzzled. 'What's so unusual about that? Army manoeuvres are quite normal – '

'Yes, but in three weeks there's a big NATO exercise in West Germany – '

'So Alexander is getting his army in shape – '

'He did that only a month ago. Second major national exercise in a month. Some of the Metropolitan police are being seconded down to Salisbury to provide extra policing. Mostly traffic control. But the whole thing must be costing a packet. And in the middle of an economic crisis.'

'I don't see how it fits,' Carteret said.

'Neither do I. But you wanted to know anything out of the ordinary.'

'Maybe it does fit. I don't know. Like a jigsaw puzzle.'

Walter Harkness rose to his feet. 'Time to go. Crime is a non-stop event. I may be needed. If I hear anything I'll be in touch.'

'I'm grateful, Walter. If you have to contact me, say nothing on the phone. I could be bugged. Just say usual place and I'll be there.'

'Right. What was that old code-name of yours? Reindeer.'

'Embarrassing to remember the past when today my antlers are falling out.'

'I may use it.'

The two men shook hands and Harkness strolled out. As he did so a newspaper boy came into the bar. Carteret waved him over and bought a paper. He thumbed through it searching for anything that might be relevant. It was in the late news column, a short paragraph.

'MAN SHOT IN GLASGOW HOTEL.'

No name given. The cold fear in him that it might be Ryder. The words stared up at him. Kneecapped, badly injured, may not live. Then with relief he was reading that the man was a local with a police record. The affair was possibly a gangland attempt at murder.

Carteret folded the paper and looked at his watch. Time for his next contact to arrive. The phone call that morning had been uncomfortable. Using the past to protect the future; that was how he justified it to himself. He'd even used the old code name to get through.

'Will you inform the Under Secretary of State that Reindeer would like to speak to him.'

Prescott's voice had come through in less than a minute. 'What is it you want?'

'A meeting this morning.'

'Impossible. I have two committees.'

'Skip the committees. I need to talk to you. Otherwise there's always Fenchurch Street.'

Fenchurch Street. The old memory between them. Now used as blackmail. It had been a Section raid in collaboration with the Special Branch on a house in Fenchurch Street, a club for men and youths with certain proclivities. It didn't matter that homosexuality had been legalised between consenting adults. It was still valuable in terms of blackmail when connected with public figures. A naval officer had been using the house to hand over information to a member of the Soviet Embassy. Hence the raid. The naval officer had been arrested and duly convicted. But that night among those apprehended had been one Suffragan Bishop, three pillars of the City, and one promising Tory MP named Prescott. Thanks to Carteret, Prescott had been released, his political career unblemished but forever beholden to Carteret and the Section.

Later when the Tories had come to power and Prescott had been offered the not unimportant post of Under-Secretary, there had been the question of whether or not he was a security risk. The Rear Admiral, as head of the Section, had made a decision.

'We are not judges of a man's morals. So simply remind him we know, and inform him we will not impede his acceptance of the post. But he will stay in line from now on.'

Prescott had survived.

Now he came into the Wheatsheaf, a worried man paying a reluctant debt. 'This is blackmail,' he hissed at Carteret. 'Now you've retired you think you can indulge in blackmail – '

Carteret was angry and showed it. 'Please be quiet and listen. I want information, not money. And it is, I believe in the national interest.'

Prescott was noplussed. 'Well ... that may be different. Perhaps I should apologise. But then again information can always be sold for money – '

'Your apologies are as offensive as your insults. Prescott, something is going on on the edges of this government. The Section is involved and may be indulging in illegal activities. I want to know about it.'

Prescott blinked. 'I don't know what you're talking about.'

'And there's another thing I have recently learnt. Why should Alexander, as minister concerned, insist on holding large scale army manoeuvres only a short time after similar manoeuvres?'

'Good God, is that why you've brought me here? Ridiculous! I believe the Minister wants to put on a show to ... to coincide with the Cabinet meeting next week.'

Carteret had heard of the Cabinet meeting. Not an ordinary session but a publicised affair, a crisis meeting at which solutions for the economic disasters of the past months were to be discussed, a last-minute bid to stop the collapse of the government's financial policy.

'But why expensive manoeuvres at that particular time?' Carteret persisted. Harkness had planted a seed in his mind. Prescott may know nothing of anything sinister but he might be able to explain the inexplicable need for further military exercises.

Prescott shifted uncomfortably. 'I don't know. Probably to distract the public from our problems. A matter of tactics. Show the country we're still a force. Give the Territorials a day out and a little extra cash. A lot of them are among the unemployed as it is.'

'That's the government's solution to the economic crisis? No, there must be another reason.'

'Alexander's showing he's got faith in the country,' Prescott muttered. 'Something like that. Nothing sinister, I'm sure. And ... and as regards the Section, indeed all of the intelligence and security organisations, nothing presents problems. Everything is smooth, we're containing the Reds –'

'We ... or the Americans?'

'The western democracies,' Prescott insisted pompously. 'Look, in deference to your security record, I'm listening to you. But I don't understand what you're getting at?'

'I have reason to believe the security services and, in particular, my old department, the Section, are running wild. I want to know why.'

'Then talk to Withenshaw. Or the Minister. I'm only a junior –'

'The Minister is Alexander.'

Prescott shook his head. 'He's a difficult man. But a good man.'

'Why can he not control the Section? What are they doing? What is the true state of the economy?'

'Look, you don't need me to tell you things are bad, Carteret. If the PM persists in going her own way, unemployment will rise still further. The World Bank won't help and the European Community is beginning to crack. The prognostication is not good. I shouldn't be saying this but it's self-evident. Now if Alexander and the PM are ensuring our security and the Section are throwing their weight about, it can only be to prevent a breakdown of the whole system.'

Prescott sat back, looking even more smug.

Carteret felt cold. The feeling, the suspicion was there.

'Could the Section be taking matters into their own hands?'

'Preposterous!' the Under-Secretary exclaimed. 'That would be high treason! They would never dare. They are servants of the Crown. Anyway of what value would it be? They have no power base. No leader.'

Then abruptly Prescott rose to his feet. 'You've used privileged information to bring me here. I resent that. But more, you are indulging in fantasy. Of course we have problems. Serious, terrible problems. But they will be solved by politicians, not secret service people. The Section could never have the expertise to deal with those matters facing the government.'

Carteret knew Prescott was right. However much the Section might behave like cowboys, there was no way that they could attempt treason. Not without a powerful figure behind them. The Section, indeed all the intelligence services, were merely instruments to be used –

Prescott cut in. 'If you'll excuse me, I'm leaving. I don't want to meet you again, Carteret. Nor do I want to hear mention of Fenchurch Street. Otherwise I will lodge a formal complaint with the highest authority – '

'If they allow you to,' Carteret said.

With one final glare, Prescott turned and walked away.

Carteret stared at the empty sherry glass in front of him. Something stirred, something he'd thought of a few seconds before. *The Section was an instrument to be used,* that was it. Martindale wasn't strong enough to use the Section. But someone else was. He found it hard to believe.

An hour later he unlocked the street door to his flat. But, for once, preoccupation took away concentration. He did not notice the man in the car across Hampstead High Street. But the man noticed him.

Some moments later the man made a call from a telephone kiosk. 'He's back in his flat. But we don't know where he's been. We lost him in Selfridges.'

Martindale replied. 'Which means he wanted to be lost. He was meeting someone.'

'We won't lose him again.'

'I wouldn't count on that. He's an old hand and he himself trained half of your people. Also we lost Ryder in Scotland. However there's no problem there. Except that he had a woman with him. A very professional woman.'

Martindale hung up. Who was the woman? Another bloody problem. And Carteret, he would dearly like to have Carteret taken out. But the old man was an ex-agent. Too many people would be alerted. No, Carteret must be left under surveillance. Next week he could be picked up with impunity. Put in a cage. The Cage. With Ryder and anyone else. With a sigh Martindale lifted the telephone again. A report would have to be made. And he himself would have to go to Scotland. He couldn't leave that to anyone else. Just as long as he was back in London in good time.

2

Jean Thurman was driving on the road winding through the hills. To the right Ben Nevis rose darkly close to them. James studied the woman's profile from the passenger seat. The ruthlessness of her actions in the Glasgow hotel both puzzled and frightened him. She had of course saved his life but her

185

wounding of the intruder had shocked him. What kind of woman could make love with affection one minute and kneecap another human being the next; and do it with a calculated determination. He couldn't provide an answer.

Some miles out of Fort William they spotted the signpost. 'Inverkeil House', indicating a narrow road leading over moorland. There was no mention of distance. They turned onto the rutted surface of what was little more than a track.

'They don't count miles in Scotland?' Jean said.

'Just the ruts in the road,' James smiled for the first time since they'd left Glasgow.

The roar of engines from behind them was unexpected and Jean tensed. James twisted to look through the rear window. Three motorcyclists on heavy machines were closing fast. Jean slipped her automatic from her handbag and laid it on her lap.

'Safety first,' she said.

The motorcycles roared past them and disappeared over the horizon, three machines bucking and leaping over the ruts.

'They do some motorbike rallies on the mountains,' James said. 'Probably locals on trial runs.'

Jean Thurman said nothing, but replaced the automatic under her jacket.

The road now dipped ahead of them and they saw the sun glinting on water.

'Beginning of the Great Glen,' James announced. 'Loch Lochy or Loch Orchy.'

The American was unimpressed. 'Seen one, seen 'em all,' she replied.

A few moments later the house appeared on their right, a spare gaunt building, three storeys high, Victorian Gothic brought to the Highlands. Jean swung the car round and they jerked and bumped along an even narrower track which served as a driveway to the slightly decaying entrance to the house.

'Does Withenshaw own this dump?' Jean asked as she drew the car to a halt among a flurry of pebbles.

'Rents it,' James replied.

They stepped from the car and surveyed the facade in front of them. It was unimpressive, the upper windows shuttered, in some cases broken and boarded over. The ground floor seemed more habitable, red curtains fringing a large bow window to the right of the door. James tugged at a large brass bell pull.

'Why on earth should a guy come from London to a place like this?' Jean asked.

'The lure of the Highlands. Fishing.'

Jean stepped forward impatiently and pushed the large door. It swung open.

'Same as the States,' she said approvingly. 'Country people never lock their doors.'

They stepped into a large hall, a bare marble floor stretching under an ornate ceiling to a broad stairway. To their right was a hat and walking stick stand, dominated by a large stuffed bear, the fur rather threadbare, the eyes, chips of green glass. On the stand was one solitary mackintosh, crumpled and stained with dried mud. To the right was a large door. James opened it.

The smell of burning peat assailed their nostrils. A fire was burning in an enormous fireplace around which were deep, sagging armchairs in a faded floral design. A bookcase stretched across one wall. The room was obviously lived-in and despite its high ceiling, had an air of comfort. Jean followed him in. A second later a floorboard creaked behind her.

'May I ask what you'll be doing here?'

The woman was small, middle-aged, wearing a floral dress not unlike the patterned furniture. Her mouth was a thin questioning line.

'We're looking for Maurice Withenshaw,' James replied.

'I'm Mrs Crathie,' the woman responded, seemingly reassured by the name. 'Housekeeper. Is the old man expecting you? If he can expect anyone.'

'Not exactly. We're friends of friends, you might say. Asked to look in on him. My name is Ryder. This is Miss Thurman.'

The thin lips formed into what could be construed as a

smile. 'The poor soul's had nobody. Except myself, the nurse and visits from the doctor.'

'How bad is he?' Jean Thurman asked.

'You'll have to be asking the doctor that one. He'll be calling this evening. And the nurse has gone into Fort William. A wee break. You can't be blaming her, the state he's in. Has to have everything done for him. Not that he's much trouble. Just sits muttering to himself.'

'Exactly what is the matter with him?' James asked, shivering slightly in anticipation of the reply.

'You don't know? Well the doctor calls it a cerebral incident but, to me, it's just a simple old-fashioned stroke he's had.'

James frowned. If it was a serious stroke, what help could they expect?

'It's bad,' the woman went on. 'One side of him's gone and his talking's all jumbled. When he does talk.'

'Speech aphasia,' Jean said.

'Call it what you like, he really can't talk. He's out in the garden at the back, just staring at the loch.'

They found him at the crest of a small hill, a hunched figure in a wheelchair staring at the distant expanse of water, a rug across his knees. He was in his late fifties, his face tanned but etched with deep lines, his expression one of comparative tranquillity. Mrs Crathie returned to the house, leaving them with the invalid.

'Mr Withenshaw?' James knelt in the grass. 'Can you hear me? Mr Carteret sent me.'

There was no reaction. Withenshaw continued to stare over James's head.

'Carteret!' James persevered. 'You remember him. He was with the Section. You knew him well.'

James thought he detected a flicker from the invalid's eyes.

'It's not going to be any use,' Jean Thurman cut in.

A feeling of despair came over James. This shell of a man desperately needed help. Perhaps the one source of knowledge as to what was happening. He tried again.

'I tell you, it's no use. You'll get nothing from him,' Jean insisted. 'I've seen strokes before in my own family.'

James straightened up but as he did so Withenshaw's right hand twitched and reached forward as if to grasp James's sleeve.

'Wait,' James exclaimed. 'I think we're getting through.'

He knelt again. 'Carteret asked me to see you. Do you understand?'

Withenshaw moved his head and his lips twisted. 'Car ... Carteret?' he gasped with some effort.

'That's it! Mr Carteret used to work for you. He says something is happening within the Section. Something he doesn't understand. They're behaving against ... against the law.'

Withenshaw moved his head again. 'The Section ... something ... happening. ... '

'Can you help us? Tell us anything?'

The invalid's eyes filled with tears. Behind the tears and the brown eyes was a desperate frustration.

'Help,' he said. 'Have to help ... will help.'

'He's just repeating what you say,' Jean broke in.

James leant forward and very gently grasped Withenshaw's shoulders. 'We need to know what Martindale and the Section are doing. Can you tell us anything?'

The man struggled, trapped within his own body and in mental agony at his situation.

'Martin ... dale. More than Martindale. Behind ... behind Martindale ... other ... other ... '

'Yes. Tell me.'

'Physical ... physio therapy ... fresh air ... '

'He's simply repeating things he's heard,' Jean insisted. 'They do that.'

James ignored her, concentrating on Withenshaw.

'The Section have killed two people at least,' he said firmly. 'Two innocent people. Why? Why?'

Withenshaw's eyes widened in comprehension. 'Killed ... killed me ... nearly killed me. Martindale nearly killed me.'

The effort was enormous but the clarity achieved was impeccable. At the same time Withenshaw's shoulders shuddered with the exertion. Then there was a sound in the distance from above them, a droning, whirring noise in the sky. Jean's head jerked up, alert.

'Withenshaw is about to have visitors,' she said, eyes searching the sky. Then she found what she was looking for. 'There it is now!' It came over the peak of Creag Meagaidh, like a large winged insect, its rotors flashing in the sun as they cut through the air. James straightened up, his eyes on the approaching helicopter.

'We're going to have trouble,' Jean went on. 'Whoever's whistled up an army helicopter wanted to get here in a hurry.'

James turned back to the man in the wheelchair. 'We've run out of time, Mr Withenshaw. If you can tell us anything, do it now!'

With a surprisingly quick movement Withenshaw reached out with his good hand and clutched again at James's sleeve. His mouth worked desperately as he tried to enunciate above the growing sound of the helicopter.

'Have to ... to watch ... Tuesday ... week. Garrison commander ... London ... the key to ... to Whitehall ... sanction ... sanction ... the act ... enabling ... enabling ...'

The helicopter, a medium-range craft with army markings, was descending now, moving down to a patch of the lawn some fifty yards from where they stood. Against the rising volume of sound the effort was too much for Withenshaw who slumped back in his chair, eyes flickering. James straightened up again, puzzled. The London garrison commander? Sanctions? Enabling? Enabling who to do what? The words had been clear enough but had the sick man's brain distorted his own intention?

The helicopter touched down on the grass. Jean Thurman was running towards the house, shouting for James to follow her. He gave one quick sad glance at the man on the wheelchair and moved after her. As he did so he saw the perspex door of the helicopter swing open and a figure drop to the grass. James caught up with Jean at the door of the house.

'It's Martindale,' he gasped.

'I figured it would be,' she replied. 'And I'd rather he didn't see me.'

190

They ran up the back stairs and into the front hall. There they came face to face with Mrs Crathie and she was no longer smiling. In her hand was a heavy Luger pistol.

'I thought you were from himself,' she said. 'Mr Martindale. But from his arrival I think you'll not be wanted. So you'll stand perfectly still and we'll wait on himself.'

From under her jacket Jean Thurman fired. It was a neat precise shot and it caught the woman in the wrist. The Luger flew in the air and fell on the marble floor. The force of the shot spun Mrs Crathie around and back against the stuffed bear. Blood besplattered its fur. Mrs Crathie uttered an oath and fell at the feet of the bear.

They ran out of the front door to the Volvo. Jean took the driving seat. Mercifully the engine roared to life at once and, as they moved off, Martindale appeared at the door followed by a large man carrying a service revolver. The Volvo started to move down the driveway at speed. Pebbles rattled against the underside of the car.

'Too easy,' Jean muttered and at once was proved right.

Across the driveway was stretched a large wooden log, part of a tree trunk. And behind the log in a line were the three motorcyclists they had encountered on their way to Inverkeil House. They sat on their machines, three black leather sentinels, waiting.

Jean wrenched the steering wheel around and the car skidded on the pebbled track engine screaming its protest. The off-side front wheel of the Volvo struck the edge of the log and the car slewed around onto a patch of lawn, heading for a clump of trees. James braced himself as Jean struggled with the wheel.

One of the cyclists moved off heading towards the car. He was moving at speed at once, too fast. Jean again struggled with the wheel of the car and it veered to the left. The cyclist drove directly in front of them and the bonnet of the Volvo struck the rear of the motorbike throwing it upwards. The cyclist went into the air and disappeared behind them. Then a large tree was in front of them. Jean twisted the steering wheel belatedly and the wing of the car hit the tree crumpling in a mass of squashed, wounded steel. The car stopped.

The driver's door flew open and Jean, with some expertise, rolled out onto damp grass. It was the classic stuntman's fall. She rolled over and over away from the car. James braced for the collision, was jerked forward and the force of contact caused his forehead to hit the dashboard. Fortunately his hands in front of him lessened the impact and, though dazed, he was able to grip the door handle and push the door open.

He staggered onto the grass, aware at first only of the fact that he was lucky to be alive and out of the car. Then, shaking his head like a boxer warding off a blow, he straightened up and looked around. Jean had managed to get up from the lawn onto her knees and was feeling under her jacket for the automatic. Then at once she froze as the sound of a shot echoed from the direction of the house and a tiny divot of grass flew up two feet in front of her. James gazed wildly towards the house. The large man who had appeared with Martindale was running towards them, weapon in hand. At the same time the two cyclists still on their machines roared towards the wrecked Volvo and took up positions on each side of them.

Martindale arrived on foot a moment later. He surveyed them in silence for some seconds as he tried to regain his breath. 'Mr Ryder and companion,' he finally said. 'You've given us a lot of trouble. All so unnecessary. Ryder, everything I know about you leads me to believe you're a decent patriotic citizen. I don't know why you should wage your own personal war against organisations of Her Majesty's government.'

James, still slightly dazed, found himself slurring his reply. 'When the actions of the Government include murder, kidnapping and God knows what, I think . . . I think even a . . . a patriot . . . might wage war. What happens now? You . . . you kill us . . . like . . . like you killed Skinner and . . . and –'

Martindale frowned. 'Skinner's death was something else. A necessary act. You'll not be killed. You and the lady will simply come back with me to Inverkeil House.'

Jean Thurman had risen to her feet now but was keeping her face averted from Martindale's gaze. The large man with

192

the revolver came up to her, reached under her jacket and relieved her of her own weapon. Martindale now turned his attention to her and she was forced to face him. His reaction was instant. His mouth opened and a look of utter astonishment came over his face.

'Jean Thurman!'

'Mr. Martindale. I suppose my being here increases the complications?'

Martindale made an effort to suppress his surprise. 'You'll have to come back to the house with us, Miss Thurman. Then we'll . . . we'll see what we will do.'

Jean smiled acidly. 'I think you've done enough to rank with General Burgoyne who lost you the American colonies.' She was now beginning to enjoy herself. 'You've certainly damaged the Special Relationship between the Section and the CIA. Aren't we usually informed of your extra-curricular activities?'

'This is an internal matter,' Martindale replied. 'No international ramifications. Still, your being here may change that. Shall we go?'

In the hall of Inverkeil House they were greeted by two young men in grey flannel suits. There was now no sign of Mrs Crathie other than a splash of blood at the foot of the stuffed bear.

'Take Miss Thurman into the lounge,' Martindale addressed the first of the young men. 'I'll join her after I make a phone call.'

'And him?' The second young man stared at James.

'Take him upstairs as we arranged when I phoned you.' Martindale smiled at James. 'As you see, we thought you'd come here. When you've finished with Mr Ryder I think it's time you brought Mr Withenshaw in to bed.'

On the second floor of the building James found himself in front of a heavily embossed wooden door of some antiquity. The grey-suited guardian opened the door with a rusty iron key.

'I should be grateful it's not a bottle dungeon,' James said lightly but the attempt at humour was ignored.

Inside the room the door slammed shut behind him and he

heard the lock turn. The room was high-ceilinged and dim, the only light filtering through the sides of thick curtains over one large window. James made out the shape of a great four-poster bed. In front of this stood the figure of a woman, hair wild, features in darkness.

'James . . . James Ryder! How did you get here?' said Nora Matheson.

'I keep referring to it as a jigsaw puzzle,' Carteret said. 'Rather a cliché. Of course life is a succession of puzzles, really, and none of them resemble jigsaws at all.'

He was sitting in the front room of a small detached house in Hornsey Rise, a comfortable, lived-in house looking onto a quiet, tree-lined street.

'I'm sorry I've landed myself on you,' Carteret went on. 'But the moment I realised I was under full-time surveillance I decided it was best to clear out. Give myself freedom to operate.'

Walter Harkness, whose house it was, leaned forward. 'You're sure they didn't follow you here?'

'Oh, quite sure. I pursued another wild route across the metropolis. Put my followers completely off my track.'

'What do you do now?' Harkness asked.

'The question indeed. If only Ryder would contact me. Let me know what, if anything, he has learned from Withenshaw.'

'And if he learns nothing?'

'Then, my dear man, I must take the little I know and place it before the ultimate arbiter. The Prime Minister. I shall need help there. From you and Prescott and any strings I can pull.' Carteret gave a small chuckle. 'I do know the Cabinet Secretary. Not well, but I know him.'

Mrs Harkness came into the room carrying a tray on which were two large mugs of tea and a plate of sandwiches. She was a pleasant-faced woman in her early forties and Carteret had been a guest at their wedding, some fourteen years before.

'I hope I'm not putting you to too much trouble,' Carteret apologised for the third time since his arrival.

'Nonsense,' said Jenny Harkness. 'We're delighted. I only hope you find the spare room comfortable.'

'You realise I'm making your home the centre of my operations?' Carteret frowned.

'Damn sight more comfortable than my office at the Yard,' Harkness responded at once. 'How about Ryder? Won't he try and contact you at Hampstead?'

'I was guilty of a small presumption there. I gave him your number should I be unobtainable at Hampstead. Anyway my line there will be tapped, I'm sure.'

'There's one thing you may not have considered, Tom.'

Carteret looked up from his mug of tea and nodded his thanks to Jenny Harkness who left the room with an encouraging smile. 'Tell me,' he said to Harkness.

'Supposing the Prime Minister knows and fully approves of all that Martindale and the Section are doing?'

Carteret looked suddenly very old. 'In that event I would have no problems since I doubt if I would be permitted to leave Downing Street other than to go to some place of detention. But I cannot somehow see the Government as a whole condoning the murder of two innocent citizens.'

'You don't know that Skinner was innocent.'

'Certainly he could have been working for an enemy. But not Mansfield. And there's Harrington. Not one to fall in front of tube trains. No, I believe the Section to be working on another initiative than the Government's. In fact it seems quite apparent who is behind this business. Although to what end I'm afraid to think.'

'Alexander?'

'The Minister for the Defence of the Realm. Also, under the PM, in charge of the security services. And the man who authorised completely unnecessary army manoeuvres next week. Incidentally I want something from you, Walter. Alexander's file.'

'What?'

'You know there is a confidential file on every minister of the Crown held by Special Branch. Primarily to trace all their connections in the event of assassination attempts. I want Alexander's. You have friends in the Special Branch.'

Harkness shook his head dubiously. 'Officially I'd have to have a reason.'

'You must not do it officially. You must simply lie.'

'Of course. What else?' Harkness grinned. 'But it might take a little time.'

'To be expected. Do you think you could let me have it tomorrow evening?'

3

'What happened?'

'They brought me here from Chester. The furthest safe house from London.'

She was there in front of him, answering questions. Nora Matheson, alive. He had become almost convinced she was dead. But he had been wrong.

'Skinner?' he said. 'What did he tell you that made them bring you here?'

She stared at him with a strangely vague look. 'When they brought me here I think . . . I think they drugged me.'

The Notting Hill process. Drugs, disorientation, destruction of memory. It takes time James thought, but they had time with her. He persisted.

'What about Skinner? You went to see him. He had information to give you. I took you to his house.'

She nodded uncertainly. 'I remember going to the house. Skinner offered me a drink, I remember that. Then . . . then they arrived . . . '

'But before they arrived, what had Skinner told you?'

She frowned. 'I'm not sure. He mentioned something about a man called Harrington falling under a train . . . then . . . then that man Martindale arrived and they . . . they gave me

196

something. An injection. After that I don't remember much until I arrived here. And there were more injections.'

With one swift action she pulled up the sleeve of her jumper. There were a number of small puncture marks on the inside of her elbow. James studied them and turned away, anger rising. Then he became aware that his hands, jacket and trousers were streaked with mud.

'Is there any place I can clean up?'

Nora indicated a door beyond the bed. Beyond the door was a small, white-tiled bathroom. Some ten feet up on the wall above the cistern was a narrow window. James looked around. An old-fashioned bath and a small washbasin. And no lock on the door.

Ten minutes later he had managed to wash the mud from his hands and brush down jacket and trousers. He re-entered the bedroom and crossed to the window. On the outside were neat rows of recently fitted steel bars.

'Like ... like the Lady of Shalott ... I feel ... ' Nora said, then a thought occurred to her. 'Couldn't Skinner tell you anything?'

'Skinner's dead,' he replied brusquely as if the statement might shock her into some reaction. It didn't. She merely blinked.

'What is it all about?' she said after a moment in a small voice. He told her most of what had happened to him since he had left her in Chester. He, of course, omitted the Glasgow hotel episode. Her eyes seemed to fill when he told her of the death of Mansfield. But there were no actual tears.

'Of course it was your diaries that gave me the leads,' he continued. 'Your notes – '

Here, she did respond. 'Ah, yes, the notes. I didn't mean to leave them –'

'I don't know whether I'm glad or sorry you did.' James gave a rueful smile.

'You wouldn't have landed in all this.'

'And maybe some people would still be alive.'

'But, James, why are they doing this? To what end?'

He shrugged. 'I was hoping you would have provided the answer to that.'

'I wish I could.'

Another pause. He studied the room. Then he suddenly felt hungry. 'Do they feed us?'

'They'll come with food.'

'We have to get out of here,' he went on. 'That might be the chance. When they bring us food.'

'There's no way. They're very careful. We won't get out until they let us go. If they do.'

Eventually he sat on a heavy armchair and Nora perched on the bed. After a time she lay back and from her breathing he knew she was asleep. He stretched his legs out, relaxing, and weariness overcame him. He slept.

He reckoned later he must have slept for two hours. He was awakened by the two young men who had greeted them in the hall. One balanced a tray on each hand, the other remaining at the door pointing a revolver at him.

'Where's Miss Thurman?' he asked, still groggy from sleep.

'Being taken care of, like you,' the first man said, placing the trays on a table against the wall. They then withdrew without further words and James heard the door being locked carefully behind them.

By this time Nora had awakened. She removed napkins from each tray to reveal steaks, roast potatoes and cauliflower. There was also a slice of gateau and two small bottles of wine. It reminded James of nothing less than a slightly superior British Railways lunch.

They ate in silence and only when they had finished did Nora speak. 'You must have found out something,' she said.

'I told you, bits and pieces. Nothing definite.' He paused and took a deep breath. 'If I can get out of here, will you come with me?'

'You won't be able to. And anyway ... I haven't the strength.'

This had been the cool assured woman he had driven to Chester. Now she was hesitant, fearful, nervous. He remembered the effects of the drugs on himself and understood.

'If I can get out, I'll get back to you, I promise,' he said.

'But how ... who ... ? They control everything.'

198

'Not quite. Carteret is still operating. You know him. His name was in your notes.'

'Yes, yes I know Tom Carteret. But he's retired ... old ... I only thought I'd get background material from him.'

'He's very active in his retirement,' James replied but did not elaborate. Instead he examined the walls of the room, and the fireplace which he discovered was blocked up.

'There is no way out,' Nora said.

He continued to examine the oak panelling of the walls, tapping them, listening for a hollow sound. His experience in antiques was useful now. But there was no hollow sound. He ended his examination of the room at the door. It was solid, the lock formidable.

He ended his examination and went into the bathroom. He stood for a moment and then he examined the tiles. They were set into cement behind which were the original granite walls of the house. No way through. Then he looked up at the window high on the wall. He felt a quickening of his pulse. They had omitted to bar this window. He estimated it to be about two feet wide and three feet high, set deep in the wall. It should be possible to squeeze through such a space. But what was beyond? A sheer drop? The side of the house, smooth, lacking in handholds? Yet he had to make the attempt.

He lifted one of the two large bathtowels and slung it around his neck. Thus adorned, he climbed onto the rim of the lavatory seat and from there onto the top of the cistern. His head was now less than a foot below the embrasure into which was set the window. He gripped the edge of the embrasure and pulled himself upwards, a stab of pain running down the side of his weak leg. He ignored it and felt around with his legs until his foot found a purchase in the wall where a tile had been displaced, allowing him to balance precariously.

The window was in front of him now and he was able to wrap the towel around his right forearm and thrust it against the glass of the window. It splintered outwards and he was able to clear the frame of retained shards with his towelled arm. He then levered himself up onto the embrasure so that his head was thrust into the dark night air. By pushing and twisting he forced his shoulders through the frame and, in the light from behind him he was able to make out part of the exterior wall. It seemed to consist entirely of rough stonework without any obvious purchase for hand or toecap. But then he perceived a stone guttering some feet below the window, uneven, eroded in part by weather, but nonetheless there, wide enough to give his feet support.

Pulling himself forward, he twisted around and lowered his legs downwards until he felt the guttering beneath his feet. A pang of fear was qualmed as the guttering held beneath him. Now he was lying flat against the wall, fingers on the window-ledge, feet on the guttering, illuminated by the pool of light cast from the bathroom window above him. What now? He could move in either direction, perhaps a foot; below him was a sixty to seventy foot drop into darkness. No escape that way. His eyes were, however, becoming accustomed to the darkness and he was able to see some distance to his right. There, about three yards away, was the dim rectangle of another, larger embrasure, a window inset in the stone and without bars. Taking his weight on one hand and on the guttering he edged his right hand along the wall seeking an opening, a crack that he might grasp.

He was soaked in perspiration now. He thought, God knows why he, a grown man – no, damn it, a middle-aged man – should be trying a Superman act seventy feet from the ground on the wall of a Scottish country house? The fingers of his right hand curled into a cavity, a hole from which a segment of stone had been displaced. Grasping the stone, he disengaged his left hand and edged along the guttering. A small hail of dirt and pebbles fell on his forehead but his grip held. One more handhold and he could swing himself into the larger window.

After a few seconds he found the handhold, not a cavity this time but a razor-sharp crack in the stonework with just the depth to give him a solid grip. From there he could swing into the window. It took him three minutes to get into this position. Behind the glass of the window he could make out heavy curtains but, James noted with relief, no light.

To have risked his neck to crash in upon a conclave of

Martindale's men would have been an exercise in futility. At least the darkness behind the curtains reassured him that he would be spared that. There was of course the danger of crashing through the glass; of ripping an artery or vein. It was a risk he had to take.

He took a deep breath. Don't think too much on disasters. He swung feet first through the window, the glass giving with one sharp crack. He felt a tearing pain in his upper right arm and then he was enveloped in thick curtains and his back jarred on a hard wooden floor surface. He rolled forward into the room and lay, gulping air, praying for silence as the final smaller pieces of glass fell, shattering on the floor.

He rose to his feet dizzily aware then of another sound in the room; of deep breathing from one side. Ahead of him, dimly outlined by light from the corridor beyond, was the door. He groped along the wall until he found a light switch. He pressed the switch and the room was drenched in light. The breathing increased. James turned to face Maurice Withenshaw lying against large pillows, bedded but awake, staring at him.

'It's all right,' James gasped. 'I've broken out of the next room.'

The panic died from Withenshaw's eyes. His mouth twisted again to shape words. 'Tell Car ... watch Commander, London ... power ... sanctioned.'

The words similar to those he had uttered earlier. James gripped his shoulder in a gesture of reassurance and, as he did so, became aware that under his now ripped jacket there was a sensation of dampness. He pulled off the jacket. His arm was covered in several superficial cuts, some of which were bleeding profusely. But there was no pulsing flow, no arterial damage. He would survive.

Nodding to Withenshaw he eased his jacket on again and, moving to the door, switched out the room light before easing it open. No need to lock Withenshaw in, he reckoned. The man was a prisoner in his own body. James moved into the dimly lit corridor and towards the stairs. A minute later, swift but silent he reached ground level. The stuffed bear stared blindly towards him. From the closed doors of a room to his right he could hear voices and behind them a radio giving the ten o'clock news.

James turned to the door leading to the lounge. Jean Thurman had been taken into that room. She might possibly still be there. Or Martindale or one of his men might be in the room. He had to take yet another chance. If he couldn't escape with Nora Matheson, he could at least try to take Jean with him. He opened the door. Jean Thurman was alone in the room sitting in a deep armchair. A tumbler of whisky was in one hand. She looked up as James entered and reacted with a smile and no sign of surprise.

'You look a mess,' she said. 'I thought you'd been locked away. But you're a resourceful kind of guy. And you learn fast.'

'I think we should get out of here,' James replied, amazed at her insouciance.

'A chase across the tundra, eh?' Her smile broadened.

'We have to find out what Martindale is doing. And I have to get back to Carteret.'

'But you haven't found out what Martindale is doing, have you? So what's the point of running back to that old man? Would you like a drink? You look as if you could use one. What have you been doing?'

His mouth was dry but he resisted the temptation. 'No. We have to move.'

She stared at him evenly and sipped her whisky. 'I'm going nowhere, James, You know for a man of forty, you're full of shit. Ladies go missing, you have to find them. So people get killed. And still you go blundering on. You guess Martindale incited the race riots in Notting Hill. You're horror struck. How dare he? How dare he blame the blacks? It would have happened anyway. All those black faces would have got tired of being pushed around and they would have started pushing. Which comes first, chicken or egg?'

'You've changed your tune.'

'The music went flat. All this gallantry, James, what's it for?'

'I thought you were on my side. . . .' His astonishment echoed in his tone.

'There are no sides! Only spheres of interest. Martindale was surprised when he saw me with you. You could hear his mind ticking over. Thurman, CIA, with Ryder? Phone calls were made, one to Langley, Virginia. I'm allowed to speak. To my operations chief. The word is stay out of it. No interference in the internal affairs of other nations ... not unless it suits us or ITT or God.'

She brushed a stray hair from her face.

'Martindale has muscle behind him. Power. We're with the power now. I've been playing the wrong game.'

James took a deep breath. 'So I go alone.'

'You don't go at all. I'm with them now.'

She reached under her jumper and pulled out the butt of her automatic. But the whisky was having its effect. She swayed and the muzzle of the weapon snagged on the wool of the jumper. She tugged at it as James stepped forward and, without thought, slapped her across the side of the face with the back of his hand. After the action, the anger rose in him. She staggered back and before she could regain her balance he prised the gun from her fingers, tearing the wool of the jumper.

Her mouth twisted ruefully. 'You learn fast, James. But then you had me as a teacher.'

She seemed to relax. And then, with surprising agility, she came at him, hands as talons, clawing at his face. He sidestepped and swung his arm around in an arc, hand clutching the automatic. The barrel smashed against her face and she went down on the carpet without a sound. He knelt beside her. She was unconscious. He was amazed at his own cool ability to hit out so brutally at a female. A few weeks before he would not have thought himself capable of such an act. But at least in her unconscious state she would be out long enough to give him a head start before alarms were sounded. He was also surprised at his own acceptance of her changing of sides. He had come to expect anything.

He straightened up, looked at the door of the room and then at the windows. Which way out, he asked himself. He chose the window.

A half hour later he was on the moor, well away from the

road leading to the house. He had reckoned on the moor as less accessible to his possible pursuers. An early fear that he might wander in circles in the dark was dispelled by a faint, distant aura of reddish light in the sky. Fort William. If he kept heading to the left of the light he must eventually hit the main road.

Of course he had not reckoned on the moorland itself. He stumbled over unseen rocks, gashed his right leg against a cutting edge of stone, sank over his shoes into soft bogland. Later on more solid ground he contemplated resting but the distant sound of car and motorbike engines from the track now far behind him were still audible in the silence of the night and he forced himself onwards. They had almost certainly discovered he was missing and the search would be on.

After they found no sign of him on the track to the house, they would certainly turn their attention to the moor. But, in the darkness, he had the advantage. They were looking for him. He giggled to himself, on the edge of a weary hysteria. The needle in the haystack, he. Fine toothcombs needed. He was a flea on Jean Thurman's tundra.

Time had no meaning. He had smashed his watch, he discovered, possibly crashing through Withenshaw's window. As he stumbled onwards, the moor seemed an infinity of blackness. Everything had lost shape and reality. There were occasional shades of darkness. And thank God, the aura of the town in the sky. Apart from the sound of his own feet, the silence was total. He pressed on, a conditioned reflex to the situation.

Then later there was a sound, a distant familiar droning, whirring sound in the blackness of the sky. At first he thought it might be in his head, some manifestation of his physical state but, as it increased in volume, he recognised it. The helicopter was somewhere over and above him. He began to imagine its shape, black, amorphous, a darker darkness moving towards him.

Suddenly from above to his right, from the belly of the machine, there was a flashing sword of light, the cold fat beam of a searchlight raking the moor. They were indeed now looking for him.

He threw himself down at the side of an outcropping of rock, curling his body around the damp stone, attempting to merge into it. The giant whirling bat of the machine dipped low and the beam of light moved over and past James's recumbent form. Some thirty feet beyond him it seemed to catch a movement within the circle of illuminated light. The light flattened as the helicopter dipped downwards. Something, perhaps a rabbit or a hare, was caught in the beam. There was the short, earsplitting-in-the-night sound, staccato, brutal, perhaps a light machine gun exploding its missiles into the moorland.

After a moment, the gunfire ceased and there was only the engine sound and the rotors beating the air. The helicopter hovered and then, apparently satisfied that whatever they had been shooting at was not their target, the machine rose and continued to move away from James across the moor northwards, the searchlight beam becoming a thinner and thinner pencil of light until it was swallowed by the darkness.

James lay for some time, resting. Then as he rose he heard a rustling sound nearby and, turning, identified the target of the helicopter's gun. Dimly he perceived the shape of a large ram, limping, one leg oozing blood where it had been hit by a bullet. The animal bleated softly then settled on the grass to endure its wound.

James moved on. He felt no emotion but simply a great weariness. He was surprised when he came upon the road, the smooth, hard tarmacadam suddenly under his feet. He limped, slower now, along the barely discernible ribbon of road. He covered two hundred yards or so before he heard the low growl of a heavy engine and saw the lights in front of him, two great eyes coming from the direction of Fort William. It was a heavy diesel lorry, its load encased in a huge metal container. James had no energy to conceal himself but limped towards it at the edge of the road. Then the cabin of the lorry drew level with him and, with a growl and a squeal of airbrakes, it stopped. A round, red face peered down at James.

'Christ, Jimmy, you look as if you've been run over by a truck.' The voice was Glasgow.

'I had a car accident,' James replied. It was a half-truth.

'Car accident, is it? Parts of you look like a piece of beef that's been through the mincer. I suppose you'll be heading for Fort William. I'm for Inverness ma'sel'. Any use to you?'

They'd be expecting him to be heading for Fort William, James thought. It was the nearest town, the place in which he would naturally seek refuge. Inverness, away at the head of the Great Glen, they would rule out. Too far on foot. The ideal place for him to go, and almost certainly a clear road.

'You're on!' he said, at once feeling cheerful.

He barely felt the aches from the wounds in his body as he climbed into the cabin of the lorry and settled beside the driver.

It was five o'clock in the morning when Carteret was awakened to answer the telephone in the narrow hall of Harkness's house.

'Mr Carteret! It's James Ryder!' The voice at the end of the line was hoarse and weary but recognisable. Carteret felt a sense of relief as he replied.

'Where are you?'

'Fort Augustus. I need help. I don't think I can get back to London on my own.'

Harkness, dressing-gowned, was at Carteret's side now.

'He's in Fort Augustus. We need to get him back here,' the old man explained.

The Chief Inspector nodded. 'Bob McGlashan. Inverness CID. He could pull him in and fly him down. And he's clear of your London Intelligence boys. Find out exactly where he is in Fort Augustus and tell him to stay there until the police come. I'll phone McGlashan.'

Carteret conveyed all this to James.

'A phone box under the shadow of Fort Augustus Abbey,' James replied. 'Listen, I saw Withenshaw. He's had a stroke but he did say something. Not very much—'

'Tell me when you get here. Now hang up, we have to phone Inverness. I'll see you in a few hours and you can tell me everything.'

A moment later Harkness was dialling the Inverness number.

There was another telephone conversation later that morning. From Inverkeil House to a house in Lord North Street.

'You haven't handled this well.'

'I could not take into account the aggressive enterprise of the man.'

'And the Thurman woman?'

'She's had her orders from the cousins in Langley. She will be returning to London with me. Her participation would never have happened had we confided earlier in the cousins. And of course Ryder could have learned little from Withenshaw.'

'Very well. But tell your people there to keep looking for Ryder. You'll be flying back at once?'

'At once.'

'Good. I need you to work with Buller. Lists have to be prepared.'

'Night of the Hummingbird?'

'I find the parallel inappropriate. And in dubious taste. Goodbye now.'

4

Harkness's lounge, some eight hours later.

James, still unwashed, clothes torn and muddy, a large brandy in his hand, sat facing Carteret. He thought the old man looked tireder, older.

'I'm all right,' he said in response to Carteret's question. 'Bruises nicks, cuts and gouges. Also strains and sprains. But no ruptures. I'm in one piece.'

'Right. Tell me all about it. And then Chief Inspector Harkness's good lady will arrange a bath and some sleep.'

James started by describing his meeting with Jean Thurman outside Carteret's Hampstead flat.

'The CIA,' the old man nodded. 'To be expected. Long noses in everybody's business. Efficiency and a touch of idiocy. A lethal concoction. Heaven preserve us from the cousins.'

James went on, describing the way his car was wired with high explosive.

'I did tell you not to go back to your flat,' Carteret said.

James then related everything else in sequence including Jean Thurman's change of attitude at Inverkeil House. He did however omit the personal moment in the Glasgow hotel. Nothing to do with the old man. And it did make him sound foolish.

'Miss Thurman's change of side indicates the way the wind may be blowing,' Carteret interrupted. 'It seems to be blowing for Martindale. Now I want everything Withenshaw managed to say. Everything. However seemingly unconnected or illogical.'

As James went over this, Carteret made notes on a small pad. When he had finished the old man looked up.

'Well then, he did give us something. And Nora Matheson, she gave you nothing?'

'I think she'd gone through the full treatment they tried on me. No memory of anything very much.'

'At least she's alive. And you, too, I'm glad to say.'

'I'm glad you're glad.'

'Mainly because of the information you've brought.'

'Thank you,' James replied acidly, anger rising. 'Do you people really care? If I'd been killed, like Mansfield or Skinner, would you have cared?'

Carteret gave a thin smile. I would have regretted your passing.'

'You're like a Government Health Warning, Carteret. The right words but no emotion. Tell me, what is happening? What's it all about? I think I have some right to know.'

Carteret's brow creased. 'Right to know? My dear fellow,

nobody in this country has a right to know anything. Freedom of information does not exist. You are only allowed to know what your masters permit you to know.'

James opened his mouth to protest but Carteret went on unflurried. 'I will however tell you. When I'm ready to do so. Because I may need you. Because my side has a manpower shortage. I will need everyone I can trust. Some policemen, some politicians, some journalists, all in untrustworthy pursuits, I grant you but needed, if they are true. True as steel.'

Eccentric, James told himself. Like Martindale and the others. Eccentric to a point of insanity. After all Martindale and Carteret are of the same breed, different sides of the same coin. The ultimate, ice-hearted professional pragmatists. Thurman had been another.

James rose unsteadily. 'I hope you don't need me too soon. Because I'm going to have a bath and sleep for a week.'

'A couple of days, anyway. And you'll need some new clothes. Before you sleep leave out your measurements. I shall attend to that personally. And don't be too depressed, Ryder. We're all of us expendable. Even six hundred million Chinese are expendable. And you. And me. You'll get used to the idea but, of course, you'll never be quite the same man again.'

James bathed and went to bed. Jenny Harkness's cool sheets were balm to his bruises and cuts. He slept without dreaming.

Downstairs Carteret sat over his notes, thinking. He had, in his long career, believed in the necessity to be utterly ruthless in dealing with enemies of the Crown. In this affair he saw no reason to act otherwise despite the enemy appearing to be actual agents of the Crown. He believed those agents to be wrong and dangerous, and though he was uncertain of their motives, they represented a threat to the institutions he revered. Those institutions had to be preserved and those who threatened them had to be dealt with, even at the cost of human life. Sanctioned. That was the word.

Sanction, the ethical meaning was a motive for obedience to any moral or religious law. The other meaning was a permit for assassination. The Americans called it 'removal with extreme prejudice'; the Russians, 'a wet job'. Whatever it was called it was murder; expedient killing in the national interest.

He turned back to his notes. Tuesday, Withenshaw had said. One week ahead. Then there was the reference to the 'London Garrison Commander'. And the word again. Sanction. The Whitehall sanction. That could only mean one thing. But would they dare? And why? Such a murder would surely antagonise the nation, unless it would appear to have been carried out by someone else. A trigger for action. Like the Reichstag fire in Germany. And then there was another word. Enabling who to do what? Something stirred in his memory. In the past. To do with the Reichstag fire, perhaps. Something in the past.

Carteret cursed under his breath. The memory of old men was not to be relied upon. He looked closer at the notes. 'Act'? Was the word a plea to do something? Or perhaps it should not stand alone. Again the stirring at the edge of memory. He paced the room. Next Tuesday it would happen, whatever it was. The Downing Street sanction, the London Garrison Commander, the enabling, the act. And next Tuesday there was a vital cabinet meeting and the commencement of unnecessary manoeuvres on Salisbury Plain, manoeuvres ordered by the Minister for the Defence of the Realm. It always came back to Charles Alexander. And the day of his unnecessary manoeuvres. Unless they were necessary to Alexander. And not simply bread and circuses.

London, cleared of regular soldiers and with many policeman away on Salisbury Plain would be an unguarded city. And those three words echoed in his head. Sanction. Enabling. Act. It was beginning to come together in his mind.

He crossed the room to Harkness's bookcase. He cursed again, this time, the fact of being away from his own home, his own books. He scanned the titles with little hope. The autobiography of a retired detective, book-club editions of popular novels, two volumes on crime; and then he saw what might help him, a tattered Pelican edition of Alan Bullock's, *Hitler, A Study in Tyranny*. He thumbed through it until he came to what he was looking for.

'Gesetz zur Behebung der Not von Volk und Reich.' 'Law for Removing the Distress of People and State.' How benevolent it sounded. Germany in economic chaos in 1933 had brought Hitler's alteration to the constitution of the German State giving him absolute powers. The beginning of Nazi dictatorship. It was also known as the Enabling Act.

Later, Walter Harkness returned from Scotland Yard to find Carteret writing, sheaves of paper in front of him.

'Lists,' the old man explained. 'Lists of possible friends. Provisional and unsatisfactory when one doesn't know who has been attracted to the other side.'

'There are sides to be taken then?'

Carteret subdued a fit of coughing and started to talk. He told Harkness everything he had deduced from Withenshaw's words. He spoke quietly and with conviction.

'This could be dangerous for you and Jenny,' he ended with emphasis.

'She knows. She trusts you, Tom. It's called faith.'

Carteret coughed. 'For God's sake, I'm not God.'

'But you like the idea,' Harkness said. 'I have something for you. SB. HMG. Confidential: not to be removed.'

He handed the slim file to Carteret. Neatly typed across the cover was 'Charles Ewart Alexander'.

'I've put myself in bloody schtuck for you,' Harkness went on. 'I only hope it's worth it.'

Carteret opened the file, sat down and started to read. Harkness went to the sideboard and poured himself a large whisky.

'Have you read this, Walter?' Carteret said.

'Skimmed it.'

'Well?'

'Well?'

'Damn it, aren't you surprised? Here. Under close associates?'

'They always list friends and ... others. If he gets into trouble, first place you look is his friends. If he has any, as a politician. Usually find the cause of trouble among friends.'

'Ours is a nasty occupation, Walter. So you aren't surprised at the lady's name here, among his . . . friends?'

Harkness shrugged and sipped his whisky. 'I'm a detective, remember. If you think about it, Tom, it could explain a lot. And of course leave even more questions.'

Carteret shook his head sorrowfully. 'It makes Ryder's intrusion into this affair quite tragic. An exercise in futility. For him. Not for us. Anyway let's talk about what I've deduced from his conversations with Withenshaw. Even though the man has had a serious stroke, he's managed to reveal a great deal. . . . '

They talked long into the night. They talked and they planned.

James slept for thirty-six hours. When he awakened it was the evening again. The evening of the next day.

A new pair of trousers, identical to the pair he had been wearing, were lying over a chair. On the chair was a new shirt, underclothes, a polo-necked sweater and a light sports jacket. On top of them was a note in Carteret's hand. 'You'll have to pay me for these. We may be able to reclaim the cost from the government but meanwhile I am an old-age pensioner. . . . '

When he arrived downstairs it was to find Harkness on the telephone, Carteret beside him listening and making notes. After a moment Harkness replaced the telephone receiver and turned to the old man. 'He doesn't believe it. But at least he's on the alert.'

'Few of them will believe it. Until they take them out. Like they took out Harrington. They're going to have to take a lot of people out. Including the Police Commissioner. Oh, I don't say they'll kill them but they'll have to hold them. Indefinitely.'

Carteret then turned to James. 'Good evening, Mr Ryder. I trust you are rested?'

James nodded. 'What happens now?'

'We are working. All I ask of you is that you place yourself under my orders. Until next Tuesday.'

'That's six days,' James replied, frowning. 'Look, I have a business to run . . . '

Carteret exchanged glances with Harkness. 'I wouldn't bother, Ryder. Not until after Tuesday. If you go to your flat, you'll find they'll be waiting for you. They daren't let up on you. You know too much.'

'I don't know what I'm supposed to know,' James exclaimed. 'All I want to do is get back to my shop.'

Carteret coughed. 'Perhaps we should let you do that,' he said unexpectedly. 'Go back to the shop. But at a time of our choosing. We may be able to do them some damage if we know when you are going and they are waiting for you. Perhaps Friday. Not before.'

'All right. Friday,' James said feeling slightly mollified. Another day or so won't do any harm. And he was still tired. And at once he felt hungry.

Carteret smiled. It was as if he could read James's mind. 'You're hungry. The kitchen. Rear door at the end of the hall. Mrs Harkness is expecting you, I think.'

James went out.

'Tom, what are you playing at?' Harkness protested. 'They'll be waiting at his bloody shop. They'll take him, perhaps kill him.'

'Exactly. Of course we'll do our best to prevent them. It will be our first offensive move. You'll have people there. Information received. You have reason to believe there will be a robbery at the shop. We'll damage them. Take at least one of their men. Bring him here. Remember I was trained in getting people to talk.' Then suddenly Carteret changed the subject. 'By the way I think I have another piece of our jigsaw puzzle. I phoned a man called Fletcher. Works at the War Office.'

'I thought you'd be keeping away from the War Office.'

'Oh, I did. Phoned him at home. Did a little discreet pumping. Wanted to know who was in command of the manoeuvres at Salisbury Plain. It's no secret.'

'Who?'

'GOC Home Counties. Sir Richard Molyneux. While he's charging around Salisbury, he retains his command. But since the Royal Family and the Cabinet are still in London, a

213

temporary post has been created. London Garrison Commander. LGC for short.'

'What Withenshaw was trying to tell us.'

'What he did tell us. And who has been appointed. A senior serving officer. Brigadier Arthur Ewart Alexander, brother of the Minister.'

'It's too obvious!'

'Of course. But Charles Alexander makes the appointment.'

'The PM would have to approve. It could mean the PM is involved.'

'No. The Prime Minister is in power. Therefore the Prime Minister does not have to take power. And she is a believer in the democratic process. No, the mind behind this is Charles Alexander. With the bulk of the army on manoeuvres and his brother in command in London, he will control the capital. He's been planning this, I believe, for a long time. Since the Rear Admiral died he's controlled the Intelligence services. That's been his power base. The man wants power. He believes the country's present torments make the time right. And of course he hasn't hesitated to stimulate these torments a little.'

'The Notting Hill riots.'

'And other incidents. The weak links were Harrington and Skinner. They wouldn't play. And they must have suspected something early on. Harrington may even have discussed it with Withenshaw. So Harrington went under a tube train. And fortunately for them Withenshaw had a stroke. Or they induced it somehow. That left Skinner. He panicked and ran. At the same time he made the mistake of trying to contact the press. Nora Matheson. Not a good choice. And Ryder got involved.'

'Like something that happens in one of those banana republics in South America,' Harkness said.

'Alexander would undoubtedly claim we have become like one of those banana republics,' Carteret mused.

'What do you do next?'

'I try and see the Prime Minister.'

PART FIVE

1

Friday morning. James was leaving the house.

Harkness said, 'You're still going?'

'Yes.' He was aware Carteret was using him as a decoy. It was the nature of the old man. 'Where is he?'

'Mr Carteret? Out. Trying to see the PM. Third try. You sure you want to go to your shop?'

'Wouldn't want to lose Mr Carteret his decoy.'

Harkness shrugged. 'You'll be all right. We haven't left you completely exposed. Some of my lads will be around.'

'I'm glad. Only thing is how do I tell them from the others?'

'Not easy in this game. If they shoot you, they're on the other side.'

'Comforting.'

When James stepped out of a taxi in New Bond Street he was greeted by a flood of sunlight, as the sun emerged from behind a cloud. The street was thronged with shoppers and it seemed to him as if, after the nightmare of the last weeks, he had returned to normality. Yet he knew it was not over and he could not resist a nervous glance over his shoulder as he turned off the street and approached the small but elegant frontage of his own establishment. The sign, 'James Ryder, Antiques' brought a feeling of reassurance.

Then he heard the voice, close to his right ear. 'Don't react, Ryder. Take it nice and easy. Just walk right into your shop as you intended. Above all don't reach for your pocket. We haven't forgotten you did have a weapon on occasion.'

The man took up a position at his side. He wore a well-cut suit but even that did not obscure the bulk and ungainliness of his body. The face was red, mottled with broken veins. James had seen it before. In Notting Hill in that past nightmare.

'Name's Buller,' the man said. 'You'll know of me. I'm the tank corps in this business.'

'You mean, the killer?'

'That kind of remark doesn't bother me. Let's just go into your shop.'

Buller had a man already in the shop and Jean Thurman was standing quietly studying a small figurine. Behind the counter the familiar figures of Anthony Cromer, James's manager, and Miss Weaver, in her forties, his saleslady stood, eyes fearful staring at Buller's man who held a revolver in his hand.

'It's all right, Anthony . . . Miss Weaver,' James said trying to hide the tremor in his voice. 'Nothing to be afraid of.'

He turned to Buller. 'Can you let them go?'

Buller shook his head. 'They'd run for the police. They wouldn't believe we're really part of the police. Let them just carry on with their work. We'll go into your little office at the rear. Tom Oswald will look after them. You met Tom in Chester and afterwards.'

The man facing Cromer and Miss Weaver turned to nod at James. Recognition was instant. Oswald said nothing.

In his office James assumed a forced nonchalance and sat in his familiar seat behind the small desk. Buller came in behind him followed by Jean Thurman. The office was small, cluttered with James's files, invoices and occasional stock. At the rear was another door leading to a toilet and then into a narrow lane, a cul-de-sac running into New Bond Street.

'Glad finally to have met you face to face, Ryder,' Buller said. 'After all we have some acquaintances in common. And we're both friends of Sybil Graham's.'

James thought, Sybil had mentioned Buller. And he had determined then that it was the end of the relationship with Sybil. Now looking at Buller he knew the meeting was definitely terminal. Sybil Graham was completely erased from his life.

'Anyway,' Buller went on, 'this has nothing to do with

216

Sybil. I'm here to take you out, Ryder. You come with me and no more Superman escapes. One small move and Tom Oswald shoots you. Understand?'

'I understand.'

'I'm curious as to why you turned up here. I told Martindale you'd keep well away. But he was right and here you are.'

'Where else could I go? Anyway what did I do? Simply tried to find Nora Matheson.'

'Your big mistake. Because of you, people got killed. Like Mansfield.'

James rubbed his forehead. Was it true? Was he responsible? 'You killed Mansfield?' he accused the large man.

Buller grinned coldly. 'A gas leak killed Mansfield. Something similar could happen to you and your friend Carteret. Unless you talk to me. You see, I never believed you were merely Sir Galahad rescuing a missing lady. You were after us from the start. Why and for whom?'

'Ask Miss Thurman. She knows the truth.'

Jean Thurman looked up from contemplating a pile of James's business files. 'He always said he was looking for Nora Matheson. Never changed his story. I kind of believe him.'

'He was well trained,' Buller insisted. 'By Carteret. Carteret was good when he was in the Section.'

'I've told her the truth,' James went on and turned to the American woman. 'Why are you here anyway?'

'Purely a watching brief,' she replied. 'I'm not involved.'

'If you let him take me out of here, you're involved.'

'No way. Not my affair.'

Buller suddenly began to exhibit signs of impatience. 'Stop wasting time, Ryder. If you won't tell me anything here, you'll tell me it elsewhere. And you might even get to live. On your feet!'

James rose. If Harkness had men around, where the hell were they? The answer came quickly.

Oswald came to the office door. 'Man coming into the shop. Customer, I think. Do we do anything?'

'We simply go out the back with Ryder,' Buller replied.

217

Oswald turned back towards the shop but at once something he saw made him bring up his revolver. Then came what seemed to James like a shock wave. Every piece of china in the shop's display cabinets vibrated. Then the roar of a gun reverberated around the shop and blew a volume of sound into the office. As if in slow motion Oswald's head jerked back and before he even managed to level his weapon he was thrown backwards and the back of his head seemed to explode in a haze of red. He fell across James's desk, face upwards, a third red eye in the centre of his forehead.

Buller moved fast, gun appearing in his hand as he moved from the door, dropping to his knees. In this crouched position he fired several shots around the lintel of the door. Three shots came from the shop in reply, two of them ploughing into the wall, the third smashing a small figurine on the shelf behind the desk. James, who had thrown himself down behind the desk, was showered with fragments of china. Jean Thurman, exhibiting genuine surprise and shock for the first time since James had known her, flattened herself against the wall of the office. Automatically she reached for the patent leather swing bag on her shoulder, heavy enough to hold a gun, thought better of it and let the bag go. Then, with a loud crash, the door behind them was kicked open and a voice shouted, 'On the floor!'

A figure in a black sweater was outlined in the doorway. Buller swivelled around and brought his revolver up, an act of desperation and some considerable stupidity. The black sweater fired not so much at the man as the movement. The noise was even more deafening as the man was using some kind of small automatic machine gun. The acrid tang of cordite filled the room. When the gunfire ceased Buller was lying, not so much against the wall as pressed into it. Across his chest were dark holes, neatly spaced, from which blood oozed out briefly. Buller was staring across at James, eyes wide open. He was quite dead.

For some minutes, James found he was deaf. The young man in the black sweater was joined from the shop by an older man, revolver in hand, in a belted raincoat. Their lips moved but James heard nothing. They examined the two

218

bodies, spoke to Jean Thurman, who also appeared to have been deafened, and searched her bag for identification. Then James found his hearing was gradually returning. The man in the raincoat introduced himself.

'Detective Sergeant Watson, working for Mr Harkness.' He nodded towards the black sweater. 'This is DC Connors. He's ex-SAS. Hence the entrance. He was a bit too keen. Mr Carteret wanted one of them alive.'

James shuddered. 'To hell with what Carteret wanted. I was his decoy.'

'They thought you were important. They sent Mr Buller after you. Anyway, you're okay, that's the main thing.'

'What if Buller had decided to kill me straight away?'

'Then you'd have been dead.'

'What happens to me now? And to her?' He nodded towards Jean Thurman.

'You go back to Mr Harkness's place. She comes with us.'

Jean straightened up. 'I'm a United States citizen with a diplomatic passport . . . !'

Watson surveyed her with cold eyes. 'I realise that, miss. You'll be returned to your Embassy . . . eventually. Meanwhile you'll be in a nice safe place where Mr Carteret may want to talk to you.'

There were no arguments. She went out with Connors.

'What happens here?' James asked, staring at the two bodies.

'We'll send the cleaners in. The word will be there was an attempted robbery with violence. But no casualties. Shall we go?'

Later that day Carteret sat staring at James and Harkness. They were in Harkness's lounge.

'It's not good. I was hoping to produce Buller as evidence. Miss Thurman will say nothing and I haven't been able to get to the Prime Minister. She left today for a conference in Washington. Comes back in time for the cabinet meeting on Tuesday. Not that she'll get anything in Washington. The Americans will sit back and wait and see. I suspect that they know about Alexander and his "Enabling Act" and rather like the idea.'

'You didn't get to anyone in Downing Street?' Harkness asked.

'Charles Alexander has friends there. And the Cabinet Secretary was unable to see me. So I was told. I suspect someone in Alexander's pocket advised him against doing so. Oh, they did say I might see the PM after Wednesday. By that time it will be too late. We'll all be under arrest. If we can be found. And we will be found.'

Carteret paused, staring bleakly at the carpet. 'I remember, at the beginning of this ... this business, after the Rear Admiral's funeral, I remember thinking, tomorrow could be worse. It seems I was right.'

'What can we do?' Harkness asked after a pause.

'Keep trying. Contact friends. Continue to tell all we know. The trouble is many ears will be deafened by the pervading silence from other quarters. In that event, I will consider a different kind of action.'

The next days were spent in Harkness's house, James solitary while Carteret continued making lengthy telephone calls, explaining, cajoling, exhorting. For the first time James felt irritation at being out of the action. Finally he broached this with Carteret.

'You may have action yet,' the old man said, suppressing his cough. 'But what you may have to do might well be worse than anything up till now.'

'What?' James asked.

'It will be our final throw, if necessary. Our ultimate act of desperation.' Carteret's hands were trembling.

'You have to be so cryptic?'

'Yes, I have to be.'

Harkness returned from duty at Scotland Yard that evening.

'I've tried to talk to the Commissioner,' he announced, ignoring Carteret's frown of displeasure at the statement. 'Oh, I was suitably enigmatic. Told him I'd received information that there might be a terrorist move against the cabinet on Tuesday. Actually he said he'd heard similar rumours.'

At once Carteret was interested. 'Go on.'

'But he'd received reassurances that precautions were being taken.'

'What precautions?'

'They were all in the hands of Intelligence. Under Martindale and using the Section.'

Carteret sat back, pale and tired, unable to hide his disappointment. 'Of course. Set the wolf to guard the flock. How classically obvious! By the time the Commissioner realises how wrong he was, there will be a new Commissioner. A new government.'

James expressed the fear written on Harkness's face. 'Then there's nothing we can do?'

Carteret didn't answer but rose and limped across the room to the cupboard in which Harkness kept liquor.

'I could use a whisky. I think we all need it. You'll both join me?'

There seemed nothing more to say. They joined him.

2

The Sunday papers were full of the imminent manoeuvres on Salisbury Plain. Photographs of Territorial Army men taking leave of their civilian existences decorated the pages. A report of the Prime Minister's visit to Washington was glowing with inaccurate optimism.

Carteret stared bleakly at the reports with ill-concealed depression. His sessions on the telephone had come to an end and later he sat, papers cast aside, gazing unseeingly at the trivia on the television screen. After a time James, who had attempted to engage him in conversation, retired to his bedroom and tried to read. But he found it impossible. His

221

mind strayed to Nora Matheson and whether she was safe and unharmed. He wondered too about himself. Once the coup was over, would he be allowed to carry on with his normal life? Or would he be arrested, as Carteret believed and simply disappear?

On Monday morning James came downstairs to find Carteret, roused, pacing the room like a caged animal.

'There's one way out,' he said. 'But I'll need your help.'

'What can I do?' James asked.

'Harkness mustn't know. Walter would not approve. But I've had to authorise such things in the past. So why not now?'

'What are you going to do?'

There was no direct reply. Carteret kept pacing. James waited.

'Tomorrow morning,' the old man finally announced. 'You and I. Lord North Street. I know exactly where. I'll do it myself, naturally.'

He looked at James. 'Will you trust me?'

'I seem to have no choice. But may I ask what you're going to – ?'

'Stop the whole thing. You see, if you cut off the head, the body is useless.'

James suddenly felt sick.

At six o'clock the next morning, they left Harkness's house and drove to Hampstead High Street in a battered Ford Cortina Harkness had hired on Carteret's instructions. James was behind the wheel. A thin drizzle of rain clouded the streets. The High Street was deserted except for a solitary milk van. James eyed it nervously.

'Forget it,' Carteret said. 'This is their D-Day. No need to watch for me any more. Just wait.'

Ten minutes later Carteret limped back across the street. He was carrying something long, wrapped in brown paper. From its shape James could have mistaken it for a fishing rod. But he didn't.

Carteret settled into the passenger seat. 'There's little morality in my profession,' he said as they drove towards the centre of London. 'But what there was, I tried to hang on to.

You see, Ryder, the excuse for every act of violence has been that it is for the greater good. Martindale and Alexander will believe that too. But I have convinced myself of my own rectitude. There's ego for you. You must also believe. Because what we will do now could also cause our own deaths – '

James said, 'Are you giving me a choice?'

'No. No choice. You must do as I tell you. You've been through a great deal. You know these people, their aims and their methods. It's not a society you would wish to live in. So you will help me stop them.'

James shivered. He was cold, the dampness of the morning seemed to permeate his clothes. He knew the old man was right. Like some cinema western. 'A man's gotta do . . . ' Yet it didn't remove the fear and revulsion he felt.

At Carteret's instruction, James parked the car in a mews adjacent to Lord North Street. Leaving the car, Carteret led him from the mews into a narrow alley. At the end of the alley was a door leading into the rear of an apartment block, an old building, the interior renovated, the exterior still belonging to another London, a hundred and fifty years in the past.

Carteret opened the locked door with a facile expertise and a plastic card and they climbed a long series of stairways past anonymous polished wooden doors. Finally, five flights up, they climbed a final stairway onto the roof. It was a flat roof, a forest of old chimneys and new television aerials. Two pigeons, disturbed by their arrival, took off with much indignant fluttering.

Carteret leaned against the stonework of a chimney, face grey, breathing heavily.

'I'm afraid I'm not the man I was.' He managed a faint smile. 'Not just the stairs. Everything . . . '

He held out the brown parcel to James. 'Take this. Over there. By the parapet.'

James could feel the smoothness of the metal through the brown paper. He moved between aerials and chimney to a small wall at the edge of the roof. Carteret followed.

'Down there,' he said. 'Lord North Street. That one. Number twenty-eight. The London residence of Charles Alexander.'

The small door at street level was set into a neat Georgian facade. The rain had stopped now and the street was shining, damp, a mirror of stone. Carteret turned back and sat on the wet stonework of the roof, an old man in a crumpled coat. He motioned to James to remove the brown paper.

James had little specialised knowledge of guns but there was something about the rifle, its lines, its sinister delicacy of form; a kind of beauty. Carteret took it from him and tested the bolt action. Then, from his pocket he drew out a clip of bullets and, safety catch engaged, he fitted the clip into the weapon.

'Keep down,' he hissed at James. 'I don't intend to be seen by accident or taken into custody prematurely. I have left a note for Harkness and after this job of ours is done he is to use it as a pretext for examining Alexander's house. I'm hopeful there will be enough evidence therein to explain our action. And indicate that the reasons for it are not criminal.'

'The patriotic act?' James said.

Carteret looked up indignantly. 'Patriotism is the last resort of the scoundrel ... Dr Johnson said it. No, this is a necessary act, that is all. Now, help me up.'

James did so and the old man placed the rifle on the parapet wall, sighting it on the door below. 'Damn! Damn, damn,' he cursed, rubbing the back of his right hand across his eyes. 'I was a bloody good shot once. Now my eyes mist up and my hands tremble.'

Then, at once, he was a shivering elderly man, body shaking with an inner frustration. 'I could do it! God rot it, I could do it. The place, the weapon and now ... now my hands let me down.'

'There's time yet.' An attempt to calm him.

'No, no, he could leave any minute. His car will come and we'll know he's coming out and ... a matter of seconds, that's all we'll have ... '

James remembered. At school on the rifle range. 'Tip of the foresight in line with and in the centre of the backsight ... '

Carteret was uncanny, he thought later. Staring at James, reading his mind.

'Could you fire it, Ryder? Not just fire it. Aim accurately? Could you do it? Could you kill him?'

The men who had gone off the flyover had died. Had he killed them? He'd resisted the thought. Yet he knew he had been responsible. Now there was another killing to be done.

'You could do it!' Carteret broke into his thoughts. 'You could kill him.'

'I could hit a target. A piece of cardboard. Not a living man – '

'You have to – '

'No – '

Carteret insisted. 'Think of Skinner. Of Mansfield. Think of what they did. It all came from the man down there. He . . . he ordered Buller to kill you the other day.'

Carteret was tugging at his sleeve now. 'You have to do it. I can't, not any more. Hands, eyes, useless . . . '

Then the rifle was thrust into James's hands and he was sighting it on the door below. There was a sensual satisfaction in feeling the cold metal on his skin. He adjusted the sights, suddenly becoming professional. No foresight, simply a telescopic arrangement with hairlines intersecting. He was concentrating on details now, turning his mind from the implications of what he would have to do.

They waited, James somehow resigned. A watery sun broke through the low cloud and beneath them its rays were reflected in fast drying puddles.

It happened quickly. A dark sedan turned into the street and drew up outside Alexander's house.

'Sight on the door!' Carteret ordered, his voice strong now and commanding. 'Sight on the door, head height.'

God, James thought, I'm going to do it. Think on Skinner in the boot of the car, on Mansfield, body shattered, keep the images, stop thought.

Below him, the door opened.

Not a man, just a cardboard target. Sight on him, hairlines intersecting. The forehead. He wasn't wearing a hat and he was laughing, a tall man, familiar through newspaper photographs.

'Fire!' Carteret, desperate. Urging. Now. 'Fire or we're all dead!'

First the acrid smell from the mechanism. Then the sound, a singing explosion against his ears, echoing below. And through the sights, the vision of the man. A small spot appeared above his left eye and below, a look of astonishment. A red haze behind him against the door. And he fell.

Then Carteret pulled the rifle from James's hands and was running a piece of cloth, a handkerchief across the trigger and the wood. There were shouts from the street below. Carteret threw the rifle down and pulled James from the parapet.

'Move!' the old man gasped.

Then they were across the roof, through the door and running down the stairs, Carteret breathing hoarsely, fighting for breath, an old man beyond his capabilities. Don't die on me, James thought, not now. I've killed a man at your instruction and I'm afraid of being caught. No emotion, no remorse, just fear and the need for the old man to survive.

They reached the car in the mews without passing a living soul. No one tried to stop them, no one seemed to see. In the distance there were sounds of police sirens, but they saw nothing. James rammed the key into the ignition and Carteret had barely shut the door beside him before they were moving.

'Head towards Lord North Street,' Carteret said.

'For God's sake –'

'A car moving away fast is suspect. Towards is good tactics.'

They were stopped at the entrance to Lord North Street by a red-faced policeman. He was joined by a companion.

'Where are you going?'

'Westminster,' Carteret said. 'What's it all about?'

The two policemen did not reply but asked them to get out of the car and produce identification. This they did. The first policeman frowned. Carteret had produced an old Section identity card.

'Will you wait here, please.'

A crowd had gathered further down the street outside number twenty-eight. The first policeman headed towards the

226

crowd. An ambulance, bell clanging, roared up from the other end of the street. The policeman spoke to a man in the crowd who detached himself from the others and accompanied the policeman to the Cortina.

'Mr Carteret? I'm Detective Sergeant Marvin.'

'I think I know you, Sergeant. The Arsenal business eight years ago.'

The plain-clothes man's deadpan expression evaporated. 'I remember you, sir.'

'What's happened?'

'The Minister for the Defence of the Realm has been shot. I was . . . ' A flush of embarrassment. 'I was bodyguard.'

'Not serious, I hope.'

'He's dead, sir. And I have instructions to detain anyone in the neighbourhood. I'm afraid you and your companion will have to come to the Yard.'

The room in New Scotland Yard was austere, benches of lightly polished wood, a highly polished floor and the usual colour scheme of civil service green. Every now and then an officer would pass the window inset into one wall and peer in at James and Carteret.

They sat for over an hour staring at each other, speaking in monosyllables.

'What now?' James asked.

'We wait.'

'For what?'

'Whatever develops.'

A pause. Minutes.

'What do they think?'

'Nothing. Had to pull us in. All depends on Harkness now.'

The door of the interview room opened and Derek Martindale came in.

'You did it.' To Carteret, a statement, not a question. 'You killed him. Assassination.'

'Ridiculous!' Carteret replied.

Martindale leaned forward until his face was close to Carteret's. 'Do you know what you have done? It was crude. Criminal.'

227

'Whoever did it, it was effective.'

Martindale straightened up and glanced at James. 'You've taken to using amateurs. Or is he an amateur?'

'Mr Ryder is an antique dealer. Nothing more.'

'I should have eliminated him early on.'

James felt cold. As if he wasn't there.

Carteret nodded. 'You should have. I would have, had I been in your place. But then I wouldn't have been, would I?'

Before Martindale could reply, Walter Harkness came into the room. 'They want you upstairs, Mr Martindale.'

Martindale frowned and went out. Harkness shut the door behind him and faced Carteret. 'You should have told me.'

Carteret didn't reply but looked vaguely around the room.

'It's all right,' said Harkness. 'The room's not bugged. Why didn't you tell me?'

'You would have tried to stop me.'

'Yes, I would.'

'And it was the only way. You know that.'

'So you shot him? Remarkable shot for an old man.'

James opened his mouth. Carteret glared at him. 'I was always a good shot, Walter. But tell me, did you go into Alexander's house?'

The policeman nodded. 'It was all there. The whole plan. A draft of the Enabling Act. Timetable of every move. I took it straight to Downing Street. Brigadier Alexander will be under arrest by now. If he'd reached Downing Street with his brother the PM and the Cabinet would have been under arrest. And Charles Alexander would have been Prime Minister. With absolute powers.'

Carteret leaned back. His face, lined and weary, was suddenly relaxed. 'Then it's over.'

'And by the way, Martindale has been summoned to Downing Street.'

'Good,' the old man smiled. 'And Ryder and myself?'

'You're free to go.'

James felt the tension ease out of him. And yet, was it so easy? Barely two hours ago he had killed a man.

Carteret rose. 'And Alexander's death?'

'Will be attributed to terrorists.'

'I've never been called a terrorist before. Except by the Russians. Oh, the rifle you'll find on the roof at Lord North Street. It is Russian made, of Libyan origin. A souvenir of my days with the Section.'

Harkness smiled. 'We'll take care of it. One other thing, the Prime Minister wishes to see you at Number Ten tomorrow morning.'

'And Ryder, here?'

'Can go home. It's over for him. After he signs the Official Secrets Act. A necessary formality. You see, none of this happened.'

All the deaths, culminating in Alexander's and none of it happened. Could be live with that? Could he force himself to forget? Perhaps it would be easy. He certainly didn't want to remember. Except for one thing.

'Nora Matheson? Is she all right?'

Harkness suddenly looked uncomfortable. 'She's under arrest, Mr Ryder.'

Carteret coughed. He coughed for some seconds. Then he looked up at James, a piercing look. 'You were very wrong about her,' he observed, stifling the cough. 'You wanted to find her. She didn't want to be found.'

'But . . . in Scotland . . . she was drugged – '

'She's a very competent actress. That was for your benefit. They wanted to find out how much you really knew.'

'She's downstairs,' Harkness said. 'I don't think she'd want to see you. You see, she's the one who was sent to Chester to find out what Skinner knew. And to silence him with Martindale's people. Buller and Oswald. Then when you became difficult they tried to silence you by putting Skinner's body in your car. You were meant to be found with it and arrested. You got rid of it too soon. When you showed such efficiency they thought you were an intelligence man working against them. They presumed you were onto Miss Matheson so it became necessary she disappear. Out of your way.'

'Why didn't they kill me at Notting Hill?'

'Again they wanted to find out who you were working for. And, as long as you were held by them they had no need to kill you. Both Martindale and Alexander wanted to avoid unnecessary bloodshed. You see, they were so wrong about you. They wouldn't believe you were an innocent.'

'But why . . . ? How did she become so involved?'

Carteret answered. 'She was Charles Alexander's mistress. It was in his Special Branch file.'

James stood, head spinning. He didn't – couldn't – understand.

'Go now, Ryder,' Carteret said. 'And forget about it. I'll be in touch.'

Harkness walked James to the foyer of the building.

'You can tell me one thing,' James asked. 'What will happen to Nora Matheson?'

'We could make a treason charge stick,' Harkness replied. 'Her involvement is all in Alexander's papers. But we probably won't charge her. She'll be released eventually.'

'Why?'

'What I said to you upstairs. It must never come out. It never happened. Oh, there will be a black mark in her file. Any sign of political activity and she'll be picked up.'

'And the deaths? Skinner, Harrington, Mansfield? Nothing will be done?'

'It's all been done. It's over, Ryder. As we told you.'

James felt an irrational dislike of them all. All those deaths and nobody answering for them.

Harkness went on: 'Something was done. Alexander was executed. You could think of it that way. And you were the executioner, weren't you? You fired the rifle. I can't believe Carteret could have done it.'

'I fired the rifle.'

'Makes you one of us, doesn't it? You'll get around to thinking we're bastards, Ryder. Cold bastards. Maybe you're right. We do what's expedient. But remember, if Alexander had come to power, there would have been bigger bastards in charge. His death was expedient. The lesser bastards survived.'

James went home to South Kensington.

EPILOGUE

Sometime later. A matter of two weeks and they had passed quickly. James was back at work and grateful for the small excitements of buying and selling.

It was in the middle of the afternoon when the two men came into the shop. 'Mr Carteret would like to see you. Won't take more than an hour.'

They were amiable but persistent. James abandoned the shop to Anthony Cromer and accompanied them into a battered Morris Minor. They took him to a house in Bloomsbury, two houses in fact, knocked into one. They ushered him past a commissionaire, signed him in at a desk behind which sat a large, hard-eyed individual, escorted him along a series of seemingly endless corridors and finally showed him into a spacious office, the walls panelled, the window expensively curtained, the desk solid, practical and almost certainly an antique. Behind the desk was Carteret. The escorts departed leaving James alone with the old man.

'Welcome to the Section,' Carteret said.

'You're back at work then?'

'Temporarily in charge. To clean up the mess. Appointed by the lady in Whitehall. She asks me to convey her thanks, by the way. Unofficially, of course. I shall only be here for six months. I agreed to that. Then back to retirement. With an increased pension. I shall be glad of that.'

'I'm glad you got something out of it,' James remarked acidly.

Ignoring this, Carteret opened one of the desk drawers and took out a bulky envelope. This, he pushed across to James.

'You too, my dear fellow. Ex-gratia payment for services and expenses. And compensation for inconvenience.'

James laughed grimly. 'Inconvenience? Having to kill someone. Yes, I suppose you could call that an inconvenience.'

'Two thousand pounds. Cash, tax free. Not a lot. But then they're having to economise in everything. The Mafia would have been more generous. Take it.'

'Stuff it! Blood money.'

'Don't be so dramatic. And quixotic. Take it. Have a holiday. Buy an antique.'

'I have one,' James said. Still it was stupid not to take the money. Carteret was right. Quixotic. To hell with it. He put the envelope in his pocket.

'Good,' said the old man.

The door opened and Martindale came into the room. He was carrying a file.

'You know Martindale, of course,' Carteret said.

James was conscious of his mouth falling open.

' 'Morning, Mr Ryder,' Martindale nodded, his face expressionless, and placed the file in front of Carteret. 'That's the Berlin File.'

'Thank you. We'll discuss it later.'

Martindale went out silently.

'He's still here?' James said.

Carteret smiled. 'Obviously. But no longer in charge. And never will be again. But he's very competent. I need him just now. And, of course, in the Alexander affair, he was only obeying orders.'

'The Nuremberg defence?'

'Martindale simply misjudged the man who was giving the orders.'

'I wonder, if you had been in his position, would you have carried out Alexander's orders?'

Carteret flushed. 'I would have checked them out with a higher authority.'

James rose. 'I'm leaving now.'

'I might have more to say.'

'I've stopped listening.'

232

They did not shake hands.

When James had gone, Martindale re-entered. 'You're letting him roam free?'

'For now,' Carteret replied. 'Perhaps later, after he has a holiday – '

'The moment he decides to disapprove, he could open his mouth – '

'Then steps would be taken,' Carteret said. He felt infinitely depressed.

Outside in the Bloomsbury street the air felt cool and fresh on James's face. He decided it was late enough in the afternoon and, hailing a taxi, went home. He planned a quiet evening. Since Alexander's death, James had little social life. As if all his contacts had been severed. As if he was afraid of contact. He opened the door of his apartment and stopped in the doorway. There was something in the air, a trace of scent, familiar, subtle. Not Sybil's. Or was it his imagination? Then he heard a movement from the lounge.

The fear came back in a rush. Adrenalin in the bloodstream. The knowledge that it wasn't finished. Something else was to happen. No sense in running; nowhere to run to; he had to face it. He went into the lounge.

She was standing with her back to him, cigarette in one hand, glass in the other. She turned to face him.

'Hello, James,' said Jean Thurman. She was smiling.

'What do you want?' he replied churlishly.

'To see you. Before I go back to America. I've been recalled. Not surprising. Someone had to carry the can for the Company's misjudgement. I was . . . sacrificed . . . with a couple of others.'

'How did you get in?'

'I think your porter downstairs fell in love with me.' Her voice still had a hoarse quality.

James poured himself a whisky and found his hand was shaking. 'I thought for a moment you might have come to finish the job Buller messed up,' he said. She was capable of it. He'd seen that in Glasgow.

She looked amused. 'You have to understand the type of work I do. It's not all homicidal. They call it Intelligence

233

though there's damn little involved most of the time. Just routine . . . and obeying orders.'

'I've heard the Nuremberg defence already today.'

'It keeps coming up. Look, James, I was on your side until my bosses in the CIA decided Alexander was worth betting on. So we got our fingers burnt and now we're back on your side. It's be-nice-to-the-British time.'

'I'm not on anybody's side. I'm out of it.'

A short silence. Then she said, 'You know if Buller had really decided to kill you I had some idea of stopping him.'

'I'm supposed to believe that?' he replied dourly.

She grinned. 'No. But hold the thought.'

He sipped his whisky. It made him feel more relaxed. 'What will happen when you go back to America?'

'Nothing very terrible. Demotion. Desk job at Langley. Maybe in time I'll get out. Marry and become one of these terrible Yankee hostesses. Try to look as plastic as Nancy Reagan.'

'You'll make it. Look exactly like her.'

'Bastard!'

'Anyway, why come to see me? Absolution?'

'I'm beyond that,' she gave a crooked smile. 'Much more practical. I don't leave for two days. Friday night. And I gave up my apartment this morning. Wasn't that stupid?'

'Tactical. You're not the stupid type. So you gave up your apartment – '

'Christ, you're going to make me ask. Okay, you're entitled. I thought you might put me up for a couple of days.'

'There's only one bedroom.'

'That's why I asked.'

He thought, could he eradicate from his mind the image of the kneecapping in Glasgow? Could he forget her coolly turning against him in Scotland? Now it seemed unreal, irrelevant. And the whisky was relaxing him. So, let it be unreal. Why not? After all the nightmare was over.

'Can you cook or do we eat out?' he said.

Some four months later the following item appeared in the inside page of a London newspaper.

HIT AND RUN DRIVER KILLS ANTIQUE DEALER

'James Ryder, well-known West End antique dealer was fatally injured last night outside his South Kensington home. Mr Ryder, who had recently returned from a holiday in the United States, died in the ambulance on the way to hospital. The police are anxious to interview anyone who saw the accident and the driver of a black saloon car, make unknown. . . . '